A WOMAN IN SEARCH OF...

LYNNE BRIGHTMAN HORN

Design and distribution by Bublish

ISBN: 979-8-986396-22-4 (paperback)
ISBN: 979-8-986396-29-3 (eBook)

ACKNOWLEDGEMENTS

I HAVE BOUNDLESS GRATITUDE TO LEE NETZER, Cindy Levy and my daughter, Kim Baldwin for their help in the production and technical process along the way. Also, thank you to others for being sounding boards for me.

CHAPTER 1

WENDY SAT IN THE WAITING ROOM FOR THE
psychologist to call her into her office. She didn't want to see a
psychologist, but she saw no alternative. Wendy's life had been shattered.
She tried to make changes to help herself, but she couldn't do it alone.

The doctor's door opened. She took a few steps toward Wendy and
shook her hand. "Hi, I'm Dr. Lewis, please come in Mrs. Murray."

"Thank you."

As they walked in the doctor indicated the chair across from
her desk for Wendy. Wendy sat at the edge of the chair her hands
clenched into fists.

"How may I help you?"

Wendy calmed herself and let go of her fists, pushing her chin
length, auburn hair behind her ears. She struggled to get the words
out. "I recently separated from my husband, Scott, and it was hurtful
and difficult. I'm not sure how to move forward. The one thing I
know I want to do is find a new job. For six years, I've been manager
of the Women's Clothing Department at Hammond's Department
Store, but I'm bored with it."

"I'm sorry about the separation. What bores you about your job?"

"The constant repetition of what I do. Since I'm starting my life over, I'd like to find work that I will be happy with and will move my life in a new direction."

"Before we go into that, please explain why you are separated from your husband."

Wendy grunted and gritted her teeth. "We were together for two years before we got married eight months ago. Six months ago, Scott found a new job and within a few months, it literally became his life. There was no time for us. We used to travel, go out with friends, and spend time together. When he was home, he didn't want to do anything, just watch TV and complain about so many things I did, like the food I made, my hair style," Wendy blurted out in anger. She closed her eyes and calmed herself. "I'm sorry, I didn't mean to yell out like that."

"It's okay."

"I tried to make improvements, really I did, but it didn't matter. Things kept upsetting him." Tears fell down her cheeks.

Dr. Lewis took some tissues to her. Wendy looked up at the nice-looking woman with deep brown eyes and long blond hair and thanked her. The doctor sat down and waited.

After wiping away the tears Wendy continued. "I considered it might have been my being overweight that made him lose interest, but he never said anything about my weight. I put up with the loneliness for a long time because I kept thinking things might change, but they didn't. I talked to him about marriage counseling, but he adamantly opposed it. I couldn't take the rejection anymore."

"I certainly understand how very difficult that was for you." Dr. Lewis took a few notes.

"It was horrible." Wendy looked away for a few seconds, turning back to the doctor. "There is something else."

"Go ahead."

Wendy hesitated before the words spilled out. "I grew up feeling the same rejection from my dad. He was fine until my mom died when I was twelve. After her death he complained about much of what I did. 'Go back to your room and comb your hair better.' 'Sit up in your chair.' He came up to my college once but never said anything nice about my room, my goals, my classes. He spent all his time with his friends and watching TV. He never wanted to have a serious talk. I felt neglected and unloved. And Scott made me feel the same way."

"So, you felt abandoned by both?"

"Oh yes. With my dad we lived together but apart. When I met Scott, he was so caring and fun to be with, I thought I had found someone to love and be loved. But when he got involved with his new job his devotion to it took precedence."

"Can we talk about Scott's job?"

"He works for an import/export company. This job takes him out of state, and sometimes out of the country. At home he was tired and didn't want to do anything, except the stupid TV. Sorry, I'm repeating myself. When I suggested doing something, he poo pooed it."

"And your marriage, can you share about that?"

"It started out great, fun times together or with friends and relatives or traveling. With the involvement in his work, it all stopped. He was all about himself, just like my dad. Finally, I couldn't take it anymore, so we separated."

"I can certainly understand what you've been through, it's been tough. You mentioned you are bored with your job. Is there something else you'd like to do?"

"Not that I can think of. My big interest is gardening but I'm not sure how I could use that to make a living."

"Maybe think about gardening and how you could develop a program with your managing experience. What else interests you?"

Wendy stared straight ahead. "I don't really have any other interests. I've been gardening since I was a child and have always loved watching plants grow and flowers bloom."

Dr. Lewis stared at Wendy and smiled. "Sounds like a wonderful hobby."

"Oh, it is."

When the session ended Wendy sat in her car thinking about all the questions Dr. Lewis asked. She leaned her head against the car seat going over the discussions about Scott and her dad being so similar with their indifference to her. As tears dribbled down her face, she thought how awful the start of 1973 had been.

Once inside her house she stared around the living room. Since Scott left right after New Year's, the quiet, empty house was disturbing and lonely, filled with terrible memories. As soon as she could put those memories away the house would bring peacefulness. She did have good memories too. She realized how truly lucky she was. Since she was an only child, her parents left her this house with all the beautiful decorations and furniture, and a comfortable inheritance. Wendy smiled when she knew her life would move on, she just needed to figure out how.

Wendy stood, started out of the living room but stopped. She opened the China cabinet near the fireplace. Scott forgot to take three old, tarnished tennis trophies. She got a bag from the kitchen, dumped the trophies in, shoving them into a closet. One less memory to look at. She returned to the living room and leaned against the arch. She admired the homey atmosphere and the attractive placement of the sofa and coffee table across from the fireplace. Wendy's favorite chair of soft blue and winter-white floral print stood near the fireplace. Against the soft beige walls were framed scenic pictures of the ocean and the mountains. They brought a calmness to the room, along with the open blinds welcoming the afternoon sunlight. 'I will not let Scott keep me from moving on,' Wendy told herself.

She changed into sweats and headed out to the greenhouse that filled a corner of her backyard. She fell in love with gardening when she was ten, spending many happy hours with her mom, dad, and cousin, Jake, working with orchids, fuchsias, ferns and other varieties of shade plants. A family hobby where they enjoyed sharing their ideas and puttering in the greenhouse. Wendy chuckled out loud when she remembered a fun time with Jake. While using the hose to water the plants, he suddenly sprayed her with water. She looked down and saw she was soaking wet. Jake and her parents all laughed...Wendy joined in.

Wendy took the trowel and clippers from the greenhouse and went outside where she weeded and picked off the remains of old flowers. The air chilled and she headed into the house leaving the gardening tools on the patio table.

She went through the kitchen, stopping at the living room doorway. Her sense of peace floundered as images of her marriage filled her head. She stared at the sofa. How often she and Scott sat on it, as they enjoyed the warmth of the fireplace, or just the warmth of each other. She couldn't stop the memories from flooding back.

"Scott, where are you?" Wendy called out as she walked into the house.

"In the bedroom."

"Hi, I just talked to...why are you packing?" she asked, looking at the suitcase on the bed.

"I have a ten o'clock flight to Hong Kong."

"How long will you be gone this time?"

"A week, maybe a bit longer. Don't know for sure until I see how things go. Would you get my white tee shirts from the drawer?"

Wendy pulled out the shirts. "I wish you didn't have to go. This is the second trip in a month."

"I have to go now because of the holiday season. It's a good time to bargain."

"Will you be home for Christmas?"

"Probably, but you never know with the import/export business."

Wendy tried to control her anger. "Why can't someone else go?"

Scott's eyes opened wide, and he gave a long, strange smile. "Because I got the offer and wanted it, so I took it."

His gruff response was menacing, but she calmed herself and tried to relax, clasping her hands in front of her. "Why can't you find a job that keeps you from traveling so much?"

Scott glared at her. "Sorry, but this is my job and I like it. Why don't you stop being bitchy and accept this reality? You were okay when I started this job."

"It's just I never expected you'd be gone this much."

"Why don't you stop complaining and think of me and my needs instead of what you want…you have everything. I need these opportunities for what I want."

"What's that?"

"A career I'm proud of and do well in so I can work my way to a top position. I need to keep pushing myself so I can be more successful."

"To me, you are successful."

"Well, I don't think so. It's not about you, Wendy. And you should be proud that I want more success than I have now."

"But we never have time to be together. All I want is for us to have time for each other. We haven't done anything together for months, including sex."

Scott turned and gawked. "You're being selfish. Find something to do while I'm gone. Get more involved in your job or go work in your garden. Quit bitching at me."

Wendy opened her mouth to speak but changed her mind. She knew any retaliation would cause her anger to explode and she couldn't handle what that may lead to. She squinted at Scott. He closed his suitcase and Wendy followed him to the front door. He didn't say a word but opened the door and left. His meanness and anger convinced her there was nothing left in their marriage.

The doorbell startled Wendy from her dismal memories. As soon as she opened the front door Cindy Rose charged in, loaded with paper bags filled with dinner. As roommates in college, they became best friends and remained so. Wendy liked their friendship because they always spoke the truth, and there was no pretense nor game playing. They shared almost everything, including their ages, thirty-two. Wendy loved Cindy's energy, her go getter attitude.

Wendy glanced at her watch as Cindy headed toward the kitchen. "I didn't think you were coming for another half hour."

"Teaching exhausted me today and I got hungry early. I'll leave and come back if you want," Cindy kidded.

"Very cute. I thought we'd eat at the coffee table."

"Groovy."

Cindy's use of popular slang made Wendy laugh. Wendy had no interest in using it.

In the living room Cindy plopped her 5'6" curvaceous figure onto the sofa. Wendy admired Cindy's looks, unlike herself. Because of her short five-foot-two-inch stature plus extra pounds she carried Wendy felt less than desirable. Scott never said anything negative about her being overweight, so she never gave it much thought…but now she wondered if that was a reason he didn't want to be with her.

Wendy sat next to her friend. "So, what happened today?"

Cindy handed Wendy a large container filled with sweet and sour chicken. "One of my eighth-grade students refused to do any work. He sat at his desk staring at the blackboard. I asked him what the problem was, and he said, "Nothing." I left him alone and he put his head down. After school I talked to the counselor. She'll call him in tomorrow and find out what the issue, or issues might be. It wasn't like him to act that way. He's usually a good and an engaged kid. I felt sorry for him. All day I couldn't get his sad face out of my mind. I was bummed out."

"I'm sorry."

"Thanks. How was your meeting with the psychologist? Dr. Lewis, right?" Cindy asked as she popped a fried wonton from her noodles.

"Yes, and it was fine." Wendy took her sweet and sour chicken out of the container and heaped it onto a paper plate she laid out earlier.

"Just fine?" Cindy swallowed the rest of the wonton and chomped on part of another one.

"I don't know how to judge the meeting. It seemed okay." Wendy took a bite of her chicken.

"So, like what did you talk about?"

Memories swirled in her head, "I really don't want to discuss it."

"Chill out, I didn't ask for your answers, just the questions. Besides, I thought we shared."

After inhaling deeply, she let it out, "We discussed the separation, but to be honest, other than that," she shrugged her shoulders. "There's nothing to share. You already know everything about Scott." She started to eat but stopped. "I still can't get over how Scott changed so much, leaving me out and devoting every hour of his day to work… his new love, or the TV. The birth control pills were a waste."

"Wendy, I…" Cindy stopped talking as she watched Wendy stare at the fireplace in front of them.

"What are you thinking about?"

Wendy came out of her reverie. "I don't know. I'm confused and angry. Where did I go wrong?"

Cindy focused on Wendy and smiled. "You didn't go wrong, Scott did."

Wendy looked at her and scowled. "You're right, I didn't, he did. I'm so angry at him. Where do I go from here?" Wendy used a napkin to wipe away the tears forming in the corner of her eyes. She took another bite of her chicken.

Cindy took a deep breath. "I think a lot of what's buggin' you about Scott goes further back than your marriage."

Wendy swallowed her mouthful. "What are you talking about?"

"You used to complain about how critical Scott was."

"So?"

"Criticism is hard to deal with and I know your dad criticized you too much as a kid. It probably made you more sensitive and even harder to deal with Scott's criticisms."

Wendy didn't want to talk about her dad. She set her plate down and headed to the kitchen without saying a word. Cindy followed.

"Well? Say something," Cindy said with concern.

Wendy stood next to the refrigerator. "That's bullshit, and a lot of Freudian crap. No one likes a husband who constantly berates you."

"True."

"What happened between Scott and me isn't about my dad, it's about how terrible Scott was to me." As Cindy leaned against the kitchen cabinet Wendy could see Cindy's mind working.

"Perhaps, but your usual way of handling a difficult situation is to avoid it, or in this case, you and Scott split. It gave you an escape from working things out."

"Thank you, Dr. Cindy. There's nothing left to work out." Wendy took a Fresca and a Tab from the refrigerator.

"Like, I'm sorry. I'll shut up."

Wendy handed Cindy the Tab. As they returned to the living room Wendy caught a reflection of herself in the tall, glass front cabinet. She stopped mid step.

"Strange time to admire yourself."

Wendy was remembering a few years earlier, when she went on a diet. She didn't lose a lot of weight, but enough, so she felt better about herself. She remembered that Scott never complained about her weight, but he did comment on the loss. Unfortunately, she put the pounds back on.

She considered her lack of attractiveness. But many people complimented her on her pretty face with its smooth complexion, cute nose, endearing hazel eyes and shiny shoulder length, straight auburn hair. Scott never said she wasn't pretty, but he rarely complimented her.

"You read me like a book. I don't know why I wanted to check myself out at this moment. Weird, huh? I know I'm overweight, but still…"

"Stop knocking yourself," Cindy said as she put her hand on Wendy's shoulder.

They headed for the sofa. As they sat Cindy broke open her fortune cookie and read the fortune. "Oh, you're going to love this, "someone new will bring new happiness.' Can't wait to see who he might be."

Wendy grumbled. "And I can't wait to find the man of my dreams cause it sure wasn't Scott. I'm sorry I shouldn't be dwelling on me."

"It's okay, you're having a tough time, I understand. Cindy tossed the fortune on the coffee table and stretched her arms. "By the way have you heard from Scott?" she asked as she started to crunch on another cookie.

Wendy winced. "No, it's only been six weeks since we separated. There's no reason for him to call and I don't believe for a minute he's become someone different."

"It could be interesting, a chance to talk."

Wendy tried to read Cindy's thoughts. "You want me to go back to him, don't you?"

"He's rad, but not unless you want to. You two should talk though."

"Talk about what? He loves his job and has no plans to leave it. He's made it abundantly clear. If he tried to get back together with me now, I couldn't trust anything he says. He's all about him."

Wendy changed the subject to avoid further discussion of reconciliation. "My greenhouse has become my solace, my escape into a world of calm and beauty. I want more of that beauty in my life. I love working in my garden and in the greenhouse."

"Yes, those have always been your favorite places to be."

After hesitating for a second, Wendy smiled and stared at Cindy, "I've decided I want more space for shade plants, so I'm going to open an indoor plant nursery especially since shade plants are the rage now."

Cindy stopped eating and gawked.

"It's one of the subjects I discussed with Dr. Lewis, my wanting something new in my life."

"Holy shit! That blows my mind. Where did this come from?"

"Dr. Lewis asked about what I'd like to do since I don't like my job. I didn't have an answer for her. But, as I drove home, the idea popped into my head. Opening an indoor plant nursery is something I know I will be good at. At thirty-two I can start over in something I love to do, garden." Incredible excitement filled her. "I'll need to find a place and think about the design for it. There will be so much to do. You know I haven't been happy as a clothing manager for a long time. This is a way to start my life over with something I love."

"Your backyard greenhouse is great, but it's not that big. I hate to play devil's advocate, but do you think you're taking on more than you can handle with a nursery?"

"Play devil's advocate if you want, but no, I'm not taking on too much. I'll work it out." Her plans bubbled up. "First, I need to find a place. After that I'll need to make calls about purchasing materials. There's the business license and insurance that need to be handled. I'll ask my attorney, who was my folks' attorney, and he'll help me with the legal end of the purchase. I'll talk to my accountant. He's been great keeping all my inheritance squared away including the stocks…so much to do, things I haven't even thought about. It will be a challenge, but the reward will be well worth it."

Cindy grinned. "I hope you don't overlook anything."

"I'm sure you'll tell me if I do," Wendy smirked back.

"Well, that's what friends are for, right?"

"Yeah, you're right." Wendy smiled, feeling calmer than she had in days.

CHAPTER 2

AFTER CINDY LEFT WENDY WALKED INTO HER
study that used to be a bedroom. There are windows so she can
see her yard. The desk is a large size so there's room to spread out
everything she needs. At the long and tall bookcase, she pulled out
a book and leaned against the shelves as she flipped through, *Shade
Plants for the Garden*. There were fabulous layouts of various ways
to arrange a garden. She could transfer those ideas to the nursery,
modify them and make them her own. She sat at her desk. She
stopped at a picture resembling a forest filled with many ferns. She
saw it as a refreshing environment. She closed her eyes to picture a
forest scene indoors. She liked what she imagined. She shut the book
but left it on the desk.

As she got ready for bed, she dwelled on the career she had now.
For years Wendy wanted to be a Women's Clothing Manager for
a major department store. She accomplished that goal and proved
successful at what she did at Hammond's Department Store, known
for their high fashion clothes. Wendy used to adore selecting outfits
from all the beautiful and stylish clothes. They were purchased by

the wealthy, including many celebrities. Seeing them added to the enjoyment of the job, especially when they complimented her when she made good suggestions like adding an accessory to an outfit. After six years of it, Wendy became bored. Because of her split from Scott, she knew this was a good time to find a different type of job.

Wendy's attitude toward her own classic clothes changed. Where she used to take great pride in putting together fashion perfect outfits, with all the wonderful accessories, now she didn't care so much. The compliments she always received about her great fashion sense, especially about her extensive variety of pant suits were always important to her. But now, avoiding many of the accessories that dressed them up was her plan and her high heeled shoes were no longer important, shorter ones being more comfortable. Wendy wanted a more relaxed lifestyle.

At work the next day, Wendy helped customers select different outfits. She couldn't wait for the same old thing to end. As soon as it did, she returned home, and sat in her study energized as she worked on plans for the indoor plant nursery. She was about to go to the backyard when the doorbell stopped her.

"Hey," Cindy said as she charged past Wendy and headed straight to the sofa, dropping into it. Wendy was impervious to Cindy's strong-willed behavior…it was a part of the Cindy she knew. Wendy sat in the chair by the sofa.

"I have something primo to tell you," Cindy burst out.

"So, you needed to rush here to tell me."

Cindy looked at her with an expression that said, Duh.

"Okay, before you explode, what?"

"Do you know what Hoffman's is?"

"Sure, a restaurant in Venice on the Goodman Canal, near Marina del Rey, and not far from your building complex.

"It's also a bar, and I went there last night. Lilly, one of the women I teach with wanted to go. So cool being that close to water and inside was far out. There's this great singer named Brad, he's awesome."

Wendy scrunched her nose. "You've never shown an interest in the bar scene, why now?"

"I don't know, but it sure gave me great fun. Who cares…it's the seventies, time to rock on. Anyway, there's this singer…"

"Listen, I'm thrilled you had a great time, but…"

"But, what? You don't want to hear? Afraid you might like it? You know you do need time to chill. Sitting around and stewing about Scott won't help."

"I'm fine. I don't need to be entertained."

"You're being myopic. Come with me to Hoffman's tonight and see for yourself. It'll do you good."

Wendy relented because she realized it was the only way to stop Cindy from continuing to pester her about it. "All right, it might be nice to get out. What time?"

"Pick me up at the back entrance of my building at eight," Cindy said as she headed out.

The warmth of the bath water soothed Wendy, and she put her head back and closed her eyes, fully relaxed. Realizing she wasn't always accommodating with Cindy's suggestions, she needed to let Cindy know how much Wendy appreciated her friendship and how she knew Cindy would be here for her. Wendy needed to be there for Cindy too. Finally, she stepped out, dried herself. She selected a pair of brown slacks to wear with a beige, long sleeved high cut blouse. Wendy tucked the blouse in, adding a brown belt. She removed the hair clips from the sides of her thick auburn hair and brushed it out. Recently she decided to let her bangs grow out, so they disappeared into the rest of her hair.

Cindy was outside the back of her building dressed in a mini-skirt with a short overtop, known as a crop top. It hit just above her waist. She wore knee high boots and looked very "in." Wendy always accepted Cindy's free-spirited styles. She, however, never cared much about being "in." Her more conservative, comfortable wardrobe looked how most of her customers dressed, although she did wear jeans and tee shirts. Regular slacks with a jacket were also comfortable.

Wendy drove the ten minutes to Hoffman's.

"Are you hyped?" Cindy asked.

"Not really. This isn't my 'scene,' but I knew you didn't want to go alone."

"Thank you, I didn't. You'll like it too, just give it a chance."

Wendy remembered many of Cindy's relationships. In college she dated a few great looking guys who paid a lot of attention to her. Having a slender and well-defined figure helped. But she also possessed a great personality. Men were attracted to her, and she relished her popularity. Wendy never experienced popularity with men. In the past her dating relationships came and went. The longest caring relationship she had before Scott only lasted four months. When she and Scott got together Wendy did feel appreciated, truly admired in the same way Cindy was. Wendy knew her lack of a lustrous body kept the type of men she wanted away. She used to picture herself with a tall, handsome guy. Scott was nice looking, and she liked when he mentioned her cuteness, but he rarely complimented her about her sexiness, obviously because she didn't look or think of herself as sexy.

There was only one other restaurant/bar on the side of the canal where Hoffman's was. There were different businesses along the way, including a law office and a realtor. On the other side of the canal were a couple of eateries and a bank and more businesses.

There were three other canals, but they were all residential. Wendy pulled into the almost full parking lot. From there Wendy and Cindy went toward the entrance where they climbed the six spiraling steps up to Hoffman's. Once inside Wendy saw a restaurant to the right and bar area to the left. It was so crowded she could barely see in. People were everywhere, standing and sitting at tall tables. To Wendy they sounded like swarming insects. The cigarette smoke overpowered her.

"This is crazy," Wendy shouted over the din.

"Oh, stop bitchin. This is awesome." Cindy shoved Wendy ahead of her through a throng of people towards the piano bar. As they approached it, the most exquisite baritone voice Wendy ever heard serenaded her with the words to, "The Impossible Dream."

"That's the fox, Brad! Isn't he boss?" Cindy announced.

Wendy didn't respond. She was eager to see the person behind the voice. They finally reached the front of the piano bar.

Cindy was right, Wendy saw a gorgeous guy. She concentrated on his enthralling voice. He strummed a guitar pressed tight against his body. Wendy couldn't tell how tall he was because he sat on a high stool. His dark brown, wavy collar length hair surrounded his handsome face, accented with large, blue eyes. You could easily see a dimple on his left cheek even without him smiling.

When he finished the song, a woman yelled out and she sashayed up to him, "Brad, how 'bout "Country Roads?" She put two dollars in the brandy snifter sitting on the bar. As Brad began, the woman picked up castanets that lay on the piano bar for any patron to use. She began to play along.

The man mesmerized Wendy. His singing drowned out the noise around her. In the middle of the song, a seat at the piano bar opened up and a woman quickly snagged it. The very attractive, slim, blonde woman wore tight jeans with wide legs. Brad smiled at her, and over the microphone he asked, "How's Tuffy?" Brad gleamed, and the woman returned the look.

The waitress came by and hurriedly took Wendy's drink order.

Wendy remained focused on the singer, tuning out every sound around her. His voice brought her calmness like the earlier bath. She was glad she came.

The choice of songs…mostly ballads, show tunes, or soft rock, with popular music from the sixties, as well as recent hits like Carly Simon's, "You're So Vain," were all impressive. As a man left the piano bar Cindy slid into the seat.

Between his songs Cindy and Brad started some flirty banter and he seemed to enjoy it. A woman who sat right in front of Brad also added cute quips.

Wendy squeezed past several people and stood to the right of the piano bar. She was uncomfortable being in the front. She sipped the wine she ordered and took a quick look around but saw nothing noteworthy. Turning back to Brad, she leaned forward and watched as Cindy stared at him with a wide grin. Wendy understood Cindy's strong reaction to Brad.

During one of Brad's breaks, he and Cindy went out to the observation deck overlooking the canal. Brad was tall, near six feet she figured, and somewhat muscular. He appeared to be in his mid or late thirties.

"Hi there."

Wendy turned to see a slender man standing next to her. "Hello."

"Come here often?"

She gave a polite smile. "No, this is my first time."

"You're the third woman who's told me that tonight. You broads really expect us to believe it?"

"I'm sorry, but it's true."

He walked away without a word. Wendy shrugged. What she resented was being called a broad.

Before Brad returned to his position behind the piano bar, Cindy introduced Wendy to him. They exchanged greetings as Brad said, "Welcome." Wendy thanked him. The intoxicating scent of Musk drifted past her. He returned to sing.

Everywhere Wendy looked it seemed as if men were hustling women, and women were hustling guys. Women were expected to be more assertive since the start of the women's movement in the 1960's. It went along with the flower power generation of free love, peace and songs of peoples' struggles. But Wendy couldn't picture herself hustling any guy. She listened as men spoke to women around them. "Do you come here often?" "I bet you're a Libra." "You live in Sherman Oaks, too bad you're GU," that meant geographically undesirable, all bullshit. None of it meant anything to her. She wondered if women there fell for those come ons.

On the way home Cindy talked incessantly about Brad. "Can you dig him?"

"Yeah, he is cool, although it seems to me, every female in the room was eyeing him."

"God, you're really encouraging."

Wendy took a deep breath and exhaled. "I'm sorry, I just don't want you to be disappointed. He looked to be doing a good PR business as he moved around and talked to so many people."

"Okay, I'll keep that in mind. But I think he's supposed to encourage people to come back."

"You're right, sorry."

"Thank you."

Wendy drove her car to the back of Cindy's building.

"Later," Cindy called out as she opened the car door.

It was two o'clock in the morning and Wendy lay in bed as she listened to Brad's voice in her head. With his powerful voice and handsome looks, she wondered why he hadn't been discovered by some record company. Suddenly Wendy's mind switched to Ron, the guy she met shortly after she and Scott separated. A friend from the gardening club she belonged to encouraged Wendy to come to the party she was having, a chance to get out and relax. Ron was so nice to her. She enjoyed the times with him. After only a couple of dates he announced his moving to Europe, quite a blow to Wendy. He was so much fun, so it hurt more.

CHAPTER 3

THE NEXT MORNING WENDY PUT ON HER PINK chenille robe and strolled into the backyard looking around her garden. It took three years to get the backyard to look the way it did, and the results satisfied her.

The sixty by sixty-foot space was a perfect size for her to manage. A large ficus tree formed a canopy not far from the end of the yard, allowing her to expand the shade plants around it. She looked down from the tree where she planted impatiens of various colors-lavender, white, pink, red, and some bi-color ones. She particularly liked the pink and white one. From spring to early winter, a magnificent kaleidoscope of colors bloomed. With spring just two months away she looked forward to enjoying the garden wake up.

The greenhouse was toward the back of the yard, a short distance from the ficus leaving plenty of room for plants, flowers, and shrubs everywhere else. On one side of the garden there was a lattice cover so she could grow ferns, begonias, bromeliads, and other shade loving plants.

From the far edge of the garden to the ficus tree, water flowed into her twenty five-foot long stream with a tranquil sound. Around the stream were low plants so you could see both sides of it without crossing the wooden board she used as a bridge. Against the kitchen wall lay a concrete patio with a canvas cover and four comfy chairs with a fire pit. She smiled as she looked around, nothing pacified her as much as the peacefulness of her garden.

She sat and watched as several monarch butterflies settled on clusters of small yellow and pink flowers on a newly awakening lantana bush. A hummingbird joined the butterflies and continued onto the bright blue salvia flowers. To Wendy nature was a consummate and unmitigated joy.

Later, Wendy called a realtor friend of hers, Lori Smith. Wendy explained she was looking for a building where she could design an indoor plant nursery. Her inheritance, especially the investments her dad made, were allowing her to buy a building and implement her plan for the nursery. She knew her folks would be pleased she was putting the money into what she loved, just as she put her heart into redecorating the house they left her. Lori said she'd check into some locations and get back to her.

At her desk in the study, Wendy snatched a pencil and ruler from the drawer and began to design an enclosed water feature. First, she drew a kidney shape that she hoped would be fifteen feet long and six feet wide. She placed it off center but near the front of the nursery. She held the paper up a bit to study it and dreamed of a soft flowing waterfall and soothing stream, with the lushness of greenery surrounding it. Wendy wanted the nursery to be as close to a natural environment as she could make it with lots of tropical and forest plants. Throughout the nursery customers could stroll on cement and bark paths while pondering what plants they wanted to purchase.

The phone interrupted Wendy's thinking.

"Hi," Scott said.

"Scott, why are you calling?"

"I wondered if you'd like to go to lunch?"

"I really don't have time. Is that why you called?"

"Well, I just wanted to know how you were. How's it going?"

She could tell he was nervous about this call, just as she was nervous when she heard his voice.

"Things are fine." To break the discomfort and to brag, Wendy announced, "I'm going to open an indoor plant nursery."

"That's a surprise. You never mentioned anything like it in the past."

"Well, time for change."

"Where will it be?"

"Have no idea."

"Oh. I hope you find what you want."

"I hope so too."

"Well, I'll let you go. Just wanted to see how you were."

In a formal tone Wendy said, "Thank you, bye."

Wendy set the phone in the cradle and stood there. The call made her distraught and unsettled. Strong resentment toward him remained. She couldn't believe he called her. Wendy remembered his anger and that horrible scene as he left for Hong Kong. However, he was unusually nice on the phone. Did he want to reconcile? Why even think about it? Why did she even care? She didn't need the angst. He couldn't have changed. He was who he was, selfish and critical. Wendy needed to forget about him and concentrate on the nursery.

The next afternoon Lori called. She found a building in Santa Monica about two miles from the Pacific Ocean. The place used to be a furniture store. Wendy wrote down the address and Lori said she could meet her there later in the afternoon.

According to Lori's information the old furniture store stood one hundred and eighty feet long and seventy feet wide. It sounded like a perfect size for the nursery.

The drive to Santa Monica was only twenty minutes from Wendy's house with the stunning beach and ocean on her left. The drive calmed her as she admired the ocean view when stopped at signals. Wendy hoped the building would be some place she could love and work with. She also knew Santa Monica was prime real estate, so Wendy's sense of confidence in her ability to afford a place in this area made her leery.

She found the address and pulled into a parking lot. Right in front of her there was a small eatery with benches for outdoor eating. She pulled her car to the left where the empty furniture store stood. The rest of the area lay vacant.

Lori emerged from her car and came toward Wendy. Lori dressed in a suit, looking very business-like. The two women acknowledged each other and turned to scrutinize the building.

"What do ya think, Wendy?"

"From the outside, it looks wonderful. I like the shingled roof, but what's it like inside?"

"Why don't we go see."

Lori unlocked the door and they both entered. They moved around to check out the inside.

The entire interior was left a mess with discarded items left on the ground including parts of a broken table. Damaged walls were obvious where hanging items or shelves for displays might have been. The very long rectangle shape impressed Wendy. They stepped to the closest end, near the entrance, where Wendy saw an office with a public bathroom sign to the side of it. She liked the fair size office. A counter in front of the office allowed room for a register, and anything else she might need. They ambled to the other end of the building and looked around, just empty space. Moving to the middle of the building they needed to step over some crushed asphalt that needed replacing.

"Well, Wendy?"

Wendy raised her hands and turned around indicating the whole area where she stood. "I love it. It has wonderful possibilities. I can already picture some of what I want to do here." She looked around the ground. "I can also see it needs a lot of work." She stared up at the concrete walls. "Some of the walls need to be repaired, definitely a new paint job, and a lot of clean up from all the junk lying around. I'll need more light…to wake up the place. I think a glass ceiling might be great, lots of light with a lattice covering below, so the sun doesn't burn the plants. But I love its location. I don't think you need to look any further; I'll take it. Well…if I can afford it. How much?"

Lori opened the folder she carried, "$65,000."

"Ouch! Do you think you could get the price down? I mean it needs lots of repairs."

"I'll see what I can do. I'll let you know ASAP."

"Thanks, Lori. You done good."

They laughed, locked up, and left.

As soon as Wendy returned home she made a scale drawing so she could see where everything might fit. Although she didn't own the place yet, she wanted to see the proportional drawings anyway. Just maybe her passion for a shade plant nursery would become a reality. Wendy knew she possessed the knowledge to do this. She learned a great deal about gardening from her mother, her father, and cousin, not to mention all the research about different plants and the trial and error in her own garden and in the greenhouse. If she could make this happen, she knew her life would move on.

She had just sat down at her desk when Cindy called.

"Hey, what's doin'?"

"I just checked out a building for the nursery. I like it. Lori's looking into a reduced price."

"Far Out! Why don't you come over, sit by the pool and tell me all about it?"

"It's sixty degrees outside, why are you sitting by the pool?"

"Because it's where all the guys are. I love to look at them and we can relax out there."

"You are the same man hungry woman I've always known. Okay, I can use the relaxation. How 'bout in an hour?"

"You live fifteen minutes from me. Why does it take an hour to get here?"

"My sitting at my desk to make a scale drawing of the building. See ya in an hour."

"Fine, an hour it is."

She used a quarter inch to a foot as the scale. She scrunched up her face as she concentrated. Twenty minutes later her eyes sparkled as she finished the outline. She drew in the office and bathroom and made a shape to indicate the pond and stream area. Wendy looked at her sketch, encouraged by what she saw.

In her bedroom, Wendy changed into a wool ribbed turtleneck sweater and corduroy pants. Before leaving she made an important phone call to her workplace. She grabbed her black wool coat and headed for Cindy's singles only complex.

She couldn't believe there were so many people outside in such cold weather. Wendy found Cindy on a chaise lounge near the pool and joined her on the edge of it.

"Glad you made it," Cindy mused.

Wendy smiled as she gave her opening comment. "I quit my job,"

Cindy sat straight. "Oh shit. When did this happen?"

"Just before I came here," Wendy sat proud.

Cindy sat back. "You quit before you even have a building? Doesn't that worry you?"

"Nope, I'm feeling great."

"I sure hope you're doing the right thing."

"I have no doubt that I am, and now without the frustrating job, a lot of stress is off my shoulders. I've been waiting for an opportunity to leave, but there weren't any until now. For the nursery, I'll need to deal with paperwork, payments, and all kinds of stuff, but my accountant, Howard, can handle most of it. I'll need to find someone else to deal with the areas he doesn't do."

Ignoring Wendy's comments, "Look at the guy in the dark trunks," Cindy said nodding in his direction.

Cindy's obsession with men was the main reason she rented in this singles' only complex. "So?"

"Isn't he groovy?" Cindy asked, as she pulled her sunglasses down from her eyes so he might see her checking him out. "What a great body, damn wish he hadn't put on a sweatshirt."

"He looks like a lot of other guys, so macho. Is there anyone here who talks about anything, but himself? I mean all the times I've been here the guys all seem to have the same M.O. They are all about themselves, what they want, what their interests are…selfish men. They rarely ask questions about you and the questions they do ask are mundane."

"You think they're all phonies, don't you?"

Wendy shrugged.

"Did it ever occur to you they're just nervous and don't know what to say, any more than you do?"

Wendy looked dubious. "You might be right, but there's never a chance to find out since most of them come on so strong. I've heard everything here again and again. They laugh constantly or are foul-mouthed, or brag about some accomplishments they've achieved."

"Hey, why are you so critical? I thought you didn't like criticism from others. The same goes for you dishing it out. You know, you can be foul-mouthed too. Where are you coming from? Honestly, you've become more of a prude in the last year than I ever thought possible. And, before you get defensive, keep in mind I've known you for a long time, so I have perspective."

Wendy opened her eyes wide, and her face contorted. "Okay, you're right, I shouldn't be critical but maybe I'm just more mature than those guys and I want a relationship with substance because I sure didn't find it with Scott."

"Why don't you give men a chance?"

"I did with Ron and look what happened. He abruptly left me."

"He doesn't mean every guy will be the same. Ask them questions so you can get to know them."

"A chance, huh?"

"Yes! There are cool cats out there."

Wendy turned to look at some guys nearby and considered what Cindy said. Cindy was right about one thing Wendy wasn't much interested in dating since she got burned by Ron's decision to leave shortly after they started to date and so soon after her breakup with Scott. Wendy didn't want to be hurt anymore. Her interest in guys had waned. All her energy went into her garden, greenhouse and thoughts of how to leave her job and find what she wanted in a new life. And now, her search ended. The plans for the nursery will fill her time.

"Okay. You're right." Wendy admitted. "I should give guys a chance, but not 'til I'm done with the nursery. I have too much going on right now."

"Okay. I'm cool with that."

CHAPTER 4

AFTER A WHILE CINDY WENT TO HER APARTMENT and showered while Wendy went to her car and brought up a change of clothes. After her shower Wendy dressed in a blue wool sweater with black pants and a matching black jacket, a favorite pantsuit. Wendy came into Cindy's living room from the bathroom, ready to go.

Cindy eyed Wendy's outfit. "Have you noticed your clothes compared to those at Hoffman's?"

"Not really. Why should I pay attention to what they wear? For crying out loud, I worked with all different styles of clothes and mine are fine."

"Yeah, but at Hoffman's your clothes are...well, dorky. They're just so business like," Cindy advised.

"They're nice and they're comfortable. I don't think they're business-like. I wear pantsuits, lots of people wear pantsuits."

"Okay to work in, but you need to think in terms of what's in style besides business type clothes," Cindy emphasized as they left her apartment. "Different clothes are suitable at different places besides you aren't working at Hammond's anymore."

"That's true, but I'm not out of style. I wear jeans and tops like everyone else."

"Not here and yours are…never mind." Cindy abruptly dropped the subject.

As they walked toward the car, "I don't understand. I never thought my clothes weren't in style, just my taste. Lots of people wear pantsuits," she said, repeating herself.

Cindy looked Wendy in the eye, "You aren't working where you need pantsuits anymore."

Wendy sighed. Cindy's point was well taken. "You're right."

Wendy was eager to go to Hoffman's this time to listen to Brad's fabulous voice and see his captivating face and great body. Her anticipation overwhelmed her. It was late Sunday afternoon, and the place was again packed. Brad began his four to nine gig which Cindy said remained his favorite time to perform. The women once again struggled to the piano bar. He began to sing, "Mariah," from *Paint Your Wagon.* Listening to his voice and watching him ignited something in Wendy she never experienced before. Brad made her wonder what it would be like to have someone like him in her life. Wendy stopped her thoughts, she needed to hold these intense feelings in abeyance.

Cindy remained in front of the piano bar, but Wendy again inched her way to the side. She looked around the room. One man came over and talked to her for a few minutes and walked away. Anyway, too noisy to carry on a conversation.

At Brad's break Cindy went to talk to him. A short time later she came back to Wendy and whispered, "Brad's coming over Tuesday night after he's done here. Tuesdays are usually slow nights. This is so rad! Can you dig it?"

With a huge grin, "I'm very happy for you."

Wendy watched as she moved away. She was thrilled for Cindy because Wendy knew how much she desired Brad, but the news brought a surprise, a tinge of jealousy.

At home later Wendy went to the full-length mirror in her bedroom and took a long look at herself. She shook her head. She didn't have the sexy look Cindy's shapely body did. Cindy's five feet six-inch body was well proportioned. Wendy's physical shape wasn't what could be considered as even good, because of the additional fifteen pounds she carried around. Her waist had a bulge, and no man would want to squeeze her butt. She knew her physical condition needed work. She stared at the long mirror and spoke. 'I need to go on a diet and find some kinds of exercises to do at home. I want to look better and maybe finally be proud of my looks.'

In the bathroom she switched on the light and looked in the mirror. From the vanity drawer she took out a pair of tweezers and thinned the undersides of her thick eyebrows. She smiled at the difference it made. She nodded, as she dropped the tweezers back into the drawer. In her bedroom, she got into her flannel PJs, flipped back the bedspread and fell into bed.

Her mind swirled as she imagined Brad in her head. Years ago, she used to dream of someone like Brad although she never thought anyone that looked like him would be interested in her. But being around him made her realize she wanted to improve herself and find a way to feel good about who she was. Maybe she'd also come out of her straight-laced shell and be more confident in herself. If nothing else Brad motivated her.

All these ideas reminded her about how good-looking Scott was. He was 5'10' with a lean build and large brown eyes. She used to admire his build and eyes. His change in behavior made his good qualities unimportant. Brad was an exceptional looking man with a great talent. Wendy wondered what Brad was really like, what his interests were, his likes and dislikes. She shook those thoughts away and closed her eyes.

The next day Wendy went to the grocery store and found food more dietetic. She cut out red meat completely, too much fat on it. Instead of buying the Oreo cookies she loved she bought fruit, vegetables and fish. No more soda either, from now on water, tea or coffee without sugar.

Wednesday night Cindy called and started to relate, in more graphic detail than necessary, her evening with Brad. Wendy's jealousy allowed only so much, but she told Cindy how happy she was for her.

A week into March Wendy made a follow up appointment with Dr. Lewis. She wanted to see Dr. Lewis because there was no one else she could talk to about Brad and her increasing obsession with him. She certainly couldn't talk to Cindy. Once greetings were exchanged, they took seats across from each other.

"So," Dr. Lewis started, "I haven't seen you in a while, how have things been?"

"I've been busy. I quit my job and put in a bid for a building in Santa Monica to start an indoor plant nursery. I'm waiting to hear if I got it."

"Wow! What great new beginnings for you."

"Thanks. I'm very excited. I hope to know if my bid was accepted in a few days."

"You seem very different from the last time we spoke. You're happy."

Suddenly Wendy couldn't stop talking. "Well, there's been some new activity socially. My girlfriend, Cindy, introduced me to a bar and restaurant on the Goodman Canal in Venice called Hoffman's.

The singer who plays the guitar intrigues me. His name is Brad. He and Cindy have started to see each other. When I first met him, everything about him impressed me…his voice, his smile, his…well, just about everything, but now I wish I could know him better. I can't stop thinking about him."

"You mean you want to date him?"

"Not sure that's the right term. From what I've observed he has a number of women he sees so I'm not sure dating works for him. My problem, of course, is he has no interest in me. I know I'm not his type and of course there's Cindy. I just don't know what to do about my feelings, they're so mixed up and I'd never do anything to hurt Cindy."

"Not his type, what does that mean?"

Wendy hesitated, not sure how to answer the question. "Well, the women he flirts with between songs and on his breaks are very… well, sexy and pretty."

"We'll come back to that, but right now, have you told Cindy how you feel about him?"

"Oh God, no…I can't say anything to her." The words tumbled out. "I'm confused about how I feel toward him. I can't seem to stop my desire for him. I've even gone on a diet to lose some weight, hoping I'd look more desirable. I want to lose weight for me too. I know now I ignored myself for too long."

"You don't feel sexy or pretty?"

"Well, I've never seen myself as sexy. Scott loved me because I was fun when I got silly during a discussion or activity. He said I was easy to be with, and he used to also say because 'you're so cute.'"

"These feelings for Brad, have you ever felt this way about another man, besides your husband?"

Wendy averted her eyes for a second and looked back at Dr. Lewis. "Not really, and I have to admit, I'm not particularly proud of them. Like I said I'd never do anything to hurt Cindy, and since he isn't interested there's no issue." Wendy clasped her hands together in her lap. "I think I shouldn't go to Hoffman's, only I'm not sure how to explain it to Cindy. And, I really don't want to stop, even though I should." She put her head down, shook it, and looked up. "I know this is crazy."

"You're tense, take a deep breath."

Wendy sat back, inhaled deeply and exhaled.

"It seems you're at a standstill. What I'm curious about is why you are on a diet because of Brad. You didn't want to go on a diet before because you wanted to lose weight for your husband, or for your health, is that right?"

"I lost weight once but put it right back on. I started to think about a diet because of Hoffman's. Cindy talked to me about my clothes and how differently I dressed from people at Hoffman's, and she was right. People there are more 'in' looking and now I envy them. I never thought about a change in my clothes style before this, but I'm no longer in the 'business world,' so why not dress differently? I want to fit in at Hoffman's." It was hard for Wendy to believe all the new ideas popping out of her mouth. "But I'm willing to explore these other possibilities."

"You have a lot to think about. Maybe also explore more deeply… write down all that's in your head. It might help you better understand yourself. For example, what would happen if Brad became interested in you? What about the other women you think he sees how does that make you feel? You need to know what you want from a relationship with this man, and how it would impact you. Will you give up your friendship with Cindy if you and Brad started a relationship, or will you see him behind Cindy's back? I ask these questions because I think you need to know all possibilities and how any decision might affect your life."

"You're right. It's just so complicated. Thank you, you've given me a lot to think about."

"I appreciate this is difficult, but you've started a whole new life for yourself. And, once you start to work on the nursery, you'll be busy."

"I know. I need to look at the whole picture more logically and try to keep my emotions intact."

"I understand your confusion, but good friendships are hard to come by. It might be a good idea to think seriously about what could happen if Brad took an interest in you. And I am repeating this, but think about Brad's other relationships, the other women you referred to. Will you be comfortable in a situation of that sort?"

Wendy didn't want to do anything she would regret. "I do have a lot to sort through, thanks again."

They said their good-byes and Wendy left. As she headed to her car, she mulled over the need to go deeper into her thoughts and emotions. Wendy knew an earnest effort was necessary to understand what she wanted and how she was beginning to see herself in a different way with a different life. All these new thoughts were mind boggling. She was glad she kept the appointment.

CHAPTER 5

FRIDAY LORI CALLED. THE SELLER OF THE BUILDING agreed to go down five thousand dollars, and Wendy agreed to the counteroffer. They agreed on a short thirty-day escrow. Wendy couldn't wait to begin work on her nursery.

Wendy knew Cindy wasn't going to Hoffman's Friday night as out of town family were visiting her. Wendy went back and forth about going anyway. 'I want to go so why not?' She wanted to get to know Brad. If nothing else she wanted to be his friend, such a different kind of man she'd ever known. She wanted to be around him and listen to how he talked to people. Maybe he'd mention what he did during his down time.

There wasn't a big crowd when she arrived, and she could sit at the piano bar. Brad smiled at her...she returned the smile. The waitress came over, took her order and returned with a glass of Chablis. While Brad sang, Wendy took the cocktail napkin from under her drink and wrote, "You have a wonderful voice," and requested the song, "Solitary Man," a great song by Neil Diamond. She signed it in case he forgot her name. As he finished his song, she handed him the napkin and put a dollar into his tip jar.

He nodded at the note, "Good song choice." He changed the music on his stand in front of him and began the song.

He put her in an ecstatic mood. When he finished singing Wendy mouthed, "Thank you."

Wendy drove home thrilled about her time with Brad and how he made her feel so welcome. She liked fitting in. She never thought she'd like the bar scene, but at Hoffman's she did.

Wendy spent the next three weeks in her own garden while waiting for escrow to close. She needed to get it up to speed for the season, so she could spend most of her time at the nursery. By the middle of April flowers exploded everywhere.

At night she worked on the design for the interior of the nursery. She drew her idea for a gazebo in the middle of the space, splitting the two concrete walkways around the nursery. She pictured how hanging plants might look inside the gazebo.

When escrow closed, and the papers were signed, Wendy got the keys from Lori. She immediately drove to the building, to her nursery.

As she parked the car, she realized she needed to decide on a name for her new business. Several names came to mind, but they weren't quite right. She let go of her thoughts and stood by the car looking at the building in front of her. She wasn't sure what kind of finished look she wanted for it. But forest green might be appropriate, and around the windows and over the door a cocoa color. The trim shape over the cocoa and on the two front windows would look like vines.

She moved away from the car and stood in front of the building for a moment and took a deep breath. She stepped forward and unlocked the door. At the counter she put down her purse and stood in the middle of the empty building. With her hands on her hips and a critical eye, she surveyed the space. The walls needed to be a pale green or maybe beige, allowing the dark green leaves of most plants to stand out. She could picture the pond area, not quite in the middle of the room, a little off center like her sketch. She sauntered around the building. She'd place small trees and shrubs around different areas so you couldn't see everything at once. People would have to move around the trees and shrubs on bark side paths to see what plants were hidden behind them. She headed down to the office. It needed a little work, but the bathroom looked gross.

As she stood by the door, she again looked around the building. Inspired by what she imagined, she left with her mind spinning with ideas. She knew a whole new world awaited her.

She needed to learn about running the business. She'd call Jim, her dad's partner in their electronics company. She knew he would help. Wendy also knew more paperwork lay ahead. She needed to find out where she could order supplies, plants, do price inventories, and she didn't know what else might be needed.

When Wendy arrived home, she called her cousin Jake. She knew he'd want to know about her new endeavor. Although twelve years older than Wendy he had always been like a big brother to her. Although divorced with a son teaching at the University of California at Berkeley, he enjoyed his life. The one person she went to when her mom died, Jake. Her dad had his own issues.

Jake liked gardening and when Wendy bought or planted something new he stopped by to see about new happenings in the greenhouse and outside of it. After her dad died a few years ago Jake remained there for her.

"Jake, I wanted to tell you I bought a building in Santa Monica and I'm going to turn it into an indoor shade plant nursery."

"That's wonderful, Wendy. What a marvelous idea, something you love to do. You were so excited to plant the ficus tree in your backyard, so you could have more shade, now you can have a whole building with shade. I'm thrilled for you."

"Thanks. I'm thrilled too."

"I can tell from your voice. You will let me know if you need any help, right?"

"Yes, thank you, but I think I'll have it covered with my friends."

"Okay but keep me posted about its progress and for sure let me know when it opens, and I'll be there in no time."

"I will, thanks."

"Your folks would be so happy for you."

"I think so. I'll call you."

"Good. Bye, dear."

Jake's enthusiasm added to the thrill of her moving on. Having his support was important to her.

She called Cindy to see if she wanted to go to Hoffman's and help her to celebrate the nursery. Cindy said yes. If Wendy needed a distraction, she knew Hoffman's was where she'd go, plus she liked the gaiety and fellowship around her.

Brad was in a good mood. Between songs his banter turned to cute little innuendoes, one directed at Cindy. Over the mic he asked, "How's Maggie today?" To the audience it could be a friend or a dog, but Cindy called a rag doll she kept on her bed, Maggie. Cindy laughed and Wendy pretended she didn't have any idea what the conversation involved, but of course, he knew she knew.

During his next break Brad circulated around the room. Girls loved to hang on him. He never stopped to talk to Wendy, but she felt relief because she had no idea what she'd say anyway. Brad and Cindy talked before he returned for another set.

Cindy whispered to Wendy, "I'm going to Brad's tomorrow."

Wendy and Cindy exchanged smiles, and then Wendy looked away as if something caught her eye, but really, she turned to hide her jealous feelings.

At home Wendy dropped onto the sofa, not particularly proud of her obsessed thoughts. She was completely taken with Brad, not just his voice, but his great body, his face, his smile, and his disposition. She still didn't know much about Brad, but she knew she loved to be around him. How could she stop her feelings? He was the man she wished she could be with...strong, handsome, and caring. She admired his happy and friendly personality.

It was a pleasant April day as Wendy and Cindy again sat poolside at Cindy's. "His house is primo. I mean, it's really something else. It's in Pacific Palisades and overlooks Pacific Coast Highway and the beach. The house is set back a bit from a cliff and you can see the ocean for miles out. When you walk out of his living room there's a patio. I'm not kidding...it's outta sight. Standing there with a cocktail...so romantic, like being in a movie. The house has lots of feminine touches. I guess he left things as memories of his mother who, of course, owned the house with his dad. His folks were killed in a car accident four years ago, really sad." Wendy frowned. Cindy rambled on, "We ate chips and dip and went skinny dipping in the pool behind the house. He is so perfect. His body is just like you imagine..."

Cindy's description aroused Wendy. "Cindy," Wendy interrupted, "Glad it was a great day."

"Hey, how'd you like to go see it, well the outside?"

Wendy sounded casual as she hid her true feelings, "Well, it certainly sounds intriguing and wonderful."

"Great, might be a fun outing and a beautiful drive, an escape. Okay, we'll have to find a date."

"Well, let me know and I'll find the time. I'll need a break from my nursery work." Wendy turned away as her face flushed. What a treat, a way to feel a stronger connection to Brad.

"The two stayed by the pool for a while longer, until they went up to Cindy's to shower and dress. They grabbed dinner. Cindy did make a few more comments about Brad, but nothing to do with her time at his house.

As they finished Cindy asked, "So, I'll see ya at Hoffman's?"

"Nah, think I'll head home."

"Okay, be cool. I'll let you know if you miss anything."

Wendy smiled and they went their separate ways. Wendy wanted time to think about Cindy's idea of going to see Brad's house. Wendy glowed when she thought about possibly seeing it. She didn't want to go to Hoffman's because Brad might make another cute innuendo about his time with Cindy. It made Wendy uncomfortable, even though she was happy for Cindy.

CHAPTER 6

WENDY SAT AT HER DESK AND WROTE DOWN some ideas for the name of the nursery. After mulling it over, the one that stood out, The Shade House. It kind of said it all. The next day she made phone calls about the lights and air conditioning. The old and noisy air conditioner needed to be replaced. She also talked to the attorney, Bob, she hired on recommendation from Cindy's brother. Wendy knew the importance of having Bob go through the necessary paperwork to make sure everything was done legally and correctly. She called some friends to see if they were willing to help her with the renovation. They belonged to the garden club Wendy attended when she could. The people she called were all enthusiastic about the opportunity to be there for her. They were always wonderful friends.

Wendy finally called Jim, her dad's partner. He made suggestions about starting up a business. He mailed the list of suggestions, along with a few other thoughts about keeping the business thriving.

The first project was cleaning the place up, especially getting rid of old debris and junk left behind by the previous owners. Some of the chipped concrete on the walls were fixed. One of the next jobs included painting the inside. The color Wendy picked out, a very pale green, gave a perfect look as the background allowed for the plants to stand out.

She enjoyed the great camaraderie with her group of friends. Carol, Judy and Mary Ann, from the gardening club, were very hard workers and were there almost every day. A few guys from the garden club also came several times and were very helpful with the heavier projects. Other members came once in a while, and she was thrilled to have them too. Wendy ordered pizza and Chinese food for lunches. It took three days to finish all the painting. When completed, Wendy hired a handyman she knew. He built the pond and stream of naturally colored concrete and on the outside were attached rocks of varying sizes and shapes. At one end of the pond a waterfall fell, and a stream flowed down and recycled back up to the waterfall.

Across from the pond Wendy watched as the handyman finished a three-foot high wooden planter to be used to transplant plants when customers bought them and wanted them placed in something other than the green plastic pots they came in. The office and bathroom were updated, and a new six-foot-long front counter was installed.

The glass roof she ordered would open and close, depending on the weather of course. Just below the roof a white lattice cover was going to be inserted to block out the strong sun. If there were no hitches and everyone continued to help, she expected the grand opening to be in two months, maybe less.

After an exhausting day at the nursery Wendy relaxed at home, ate dinner, cleaned up and changed into a pair of navy-blue slacks and tucked in a beige blouse she rarely wore. She finished it off with a navy belt. She looked in the mirror definitely a more casual look than her business attire and a little more in-style, a better fit for Hoffman's.

Of all the days at Hoffman's, Wendy thoroughly enjoyed Sundays, well the few she'd been to. The upbeat crowd moved about with lots of conversations and laughter. People seemed so laid back.

Cindy and Wendy worked their way up front, and Cindy grabbed a seat at the piano bar as a man left. Wendy moved to the side being uncomfortable with the encroachment of so many people in front. Brad paid a lot of attention to Cindy as well as another woman near Wendy.

"You don't talk much, do you?" a man asked as he appeared next to Wendy.

Wendy turned and found herself face-to-face with a very friendly smile. "Yes, I do, but it's pretty hard to talk in here."

"That's true."

Wendy turned to watch Brad.

"My name is Marty."

She turned back to him. "Hi, I'm Wendy."

They both watched Brad.

Marty crossed his arms. "He has a good voice."

"He sure does."

Marty leaned into Wendy. "I must admit when he sings ballads his voice makes me feel pretty relaxed. His fast songs are great fun."

"I agree."

Marty seemed to appreciate Brad's talent.

Brad started a break. "Could I interest you in talking on the deck?"

Wendy liked his attitude and his appreciation of Brad. He was about five foot six inches and nice looking with brown, curly hair, dark brown eyes and a slender build. "Okay."

They walked out to the deck surrounded by plexiglass to keep people safe. They stared down at the dark waters of the Goodman Canal.

"I've seen you here before. You're a friend of Cindy's, right?"

"Yes, how did you know?"

"I pay attention. No, seriously, I talked to her briefly a couple of times. Cindy and Brad have a thing goin', huh?"

Before she could tell him, it wasn't anything she'd talk about, he said, "You come here to keep her company, right?"

"Actually, I do, and I like the music." Wendy thought Marty looked out of place on a Sunday with a blue suit, white shirt, and tie. He went on to tell her he graduated from Stanford Law School and had lived in West Los Angeles for the past three years. Wendy told him she went to UCLA and lived in Mar Vista.

"I know I look a bit odd for this place," he said as he fiddled with his tie, "but I just came from a business meeting.

"A business meeting on a Sunday?"

"Unfortunately, yes. I work for Hilstrom Corporation and, once in a while, one of the big wigs from New York comes to town and we work around his schedule."

"That makes sense. What's Hilstrom Corporation?"

"It builds and runs restaurants around the country."

Wendy wasn't sure how to continue the conversation. "Finally, is it interesting work?"

"It is. I enjoy the legal end."

"You're their lawyer?"

"Well, one of them, they have quite a few."

A breeze came up. "I'm sorry. Could we go back inside? It's getting chilly."

They returned from the observation deck and moved toward the piano bar. "Thought you two forgot us," Brad announced over the microphone. Marty smiled at Brad and glanced at Wendy. She tried hard to hide her embarrassment at being spotlighted. Seemed like Brad knew Marty, or he wouldn't have said anything. It was the first time Brad had acknowledged her out loud. Wendy liked the attention, even though uncomfortable with it.

Wendy enjoyed visiting with Marty. Before he left, Marty asked for her phone number and with a flushed face she gave it to him. What attracted him to her she had no idea, but quite a compliment from such a nice-looking guy.

The next day Wendy received the list from Jim about ideas of how to manage the business and make it a success. First on the list, keep track of inventory so she'd know when to re-order. Jim told her she needed to contact her accountant periodically to determine how much money she had to work with. She needed to figure out where were the best areas in the nursery to invest the most money. She immediately considered the pond and stream. The gazebo came to mind too.

Two days later Wendy went to the appointment she made with Dr. Lewis. She wanted to talk about the nursery and Marty.

"Every day I go in something new is being worked on. The concrete coloring, the pathway rocks, and the finished façade in the front looks great."

"That's wonderful. What are you calling it?"

"The Shade House."

"That's certainly appropriate. You must be under a lot of pressure to get it ready."

"I am, but it satisfies me to watch it take shape."

"Nice things are happening for you. It's good to hear."

"Thanks." Wendy hesitated but decided in this session she'd share something more. "I wanted to talk to you about…well, criticism."

"What about it?" Dr. Lewis asked.

Wendy took a deep breath as she tried to relax the knot in the pit of her stomach. "When I first told Cindy about the nursery, she became critical of my taking it on. She meant it to be helpful, but it bothers me she saw me as unable to handle the responsibility. Criticism has always been difficult for me to deal with. As you know my dad was always critical as well as Scott. With so much happening I want to be able to handle anything coming my way without getting angry."

"What do you see as the issue?"

A thought buzzed in her head. "Well, as a kid, I never felt confident, always afraid of disappointing my parents. They were often critical of my choices. Now, I'd like to find some way to accept criticism and acknowledge, well…maybe I deserved some of it."

"Perhaps it would be helpful to think about whether what is being criticized about you is true, or not. You should be honest with yourself."

"Hmmm…I want to be. To tell the truth, I think I do a fair share of criticizing myself. I guess I need to think about others' viewpoints before I criticize them for things I disagree with."

"Learning to accept peoples' differences is important to all relationships. Your attitude is good."

After a pause Dr. Lewis asked, "Do you still go to hear Brad sing?"

"Oh yes, and each time I go to Hoffman's I want so much to talk to him, but I can't. There's no way I can do it comfortably, mostly because I don't know what to talk to him about."

"It may come to the point where your primary concern is Cindy."

"I know. Cindy went to Brad's house and described a beautiful home overlooking the beach. It thrilled her."

"How did it make you feel?"

"I was happy for her, but I wished it was me."

"I would be remiss if I didn't repeat if Brad starts to like you, you're going to find yourself in a difficult position."

"I know. I have been thinking about the list with the pros and cons of everything like you suggested. I'd never do anything to hurt Cindy, so Brad may remain only a vision to see and hear. I do have something else to tell you."

"What is it?"

It's about a man I met at Hoffman's. His name's Marty. We talked for a while on the deck just outside of Hoffman's, a quiet place to talk without music and all the people rambling about…anyway, he seems very nice. He took my phone number."

"Well, that's wonderful. How do you feel about him?"

"I'm not sure. He was interested in talking to me and he asked for my phone number so there must have been something he liked about me. He's an attorney for a large corporation called Hilstrom."

"I'm not sure why you made the comment about something he liked about you."

"Well, I know it isn't my figure, so I'm curious what he saw in me."

"You have good qualities. Do you think about those?"

She shrugged, "Not really."

"It might be a good idea to give them some thought. Maybe Marty will work out for you." The doctor looked at the clock next to her. "Sorry, our time's up. You have some good things going for you." Dr. Lewis stood.

Wendy did the same and moved toward the door. "I know. I'll concentrate on those."

"Hope you have a good week."

"Thank you."

Wendy headed home thinking about what Dr. Lewis said about her good qualities. She never really gave them much thought. All she knew for sure, she was a caring person. Marty's interest in her made her want to understand what interested him in her.

CHAPTER 7

THE NEXT MORNING WENDY HEADED TO THE Shade House. The workers' installation of the glass roof and the lattice to be placed just below the glass appeared ready. Carol and Mary Ann worked on stacking some newly arrived ceramic pots.

Carol met Wendy in the center of the nursery.

"It's so rad," Carol said. "I feel like I'm in a forest and I don't just mean the forest area, I mean all of it. I worked at a nursery when I lived in Sacramento and I've been gardening for years so I've seen a lot of nurseries, but none compares to the naturalness of yours."

"You have helped make it look good, along with Mary Ann, Judy and others." Wendy placed her hands on Carol's shoulders. "I couldn't have done it without you guys. I can't thank you enough."

"You're welcome. We loved to help."

"I didn't know you were experienced at gardening."

"Yes, I love it a lot. I have house plants in my apartment, but wish I had a balcony for more plants."

"I can understand your desire." Wendy hesitated, "I remember you said you were between jobs, is that right?"

"Yes, I was let go about a month ago."

"I'm sorry to hear that." Without hesitation, "Would you be interested in working here?"

"Really?"

"I'd love to have you help out."

Without a moment's thought, she blurted out, "I accept your offer."

Wendy smiled. "Wait, you don't even know the wage."

"I'm sure it will be fair."

"Thanks, Carol." Wendy leaned forward and gave her a hug.

Carol went back to finish the pot area with Mary Ann.

It excited Wendy to have Carol onboard.

Later that day Wendy toured the nursery, starting at the right concrete walkway near the register until it curved around taking her to the other side of the walkway and back to the register area. On the way she checked the many bark paths leading inside the walkway. Everything would be finished tomorrow, and she couldn't wait to be there alone and enjoy the work she wanted to do. She'd find just the right places for the plants sitting around, including the hanging ones.

Carol and Mary Ann finished the potting area. Below a long shelf hung Wendy's hand tools--clippers and several trowels and two pair of gloves. A couple of bags of potting soil, oak leaf mold, bark, and perlite were on the floor next to the area.

The space at the far end, near the emergency exit, was the forest area. To create the look she wanted she included many ferns. A few tall plants were toward the back of the area with some shorter plants in front of them. She'd add and change plants as new ideas came to her.

In the evening Wendy was in the living room on her hands and knees doing stretching exercises when the phone rang. She flopped onto the floor, took a calming breath and crawled the short distance to the phone.

"Hello."

"Hi, it's Marty."

Wendy lifted herself up and settled into a chair. "Hi."

"How's it going?"

"Very well, the nursery is close to being finished."

"Wonderful. May I interest you in going to dinner tomorrow night?"

Although apprehensive about dating again, Wendy felt she should give him a chance. "Yes, I'd like to, thank you." She gave him her address.

"I'll see you at 7:00, okay."

"Okay."

After they hung up, she surprised herself for accepting his offer so readily. She worried about being hurt again, but she needed to move forward. Finally, she shrugged and went back to her exercising.

The next afternoon Wendy scanned through books and old magazines about gardening. She found some new ideas using tall shrubs and trees. She could borrow the ideas, but on a smaller scale, with dwarf trees and shrubs. She dog-eared the pages.

An hour later she showered. At the mirror, she put on eyeliner, something she rarely used, then mascara, and some pressed powder to her face. She decided to wear a pair of black cotton slacks with a short sleeved burgundy top tucked in with a gold-colored belt. Around her neck, and down the top, hung a long gold chain. She looked at herself in the full-length mirror, gave a sly grin, and grabbed a black jacket, setting it with her purse in the living room.

There were a few minutes before Marty's arrival, so she went to her study to look at the detailed sketch of the nursery. Ideas about hanging items and rustic signs interested her. The doorbell rang. She dropped the book and rushed to the door but stopped and cringed as she wondered how to be comfortable with a new man in her life.

After opening the door, Marty greeted her with a big smile. He helped her with her jacket. They headed to The Blue Whale, one of Hilstrom's restaurants.

They sat in a quiet booth and studied the menus. The waiter brought water, and Wendy ordered white wine, Marty red. She told him about the nursery. It easily started the conversation.

"Your nursery sounds very cool. Maybe I can stop by and see it."

"Of course."

"I have to admit my place could use some greenery or something. I guess a few plants inside might be a good idea."

"I'm sure plants will be a cheerful addition." Wendy tried to control the angst she was experiencing. "Where are you from?"

He waited while the waiter set their drinks down and took their orders. "I'm from New York, but I've been on the coast about ten years."

"Where's your office?"

"Beverly Hills."

"How nice."

"Yes, Hilstrom hired me full time about three years ago, so I closed my own office in Culver City, and now I work out of Hilstrom's building."

"What kind of cases do you handle?" Wendy stopped. "I'm sorry, am I asking too many questions?" She felt uncomfortable trying to carry on a conversation with a man she didn't really know.

"No, of course not. We didn't have much time to talk at Hoffman's, but maybe now we can get to know each other better," he said with a deep smile.

Awkward was how she saw herself. "I'd like that," she said returning a smile.

"On the side I do volunteering as a legal aid. I like my volunteer work. It can be a challenge, but also it keeps me on my toes."

"That all sounds wonderful. Volunteering is important."

Wendy explained the commitment to her causes. "Remember during the Viet Nam War when thousands of people protested and marched against it, trying to make a difference in the world?"

He nodded.

"I was one of them. Thank goodness for the peace talks that are now on going. There is still so much political and social unrest. I want to help bring equality and fairness to everyone, including women. Unfortunately, there are opponents to a lot of this, so protests against and for continue."

"Wow, you're quite an activist."

"I used to be."

"Used to be? Why'd you stop?"

"When I started dating my now estranged husband, he wanted me to spend the time with him," she cringed as she answered. "I'm sorry. I didn't mean to talk about him."

"No, it's fine, really."

She liked his response. Her activism was a good quality. That reminded her she should add it to her list. Later she'd think about what other good qualities she possessed things that might help her appreciate herself more.

"Anyway, I played a small role during the sixties in the women's movement. I worked with a group of women who made banners and signs. We also designed handouts and xeroxed them so we could pass them out on street corners. I also heard Gloria Steinem speak…so inspirational."

"She definitely made a headway with the women's movement. I admire your concerns for others," Marty complimented.

"Thanks, I haven't done anything for a long time, but I'm glad I accomplished something."

When they finished their dinners, Marty drove them to the Santa Monica Pier where they sauntered out to the end, as the soft, night breeze passed by them. Leaning against the railing they looked out at the Pacific Ocean, admiring the reflection of the moon off it.

"This is very nice," Marty said as he turned toward her.

"It is. I like to see places of serenity and this ocean view is certainly one of them."

They watched for a while until he clasped her hand. With admiring eyes, she looked up at him as they walked back along the pier to where they started.

Wendy saw characteristics she admired in Marty... his romantic spirit, his good attitude and interests they shared. She liked the way he was so laid back. Marty showed no pretense, he seemed like a regular guy. At least she knew he was against the Viet Nam War. She needed to know his other values. Marty made Wendy remember Scott's lack of interest in being an activist.

They stopped at the carousel and watched as it circled in its charming way. It was beautifully lit, and a calliope played as the carousel turned.

"Shall we head out?" he asked, his voice pulling Wendy out of her pensiveness.

He parked in front of her house.

"I like your enthusiasm and your ambition. They're really great traits," he complimented as they walked to her front door.

"Thanks, Marty. I'd like to hear more about you and your work and what you do for fun."

"I thought I'd go to Hoffman's tomorrow night after work. Will you be there?"

"Yes, I think so."

His eyes met hers. "Good, I'll see you then." He leaned down and gave her a light kiss on the lips which she readily accepted. Happiness danced in her eyes as they smiled at each other.

Marty headed back to his car as Wendy stepped into her house. Once inside she reflected about how genuine he seemed. She mulled over Ron and how much she liked him, and how he quickly moved away, and, of course, Scott and his dismissal of her. She hoped Marty wouldn't be like either of those men.

CHAPTER 8

WENDY ENJOYED WALKING THE ALMOST completed nursery, impressed by what she saw. As she wandered the paths, she took notes where small trees and shrubs might fit.

She made a good choice having the main concrete path move around the nursery. The path split near the entrance and went to the right or to the left with the gazebo between them. Each path meandered around where you could step into bark side paths to look at the plants.

Going around to the cash register behind the counter she looked to make sure everything was in order. The installed phone looked great on the counter and all lights were placed as she directed them. The finished plumping ended the major needs.

All the labor and drudgery finished around two. She talked to the workers for a while. When the conversation finished, they went to the door where they handed Wendy the key. She followed them out and thanked them again for all their hard work. They nodded, smiled, and left. Wendy turned and studied the vine trim around the door. Smiling and acknowledging the welcoming look, she knew the hard work paid off and the frenzy ended.

She returned inside and moved next to the counter where eight large plants were on the ground. She placed them onto a wooden cart. She rolled it around the nursery and stopped when she found places for each one of them. She spent almost two hours moving plants around and finally went to her office to unwind. Another delivery of plants was expected. She nibbled on a bologna sandwich she brought. Finally, at five there was a loud banging on the door.

A driver brought six dozen more plants. There were gloxinias and streptocarpus with their beautiful flowers. More ferns, bromeliads, begonias, donkey tails, dracenas, and other shade loving plants, all part of the mix. The driver unloaded the plants inside and left. Wendy started to take the paper plant sleeves off of the six and eight-inch pots. The four-inch plants were in cartons. Standing back, she smiled at the great array of greenery. Temporarily she set them all together around one side of the pond.

Being exhausted she decided tomorrow she'd place them. She took her purse from the office and stood near the door to listen to the waterfall as it gurgled from the top level down into the stream. After another look around, she turned off the lights and went outside. She locked up and again faced The Shade House sign. The capital letters above the door were black and eight inches tall. Below the sign were the wooden ivy pieces that went down from the sides of the door to the bottom. She couldn't wait to see the door lit up when the front lighting was installed tomorrow. She turned toward the street. This property on Santa Monica Blvd. where traffic flowed, and people walked around shopping, she hoped would bring them to this new business.

She took a long rest before she prepared for the visit to Hoffman's. She read her mail, ate a light dinner, took a quick shower, dressed and left.

Hoffman's was its usual noisy place. As Wendy approached the side of the piano bar, she heard Brad announce, "It's a little early but the sun will be up soon," and he sang The Beatles *Here Comes the Sun*.

A woman at the piano bar picked up a wooden shaker and swayed to the music as she played along. The next song, *Delta Dawn*, was rapturous, and the shaker became faster and louder.

Wendy noticed Cindy wasn't there yet, but Wendy smiled as Marty came toward her.

"This place is really jumpin," he stated as he stood next to her.

She laughed. "It sure is. How are you?"

"Great, a good day at work."

"Glad to hear it, me too."

They stood, listened, and watched.

Cindy touched Wendy on the shoulder. "Hi guys. This place is wired." Cindy ordered a drink as the waitress passed by. "So, what's new with you?" she asked Wendy.

"The nursery is almost done. Not long before it opens."

"That's far out."

Just then, Brad started his break. "I need to chitchat with him," Cindy announced and moved away.

Marty looked around. "Everyone seems in a good mood…a lot of happy faces." Without hesitation he asked, "What are you up to for the weekend?"

"Just goin' to finish whatever I can at the nursery."

"Is it okay if I come by and see it?"

"Sure. I'll be there tomorrow about ten until I don't know when, maybe four. Just knock on the door.

"Thanks, I'm looking forward to seeing it."

Wendy couldn't wait to get Marty's opinion on all the work, an objective viewpoint. She excitedly described the nursery layout.

Brad returned from his break and started his next set. Cindy came up beside them, raised her eyebrows and smiled at Wendy. She knew what the look meant.

An hour later Marty walked Wendy to her car. "How about I come tomorrow around four and we could go to dinner after I visit?"

"I'd like that."

Wendy locked up and they went outside. As they said goodnight, they lingered in a long and arousing kiss. She unlocked the car door. Marty opened it and Wendy slipped in. He closed the door. As she drove away, her face lit up when she realized how much she liked Marty.

At home she put on her night gown and got into bed, leaning against the quilted headboard. For whatever reason, after she replayed the evening with Marty, her thoughts flashed to Brad's Pacific Palisade's house. She had been too busy to go see it after Cindy's suggestion, but she could now.

It was a little late, but Wendy called Cindy. There were short hellos and Wendy went on. "I was wondering about your suggestion to see Brad's house. I know I've been busy with getting ready for the nursery opening, but I could use a break and that would be a good getaway if you have time and still want to go." Wendy gave a short laugh. "Maybe I will picture you as you stood there, looking down at the Pacific Ocean with Brad at your side and drink in hand."

"Sure, you don't have to convince me. I've been wanting to drive there and thanks for the reminisce…sweet thought. I'd love for you to see the outside. I guess we could park on the beach side and look up at the patio where it overlooks the ocean. Yeah, I like the idea. When?"

"Sunday, around ten, okay? We could go to lunch afterwards. What do you think?"

"Sounds primo to me."

"Great."

Once off the phone Wendy whirled around and hugged herself, excited about this chance to feel a different kind of closeness to Brad.

The first thing Wendy did when she got to the nursery the next day was take the wooden cart and place two of the heavier plants onto it. The weight made it difficult to lift them onto the cart, but after struggling for a few minutes she was able to drag them on board. She pulled the cart down the paths until she found places for a schefflera and a palm. Wendy returned to put a Norfolk Star Pine and a short fir tree onto the cart. She later placed smaller plants on tall plant stumps so plants could hang down the sides of them. The shorter stumps held non hanging plants. Along the concrete walkway, poles with hooks were installed for a few hanging plants.

She stopped and looked at the entire nursery. Around the inside ledge of the pond, she placed a few small plants. She could see the need to play around with their positions but at the moment she wanted to look at the fuchsias she brought from home. Her mother loved fuchsias and spent years trying to propagate a fuchsia with a blue hue.

"Do you think it will be hard to get the blue," Wendy asked her mom as they worked in the greenhouse."

"Maybe, but I really think a blue toned fuchsia would be ideal for the fuchsia family. I'll keep pollinizing until I've tried everything I can."

Since her mom's death, Wendy tried to accomplish the same goal. She wanted to continue to find a way to make a shade of blue…a tribute to her mother's memory. She set the fuchsias on a shelf above the worktable. She'd work with them tomorrow.

She went to the far end and stared at the forest area. The total space was twenty feet wide by eight feet deep. At this point, the forest section blended into the tropical plants around the area.

The short paths in and out of the concrete were also covered with walk on bark. Next to the paths were a couple of five-foot shrubs. Patrons could move around them to see the other side, like ducking around trees in a forest. In the summer she would have green and yellow hostas, flowering foxgloves and primroses, with more flowering plants. The rest of the year green plants, but also variegated ones for contrast. She stood back about six feet, so she could take it all in. She beamed.

She went to the counter and cleaned up where she put the office supplies: pencils, paper, scratch pads, calculator, and plant tags. A new file cabinet replaced the old rusty one. She made several price charts for the different plant sizes and placed them around the nursery. The trees and big shrubs were marked individually on brightly colored plant tags. The opening loomed close.

CHAPTER 9

WITH SO MUCH MORE TO TALK ABOUT WENDY was downright anxious for her appointment with Dr. Lewis. Dr. Lewis always provided interesting, insightful and helpful comments or asked questions Wendy wouldn't have considered asking herself.

She sat opposite the doctor as usual.

Dr. Lewis' eyes lit up. "Is the nursery open yet?"

"No, but in a week, I hope. Actually, I'm here to talk about Marty. I'm not sure how to deal with him."

"Deal with him? What does that mean?"

"Well, I like him, but I'm apprehensive, afraid he will just be another man to hurt me. I couldn't handle it again."

"Have you gone out with him?"

"Yes, we went for dinner and walked the Santa Monica Pier. We talked a lot about the nursery and his job."

"What did you like about him?"

"He's kind and has a laid back manner making me comfortable to be with him."

Wendy's eyes followed the doctor as she went to the coffee pot, picked it up, and held it out to Wendy.

"Yes, please."

The doctor handed Wendy a mug and returned to her seat with her own mug. Wendy took a sip.

"You are concerned about something that hasn't happened yet. You can protect yourself by not continuing the relationship, but it means you may not find out if he's someone you might want to be involved with."

Wendy set her mug on the table next to her. She sat up listening carefully.

"I know you're afraid of being hurt again, but this is a decision only you can make. Is it worth taking a chance you might be hurt again, or stopping the relationship before it moves forward? Those are the choices I see."

Wendy glanced out the big window behind the doctor's desk and looked back at her. "I know. I guess I wanted you to tell me which is the right choice for me. I know you can't, but what you said makes sense."

"How's the Brad situation?"

"Nothing's changed." But she wanted Brad to care about her, to make her happy, wishful thinking. "Maybe Marty would be the someone to take my mind off Brad." She did not mention her going to see Brad's house.

"Sounds like something to explore. Your thoughts toward Scott now?"

"At the moment I'm confused about whether my marriage to Scott was really for love or the need for security. How can anyone tell the difference? Isn't love feeling secure? And isn't being secure feeling loved."

"Of course, but there are different types of love." The doctor's open hands stretched toward Wendy as she spoke, as if the words were floating to settle in Wendy's lap. "Did you feel secure as a child? By this I mean, did your parents make you feel loved?"

"I think so. As I said, my critical dad made it hard to know how he felt toward me, especially after my mother died. Sometimes, I wasn't sure if he loved me." Wendy had a hollow feeling inside her.

"What about your mom, do you feel she loved you?"

"Oh yes. She tried to come to my defense whenever my dad picked on me. She'd tell him to leave me alone, but he didn't listen. They argued a lot, but she was there for me." Wendy hesitated. "She died when I was twelve, and that made matters worse between my dad and me."

"I can understand. Too much criticism can make you feel insecure. But did you feel your dad loved you?"

She hesitated but nothing came to mind. "I don't know." Wendy tried to remember any times when he made her feel loved, maybe when she was a small child. She looked down at the carpet, and up at the doctor. Nothing came to mind. Wendy shrugged. "I think he did."

"Sometimes parents don't realize how much their criticism can cause problems later on. So, is there a possibility your father's criticism, plus Scott's, made you feel unloved, and this was the reason you wanted the separation. In other words, it wasn't just about his job."

Wendy's arched her eyebrows and gritted her teeth. That revelation shocked her.

The doctor's phone buzzed. "Excuse me." A few seconds later she hung up.

"I'm sorry," Dr. Lewis said. "I have a patient in the emergency room. I know this isn't a good place to stop, but the woman is asking for me. I'll owe you some time."

"I understand."

Once outside Dr. Lewis' door Wendy stressed by the deeper look into criticism and her dad's behavior. Wendy entered the elevator, leaning against the back wall. Tears swelled as a memory filled her head…her dad hitting her mom. Why didn't she remember it until now? The idea of her dad being abusive filled her with indignation. She must have blocked out the repulsive incident. She tried during past years to reconcile with her dad, but he never wanted to talk about the past. His death, a few years ago, left her without the opportunity to clear the air. After leaving the elevator, she stopped, folded her hands and knew she never felt loved by her dad.

Wendy drove straight to the nursery. All the way she obsessed about what she wanted. Would she keep Marty at arm's length emotionally so she wouldn't be hurt? The passionate kiss they shared made her think he truly cared for her, or did he just want to have fun times without deep involvement?

She turned on the lights and the waterfall switch as she entered The Shade House. The completed look made her ecstatic. It was everything Wendy wanted it to be. She watched the water drop into the stream and move through the pond. She roamed around the entire nursery and stopped occasionally to change the position of plants. The pale green walls were a good choice. The plants were prominent.

Her energy surged. The wait for her dream to be completed ended. Wendy picked up the remaining plants sitting on the ground below the pond. Along the inside ledge of the pond, she intermittently placed an array of plants including begonias, streptocarpus, bromeliads, and more ferns. She loved the small red, pink, and white flowers on the different wax begonias. She held up one of the four-inch pink begonias and admired the color against its bronze leaves, finally setting it down. The begonias brought variety to all the green plants, along with the variegated and wavy leaves of the begonias, and the colorful red, gold, and green leafed crotons. Plants on top of the rocks lined the stream and at the head of the waterfall stood one of the colorful crotons.

She moved to the front of the counter. She looked at the start of the two main concrete pathways that went around the nursery. The small white gazebo, built to Wendy's specifications, separated the beginning of the two paths just like she planned. Different hanging plants lined different paths, among them were pothos, donkey tails, fuchsias, all extended from hooks. Her thoughts were stopped by a knock on the door. It had to be Marty and she couldn't wait to hear his opinion of the nursery.

"Hi Marty," she greeted him as she opened the door.

"Hi, I love the outside with the vines, a very woodsy look." As soon as he came inside, he looked around and gasped. "Wow, it's bigger than I thought and beautifully done."

"Thanks, glad you like it. Want to walk around?"

"Sure."

As they made their way around the nursery Marty stopped and asked questions about different plants. They ended up by the waterfall.

He looked at her and asked, "Is this your dream come true?"

Wendy grinned ear to ear. "It is. I have a greenhouse at home, but it isn't big. Since I like plants so much this seemed like an even better way to enjoy them. Now it's done and it's all I imagined and more."

Marty took a long look around. "You're very creative. The place is exceptional, very unique. People will love to come here because it's like an escape from reality."

"What a good way to look at it. That's nice." Her eyes sparkled up at him, and he flashed a big smile.

"May I interest you in an early dinner?"

"Love to."

Wendy grabbed her purse and sweater from the office. She took another look around before she shut off the switches and locked the door behind her.

CHAPTER 10

WENDY LEFT HER CAR IN THE PARKING LOT AND climbed into Marty's new white Camaro. He drove them to The Tiger's Den. The restaurant's entrance was compelling with dark brown velvet walls. They followed the host into the restaurant where the lights were low and the signs on the walls were in French. Hanging pictures included the Eiffel Tower and Parisian city sites. Once seated at a small round table in the center of the room the waiter left them menus and soon returned with water and took their drink orders.

"This is exquisite, Marty," Wendy said as she scanned the room.

"I've always liked it because it's cozy and they have live music in the bar at night."

"Sounds nice."

They looked at the menus and made their decisions.

"I was wondering, and you don't have to answer if you don't want to," Wendy started, "but did you see anything at the nursery you'd add or change? I can take criticism. I want to make it the best it can be." It surprised her when she chose those words, but they just popped out. She relished the idea she could accept his criticism of the nursery.

His eyes widened. "I've never been to an indoor nursery, but yours was impressive. I can't imagine many indoor nurseries look so much like the real outdoors."

"You aren't just saying that, you know, to be kind?"

"No, I tend to tell the truth. That's one thing you'll learn about me. I don't like lies. If I have something to say, I'll come right out with it. Of course, I'll do it without hurting anyone's feelings, at least I hope I wouldn't. Are there other indoor nurseries around here?"

"Regular nurseries have indoor sections, but no, I don't know of any similar to mine." The waiter brought their drinks and took their dinner orders. "I'm glad you told me about the truth being import-ant to you. I feel the same way. Could you tell me some more about yourself?"

"Well, what do you want to know?"

"I don't know, what did you like to do as a kid?"

He laughed. "I played baseball and collected baseball cards. As a Boy Scout I did all the different activities that came with the Scouts. How 'bout you?"

She chuckled, "I was a Girl Scout."

They laughed at their shared interest.

Wendy continued. "I liked to play jacks and pickup sticks. I loved Hop-a-long Cassidy and owned an outfit like his, only it was a skirt and top. I liked to swim in my aunt's pool. She used to call me a fish because I preferred swimming underwater," Wendy proclaimed with a playful smile.

"Hoppy was fun, and how about The Lone Ranger?"

"I forgot about him, never missed it."

She figured she'd shared enough about herself. She leaned her elbows on the table and looked Marty in the eyes. "So, tell me exactly what do you do as Hilstrom's attorney?"

Marty leaned back. "A lot of different things. It's hard to be specific. I just try to keep everything organized and make sure the restaurants all follow the agenda we set down."

The waiter brought their orders, and neither of them spoke for a few minutes as they began to eat.

"You didn't mention how good the food is here," Wendy said as she took another bite of the roasted chicken.

"It is, isn't it?"

As soon as they finished their dinners, Marty surprised her, "Would you like to come to my place for an after dinner drink?"

"I'd love to." Wendy glowed as she thought about this new relationship. At that moment she decided not to worry about what might or might not happen between them. She enjoyed his company and his sharing, something Scott stopped doing.

They drove to his apartment in Brentwood, a very nice area above West Los Angeles.

"Wow! Love your decorating style," she remarked as soon as they stepped inside. "Did you do it yourself?" The living room walls were painted off white with beige carpet and light gold upholstered furniture, the popular Danish Modern style. Light weight wood was used, and the arms of the chairs and sofa were narrow and metal.

"Thanks for the compliment, but no, a woman friend did all the work. I like her tastes. She did a good job."

"Yes, she did." Wendy again looked around.

Marty headed toward a built-in bar on one side of the dining area. "So, what's your pleasure?"

"A screwdriver, please."

"One screwdriver coming right up."

Wendy sank into the sofa. Marty came over, handed her the drink, and sat next to her.

Wanting to know more about Marty she asked, "What do you do for fun?"

"Well, I used to have time for hiking, but not as much anymore. I do love being out in nature."

"Where did you used to hike?" Wendy sipped her drink.

"I loved the trails in the Santa Monica Mountains."

"I'm not sure I've ever thought much about the Santa Monica Mountains unless, unfortunately, a fire happened."

Marty took a swallow of his drink, "What interests you about life?"

"Wow, a philosophical moment." Wendy set her drink down. "Hmmm…people who care about others. That's why I opposed the war. Our soldiers died for a war we shouldn't have been in. I hate war, and I hate hate. Like I said last time, I was thrilled when the January Paris Peace Accord happened."

As she finished her sentence Marty set his drink down on the coffee table. He took her in his arms squeezing her to him with an ardent kiss that lingered. Without speaking he stood, took her hand and she followed as he guided the way to his bedroom.

Wendy stood still.

Marty unbuttoned her blouse and unhooked her bra. They looked at each other, removed the rest of their clothes and crawled onto the bed. When they finished their love making, they slid under the covers.

"That was wonderful, Marty," Wendy whispered as she turned toward him.

"I agree. Your body is enticing. I like how you looked in your slacks and sweater, but you should wear clothes to show your body off more."

The subject shocked her. "You're kidding, like what?"

"Crop tops would look great on you with hot pants."

It surprised her that he found her body attractive because she didn't see it that way yet. She raised her head on her elbow. "That look isn't me."

He sat up, "Why not? You shouldn't be uncomfortable to have people take a lingering look as they admire your body."

She sat and looked at him…he admired her body. "Maybe if I lose some more weight…I'll think about it, but I don't know." She already dropped eight pounds and lost a few inches and looked better, but it wasn't enough. She needed to lose more. "I've never thought about people viewing me in any special way as you're suggesting."

"Well, just something to think about. I'll get our drinks."

Wendy couldn't get over his comment about her body. She blinked and watched him walk away admiring his five foot ten-inch sleek body.

He returned and handed Wendy her screwdriver. "You okay?"

"Yes, but why did you ask me about my clothes?"

"I don't know, it just came to mind. I think I threw you off with the crop top comment."

"Well, I was stunned. A man has never talked about my clothes."

"Not even your husband?"

"Rarely."

"Well, I just want you to know you have a nice figure and should be comfortable showing it off."

"Thanks, Marty."

Wendy took a sip of her screwdriver. It thrilled her that her dieting with exercising was already successful. Marty made her feel desirable and sexy. She'd have to think about changing clothes styles.

After setting Wendy's drink on the nightstand, he gave her a deep passionate kiss, which she eagerly returned.

They fell together on their sides, "This was a great evening," Wendy said as she brushed some hair back from his forehead.

Marty gave her a short kiss. "I thought so too." He shook his head. "I hate to do this, but unfortunately I have an early morning meeting."

They got dressed and Wendy grabbed her purse from the living room. In the bathroom she brushed her hair and put on fresh lipstick. She looked at herself, shook her head and smiled, still surprised at his compliment.

Marty drove her back to her car and opened the door for her. "Thank you for a great time."

As an answer Wendy hugged him and gave him a prolonged goodnight kiss. "Me too," she added as she pulled back.

What a coincidence, on the way home, the second song the radio played was a song by The Carpenters, *We've Only Just Begun*. Wendy took that as a message.

CHAPTER 11

 Wendy reminisced about the night before. Marty's traits and interests were equal to hers. He was fun, gentle, and with a wonderful personality. He also let her say what she wanted without criticizing her. Wendy never received the kind of compliments he gave her. Plus, it pleased her that he appreciated nature, so she knew his enthusiastic response to her nursery was genuine.

The one thing that interested her was why he thought she should change her clothes style…the same idea as Cindy's. She never thought about crop tops and hot pants for herself. The idea of her tummy exposed made her grimace, but maybe she'd consider it with more weight loss.

After breakfast Wendy looked through her closet. Most of her clothes were pretty ordinary, pant suits, slacks and one pair of jeans. She shook her head and closed the closet door. Maybe Marty was right, she should at least check into how she might look in more "in" style clothes.

Wendy leaned back in her comfy chair by the fireplace and closed her eyes as she visualized her completed nursery. She took herself down the paths and saw the variety of plants: tall ones and short ones. It also pleased her about putting plant wall pockets in several places. The pictures of Yosemite and different woodland areas made her smile. Wendy opened her eyes, smiled slightly knowing the completed look was as she wanted it.

Thank goodness her accountant and attorney controlled all financial and business matters. She appreciated all the work they did for her. She excitedly anticipated the newspaper ads about the opening being in a few days.

She changed into her gardening pants and an old tee shirt. In her backyard she trimmed shrubs and a few overgrown plants. The May weather welcomed her and many of the newly planted annuals were in bloom. Soon more plants would show their budding colors. She stared at the columbine plant next to her. The red and yellow flowers were gorgeous. Always entranced by the unique color combination on the small bloom, she took a flower in her hand. She wasn't sure why she remembered her mom and dad arguing over the placement of a similar plant when she was a kid. They became so disgruntled her mom walked away while her dad took the plant and put it where he wanted it. Wendy shook her head and kneeled to pull weeds, followed by hosing off the concrete patio. As she worked nearby, she absentmindedly thought about the trip to Brad's house.

After lunch she showered, changed clothes, and went to Century City Mall to look at different clothes styles. Cindy once mentioned Judy's as the best store for popular stylish clothes. She searched the mall and found the store. Wendy walked around inside until she came to a section with hot pants. She held up a pair and realized she couldn't have worn these even two months ago. With the inches she dropped and with her diet and exercise, maybe she'd give hot pants a try. Wendy walked to some blouses to try on. She returned to get three different colored hot pants she hoped might work with the tops.

"May I help you?" a saleswoman asked.

"I was trying to decide what tops went best with each pair of pants."

The saleswoman perused what Wendy was holding. "Good choices. Maybe try them on to see which ones you want," the woman suggested.

"Thank you, I will."

In the dressing room Wendy first tried on brown cotton hot pants with a white top. "I like them," she said aloud. She looked in the mirror, turned to the left and to the right. She smiled. They weren't short, short hot pants, but her thin legs looked good in them, so she would be comfortable if people stared at her. She tried on another pair…too tight. The third pair was good. After trying on crop tops, she decided she looked okay with the ones that hit slightly below her waist, so she decided to buy a navy one as well as a white one to go with a pair of new navy hip hugger pants, she grabbed before coming into the dressing room. After leaving the dressing room she walked around and took bleached and stonewashed flared jeans. She returned to the dressing room and loved them all. She left the store loaded with packages and enthusiastic about her purchases.

She stopped at Leed's Shoe Store and bought a pair of black, over the knee boots, and some shorter white ones. Boots were new to her wardrobe.

She returned home and tossed the packages on the sofa. She stood for a moment until her mind zoomed to Brad's house. She hoped by seeing the house and picturing him there, she could picture herself standing next to him. She called Cindy to confirm when she was picking Wendy up…forty-five minutes.

The time gave Wendy a chance to unpack the purchases. She took all the clothes and matched up what she preferred. She could get five outfits when she mixed them. After putting everything on hangers she pushed her pantsuits to the rear. The new clothes stood in front.

The drive to the Pacific Palisades home along Pacific Coast Highway was beautiful. The sand on the beach looked smooth, and the water calm with only small ripples in the waves. There were people sitting on blankets or standing next to the water edge. Cindy and Wendy chatted about Marty, Brad, and The Shade House.

As they approached the area near Brad's house, Cindy told her, "It's three houses down. I think we'd better not park too close because he may be home and if he walked out and saw my car…you know, I'd feel like shit."

"No problem."

The house stood at a side angle from where they sat with no front look to see.

"What do you think Wendy?"

"Wow, it's much more inviting than I thought it'd be. I see what you mean about the patio area overlooking the beach. He looks straight out from the patio with the beach and the ocean as his backyard or is it the front yard?"

"No, it's the backyard, the front has the pool."

"In the center is a very small fire pit with space for a small dish or drink along the edge. You can't see it but there's a Jacuzzi to the far right of the table."

"I'm impressed. Great look and a view to die for. You're so lucky."

"Thanks."

"I can picture you standing near the edge of the patio with Brad and a drink in hand, just like I said."

"Oh, shit, he's there, duck down. I hope he doesn't look this way. I'd never be able to explain why we're here. I mean it would sound asinine."

"Don't flip out."

"Wendy, can you look up a bit and see if he's gone yet?"

Wendy slowly lifted her head in time to see Brad's back as he moved into the house. "It's clear. We better split."

"For sure."

They drove toward Wendy's laughing about how silly they were. They grabbed an early dinner and talked about the adventure they experienced. Both agreed it was a hoot, especially since they didn't get caught.

The next morning Wendy arrived at The Shade House by nine. She once again walked the paths. She stopped at the gazebo and stepped inside where a small, white wrought iron table stood with two chairs if someone wanted to sit for a while. There were several benches around the nursery also. Wendy wanted people to linger and enjoy nature.

She sat in the gazebo and considered the advertising she put out and hoped all of it reached enough people. Hopefully, word of mouth took over. A week ago, she put ads in the Los Angeles Sun newspaper and the Santa Monica Morning News. She also put flyers in grocery stores and Cindy put some in the rec. room of her building.

When she got home, Marty called. She didn't tell him about the clothes, she wanted to surprise him. She invited him to come over for the evening, so they could watch *All in The Family* together and afterwards go to Hoffman's. Wendy found the show totally outrageous, but funny. Archie Bunker, the father of the family, was so ridiculously prejudice. His son-in-law, on the other hand, who Bunker called Meathead, and his daughter, were complete liberals. It made for interesting comedy.

Wendy dressed in her new beige hip huggers and navy crop top. She stared at herself in the mirror. She couldn't get over how different she looked in these *Mod* clothes. Logical and practical were how Wendy always visualized herself, but not anymore. The doorbell rang. She took one more look in the mirror and grinned.

As soon as Wendy opened the door Marty's mouth fell open. "What a super outfit!" he exclaimed as he came in and looked her up and down.

She turned around. "Glad you like it. I did some shopping."

"Holy shit. I can see, and you have great taste. I'm glad you decided to try the change. You really look fantastic in this outfit."

"Thanks. I bought some more outfits. It's going to take time for me to get used to these clothes."

"I can't wait to see 'the more.'"

They watched an episode of the Bunkers with Latino prejudice showing its ugly face.

"So, what did you think of this episode?" she asked as they watched the credits roll.

"I like the characters a lot and the acting…very cool."

"What about the message dealing with Latino prejudice?"

"The idea was to make people think. Some of them will be Archie, but some will be Meathead…they make the world go round."

"But prejudice is surely an important topic."

"I agree, but let's not get too heavy about this topic for now. Let's just appreciate the moment."

"Okay." Wendy dropped the subject.

"Are you ready to go?"

"Yeah, I am."

Hoffman's wasn't as crowded as she expected. As they approached the piano bar a couple left their seats. Wendy and Marty grabbed them.

Brad said, "Welcome," as they sat. Wendy mouthed thank you and Marty nodded.

The waitress came around and took their order. A maraca sat on the bar. Wendy had never tried it before but decided tonight would be the night. It wasn't loud but had a nice sound. Wendy played as Brad sang, Peter, Paul and Mary's hit, "I Dig Rock n' Roll Music."

Cindy came in just as he finished his set. "Hey, how are you, cats?"

Marty answered, "Everything is bitchin'."

Cindy noticed Wendy's clothes. "Far out, great change."

"Thanks."

Wendy, Marty and Cindy chatted during the break. Brad came back for another set and talked to a woman Wendy knew who came from the San Fernando Valley, at least forty-five minutes away. Brad leaned over his music stand in front of him to talk to the woman. Her long, black hair, and big dark eyes, gave a very sensual appeal. As Brad began to sing, Wendy noticed Cindy still starring at the valley girl. The woman showed a very friendly expression, Cindy didn't.

CHAPTER 12

THE NEXT DAY WENDY RETURNED TO THE NURSERY long enough to check everything. She stood at the pond area. The soothing sound of the waterfall and the gentleness of the stream made her reflect on the beauty now showing in her nursery.

Carol's willingness to work there thrilled Wendy. Wendy could talk over concerns about the nursery with her. She knew she picked a good worker. Carol carried herself with self-confidence and her charming personality would encourage people to come back and be around her as well as the nursery.

At home Wendy called her cousin Jake to tell him about the opening of The Shade House.

"Hi Jake."

"How are you?"

"I'm calling to tell you about the nursery opening?"

"Wonderful. I can't wait to see your creation."

She gave him the information. "So, I'll see you at the opening?"

"Definitely."

His enthusiasm always encouraged her. Wendy turned on the TV and listened to more information about the Watergate scandal. The news revolted her. The burglary of Democratic National Committee headquarters involved spying and sabotage conducted on behalf of President Nixon's re-election campaign. If it came out Nixon was in any way connected to the break-in impeachment would be imminent. Now, the country waited to find out. It may be big news, but Wendy decided working in her garden would be even better than the news.

Later she called Cindy suggesting they go for dinner. Cindy agreed. They met at Hamburger Hamlet.

Already seated in a booth when Wendy arrived Wendy scooted into her seat as they exchanged greetings.

"So, how was Hoffman's for the rest of the night?"

"It continued to be great, but did you see the way he looked at the exotic looking woman with the long, black hair?"

Wendy could understand Cindy's jealousy. "She's been there a few times, you never noticed her?"

"No, I would have remembered, but..."

"Cindy, you know he sees other women, so why does this one bother you more than the others?"

"I've tried not to think about the others. It doesn't make me feel very special, makes me feel shitty."

"Well, it shouldn't. Look at it this way, he picked you to be one of the women he finds attractive...he was impressed with your looks, and I'd imagine your personality too, so you should feel good."

"I s'pose. It's just such so damned exasperating."

"Just feel appreciated. You look wonderful! You have a great body and beautiful dusty brown hair." Wendy touched the sides of her hair. "Your clothes are impeccable and, of course, you are sexy. He must enjoy your time together and your talks."

"Actually, there isn't a lot of time to talk. His visits aren't long." Wendy decided not to comment.

A waitress took their drink orders, and they checked the menus.

"If you don't mind, I wondered what do you and Brad talk about, I mean when you talk?" Wendy asked.

"We talk about people at Hoffman's, movies, football, just different things, nothing deep. Come to think about of it, pretty much surface topics. Like I said, we don't have much time to talk. Why did you ask?"

"I don't know." Wendy leaned against the table. "I've often wondered what interests him, what kind of person he is when he isn't performing."

The waitress set down the drinks and took their orders.

After the waitress left, Cindy leaned into Wendy, "I think you mean fucking."

"Haha, so what's he do when he's not involved in singing or fucking?"

"Mostly watches sports and listens to music and practices."

As they enjoyed the wine, they chatted about who they thought some of his other women friends were.

"I know I'm one of, I don't know how many, so I do accept whatever time I have with him. When we're together he says sweet things and makes me feel special, so desired."

Wendy reached across the table and touched Cindy's hand. "Cindy, you're special anyway."

"Thanks, I do feel good being part of his life," Cindy admitted.

They started to eat as soon as the food arrived and continued with small talk throughout dinner. After dinner they went their separate ways.

At home, Wendy thought about Cindy's attitude as a good way to look at the situation. He must be something great for Cindy to have such deep convictions about the relationship.

Wendy watched the unusual May rain as it drizzled outside her back porch. She opened the door and listened to the soft sound of the raindrops dropping onto the concrete patio. While watching "The Mary Tyler Moore Show," Wendy ate dinner. She loved the comedy and the great social comments Mary made. They concentrated on how women were treated in the workplace, which wasn't always good.

Marty left for a business trip to San Francisco and Cindy didn't say whether she would be going to Hoffman's or not, but Wendy put on her new pair of stone washed jeans and a wheat colored long sleeved blouse with ruffles at the wrist. Wendy knew Cindy's reaction, "You look funky." She liked this change, especially the fact people she knew at Hoffman's made so many positive comments about how good she looked. Everything she had been doing to make herself look better paid off.

She loved the center piano bar seat, and it was available when she arrived at Hoffman's. A woman next to her took the maraca and started to play along with the music. Wendy took the four-inch-long wooden instrument to shake and joined in. She laughed a lot and became silly, joining in with people around her. Being outgoing at Hoffman's made her feel right at home and she enjoyed the enthusiastic participation as everyone else seemed to. Wendy now belonged in a comfortable space.

Cindy came in and stood by Wendy. They nodded to each other. A few minutes later Brad took a break. Cindy and Wendy were talking when Wendy noticed Brad visiting with an older looking distinguished gentleman dressed in a white shirt with a tie and wearing a sports jacket. Wendy mentioned it to Cindy who looked over.

"I think it's his agent. Brad mentioned he might stop by. Brad hired him a couple of weeks ago to see if he could find some out of town engagements for once in a while."

Before Wendy could ask what kind of special engagements, Brad returned for his next set. The agent stayed for a short time.

Wendy stared at Brad. She loved the way his white, satin shirt was open with his chest hair exposed. She pictured what Brad's naked body might look like. The disturbing, but incredible picture, escaped into her consciousness without warning.

Wendy left after the set. Feeling happy and sad, she needed to get out of there. As she drove home, she tried to understand her mixed moods. Wendy was very happy for Cindy. So, why did Wendy feel happy and sad? More than ever, she loved that Marty made her feel appreciated, special and calm. But when around Brad, he brought a different kind of calmness with his looks, his body and talent. All those traits made her desire him and want to be in his life. The craving for two men triggered confusion and anguish.

CHAPTER 13

IT WAS THE LAST DAY OF MAY AND A BEAUTIFUL
morning for The Shade House kick-off. The skies were powder
blue with light fluffy clouds and a beautiful sunny greeting. Wendy
arrived at the nursery at eight o'clock. The nursery opened at ten and
closed at five.

Once out of the car, Wendy went to the entrance and stood back.
The cocoa painted sign with wooden ivy above and around the door
was the right image. She opened the door, turned on the lights and
waterfall, and continued to her office where she put her purse and
her packed lunch on the desk. She went around to the front of the
counter, staring at the wonderful new roof as she pressed the button
to open the lattice covering to let the low morning sunshine down
on the plants. With an enormous grin she shouted up, "Thanks mom
and dad." She stood still and let her eyes wander as she cherished the
length and breadth of her wondrous accomplishment.

Carol came in dressed in stonewashed jeans and a long-sleeved
dark navy tee shirt. Wendy dressed in dark blue jeans and a plaid
flannel shirt. Good comfort for the day. The two of them set up a

table near the front door with lemonade, cheese and crackers. Wendy turned on a radio station where soft instrumental music played. There were two speakers, one near the front and one toward the rear.

"When the people start to come in just walk around and see if anyone has questions or needs help. But move away to give them space if they don't seem interested."

"Okay."

At five minutes after ten the first customers came in, two women.

"Good morning," Wendy greeted.

"Mornin' to you," one of the women responded looking around. "Very nice place."

"Thank you. Feel free to help yourself to the lemonade and treats."

"Thanks, we'll take a walk first."

"Let me know if you have any questions." They nodded and moved away.

Wendy needed to stay near the door for a while to welcome everyone. Carol moved around to help where she could. The next time the door opened Wendy turned to see six people come in. Wendy offered the refreshments. A few took a glass of lemonade and they soon split up and started to explore.

Mary Ann and Judy came to see the finished product. As they approached Wendy, Mary Ann said, "It looks great Wendy." Judy agreed.

"Thanks. I owe a lot of it to you two. Did you know Carol's working here?"

"She mentioned it and that's good," Judy commented, and Mary Ann nodded. They wandered off.

Wendy watched as customers stopped to admire a plant or check the plant label to see the name. A woman in a bright pink dress came to the counter carrying a Chinese evergreen plant. She had already put a couple of other plants on the floor near the counter. Her friend clutched an orchid to her bosom.

"Are you interested in different containers for your plants? We repot them for free."

"Let's see," the woman said as she tilted her straw hat sideways. "This one is a gift, so maybe a decorative pot is a good idea."

Wendy showed the woman and her friend the pots in the alcove near the potting bench. Wendy stepped back so they could examine all of them and returned to the register where she waited.

"That's a wonderful choice," Wendy complimented as she held up the straw hat woman's choice, a light gold terra cotta pot. The other woman didn't want a new pot for her orchid.

Wendy potted up the Chinese Evergreen. She scattered small wooden bark on top to give it a finished look and wiped some clinging dirt from the sides, handing it to the woman. Other plants they bought Wendy placed into paper potholders to protect them. They paid for their purchases and thanked Wendy.

"I love this place," the orchid woman said, as they turned to leave.

"Thank you," Wendy handed them each a business card in case there were any questions about their plants.

"Thanks, we'll be back."

The women left. Their words were encouraging. Wendy made a note to create a list of all the plants with their care.

As soon as the women made their exit, her cousin Jake came toward her. He was a burly, short bald man whose expression read happiness. She went straight to him and gave him a big hug, he gladly returned. He pulled back and looked at her.

"You look wonderful sweetheart. You've lost a lot of weight."

"Thanks, I've been working on it."

"It's good. He turned to see the depth of the nursery. This place is fantastic. It's huge. I had no idea it would be so big, and I love it. You've really created a place of solace here."

"Thanks, sounds nice. Want to walk around with me?"

"Of course."

They ambled for a few minutes until Jake stopped and walked into a bark path inside the main walkway. He ducked his head as he came out next to a short tree.

"I'm speechless. Really Wendy, you've done a superb job with the design. I love the paths and there's such a great variety of plants. I don't recognize most of them."

"Thanks again, Jake."

"Let me show you my favorite spot, well, one of my favorites."

They went to the forest end. "I loved the lushness of greenery, so I designed this end to look like a forest, well as close as I could come inside a building without tall trees."

Her cousin glanced around and nodded. "Amazing, I don't know what else to say, just an amazing job. Great atmosphere. I'm so proud of you."

"I really appreciate hearing that. You want to follow me to the other side, and we can head back to the stream and pond you may have noticed when you came in."

"Actually, I spotted you, so I only glanced at the pond, but I can't wait to see it up close."

They moved around the concrete walkway and stopped at the pond.

"I'm stunned, my dear. This is extremely soothing to listen to and to see. You have such wonderful creativity."

"Thanks. This is another favorite of mine. I have a lot," Wendy conceded.

"I would think so."

"Want some lemonade?"

"I wish I could, but I can't stay."

Wendy went with him to the door. "So glad you like it."

"You were creative when you designed your backyard, so I'm not surprised with this wondrous nursery. You are one helluva of an artist." He looked around again. "Your folks would love this and be so proud of your accomplishment." He gave her a kiss on the cheek as they exchanged good-bye hugs.

As she watched him walk away, his enthusiasm sparked great pride in her. They were cousins and friends since the greenhouse days…always in touch. She truly appreciated his enthusiastic reaction.

Carol came to the counter with a gentleman who wanted to know more about the Piggyback plant he held in his hand. Wendy explained the outstanding traits as she pointed to its fuzzy leaves and their unique shape. "Perhaps you'd like to pick out a nice pot for the plant? We re-plant them for free."

"Yes, thanks. That's a great service. This is a surprise for my wife, so a different pot is a good idea."

Wendy pointed the way to the alcove. The man returned and Wendy went with him to the potting area where she planted the Piggyback plant in the green, glazed pot he picked out. She wiped the outsides and they returned to the counter. She handed the plant to the gentleman in an open box Wendy took from behind the counter.

He paid her, and as he was about to leave, Wendy called out, "Thank you for visiting, hope your wife likes the plant."

"My wife is going to love this place," he said as he looked around and walked out.

Cindy came in near closing to see how the day went.

She looked all around her. "This place is really outta sight. I love it."

"Thanks, Cindy."

Wendy locked up a few minutes later and Carol, Cindy and Wendy briefly talked outside, and Cindy left.

Wendy turned to Carol. "I'm so glad you will work here."

"I really do enjoy nature, and your nursery is a treasure in the middle of a bustling city."

Thanks so much. They hugged and headed out.

Wendy returned home at five-thirty. Feeling completely exhausted, she flopped down on her bed and reviewed the day. She was so glad the opening went so well. At least thirty or more people came through, along with some of her friends.

Marty called to see how the opening went and they chatted. She couldn't wait for him to get back from San Francisco, she missed him.

By the end of the week, she revelled in the fact so many customers visited. Her nursery was off to a good start.

CHAPTER 14

AT TIMES THE TELEVISION WAS WENDY'S companion, but sometimes her enemy. The Watergate scandal exploded. President Nixon fired the White House Counsel, John Dean, and the attorney general resigned, along with two staffers. Nothing like this ever happened in American history. Wendy always loved American history in school, and continued to read books about it, but she hated what might become of this ugly chapter in its history.

She turned off the TV just as her phone rang. Marty was back. He wanted to pick her up for dinner, but she explained she was tired and asked if they could do dinner tomorrow instead. They spoke briefly about his trip, and he told her he'd pick her up at seven.

In the morning Wendy drove to May Company in search of some gold clip-on earrings she decided might be great with several of her outfits. She went directly to the jewelry area where she found several pairs of clip-ons. As she admired them, she turned and watched a woman pierce the ears of a young girl. Wendy only watched for a second during the piercing and quickly turned away as the girl called out, "ouch." When it was done the girl smiled into the mirror the mother held for her. Wendy decided she wanted her ears pierced too.

She stared at the earrings she picked up, put them down and picked out pierced earrings. She couldn't decide between the gold hoops she held, or a pair of pearl drop earrings in front of her. They weren't real pearls, but Wendy liked them just the same. She decided on both, always good to have choices. She went back to the counter where the woman who pierced ears stood, and Wendy asked to have hers done. Wendy watched as the woman prepared the materials needed for the piercing. As the woman's hand moved to Wendy's ear Wendy closed her eyes and cringed at the sharp poke. She did the same with her other ear. Afterwards, she held up the mirror and admired the hoops. She'd no longer have to worry about clip-on earrings falling from her ears.

At home Wendy put on a new, short white top and a black wide legged pants. She looked in the full-length mirror and grimaced. To get her body into even better shape she recognized the need to exercise more along with her continuing diet. But still, Wendy thought she looked damned good. She admired her long, auburn hair as it hung straight down her back, but with a center part instead of a side one she usually wore. She applied mascara and put on lipstick. Wendy stared at herself in the mirror, moving closer to see her new earrings better. She smiled.

Marty arrived wearing a business suit.

"Holy shit, you look fantastic!" he exclaimed as Wendy opened the door. "Every time I see you, you look great."

"Thanks. Glad you're good with it."

"Of course, and I'm glad you decided to give it a go." He stood back to get a complete look.

She turned around.

"You look sensational." He took hold of her butt and squeezed it, pulling her to him. The kiss was intense.

Wendy pulled back. "I'm really happy you like it. You always look good in suits."

"I didn't have time to change."

"I figured. I'm starved. Where are we eating?"

"There's a place called Pirate's Cove, thought we'd try it. It's in Venice on Lincoln, a short distance from Ocean Front Walkway and the ocean. Have you ever been to Ocean Front Walk?"

"No, I haven't."

It's very long with all kinds of shops and food stops. It's a fun place.

Pirate's Cove resembled a hideaway, a cozy place with a few fishing nets and a couple of buoys. As they walked in, they moved to a bar straight ahead against the back wall. Wendy turned to the far left and across from the bar, she saw a piano bar with ten high back stools. A small musical group sat behind the piano bar with a drummer, piano player, and a singer with a guitar. There were tables and chairs on the main floor and to the right and up two steps was a railing with a few more tables and chairs. This area also had a dance floor.

Wendy followed Marty up to one of the tables near the railing. As soon as they sat a waiter came over and took their drink orders and left the menus.

Wendy crossed her arms on the table edge. "So, tell me more about your trip."

"A good trip with some changes to come."

"Good changes, I hope."

"Well, the changes are still being finalized, so we'll see."

They previewed their menus.

The waiter set their drinks down and took their orders.

"I missed you," Marty said as the waiter left.

"That's really sweet. I thought about you a lot especially the many things we have in common, and I like that you're supportive of equal rights for women."

"It isn't just women's rights. I think there should be equality for everyone."

"I totally agree, Marty."

"As long as we're sharing our thoughts…I have to tell you how special I think you are…your personality, your kindness, your smarts, your hair," he said as he ran his fingers down the side of it. He leaned into her. "And you're so pretty…" he stopped, moved her hair aside and stared at her face, pulling back, "Did you have your ears pierced?"

"Yes, this morning."

"Well, you dazzle all over."

She demurred. "I don't know what to say, except thank you. And you, your eyes, your beautiful blue eyes always entrance me." She gazed at them. "They entice me to see more."

He smiled, "I thank you, and I'm in total agreement about wanting to see more."

They smirked at each other as the waiter set their dinners down. "Let's eat and I'll tell you more about sites I got to see while on the trip."

"Okay."

They chatted as they ate. Marty shared his time on Pier 39. As he finished talking, Wendy related the happenings at the nursery with so many customers. They stayed after they ate and sat back enjoying the music. After a while they decided to go back to Wendy's.

Walking into the living room Wendy asked, "Wanna a drink?"

"Sure, scotch on the rocks."

Wendy went to a buffet she used as a bar. She got out the scotch and vodka and went to the kitchen for ice and orange juice for her screwdriver. She put the ice cubes in both of their glasses, returned to the buffet and poured the scotch and the orange juice.

She took their glasses to the sofa, where they toasted each other.

Wendy's eyes penetrated his…her desire for him increased with an urgency she never experienced before.

He must have read her thoughts. "Should we take our drinks into the bedroom?"

"What a good idea."

With one hand Marty pulled Wendy up. Once in the bedroom, with a little help from Marty, she quickly undressed. He wasted no time as he undressed while Wendy sat on the edge of the bed and watched. He sat next to her, pulling her onto the bed, cozying next to her. He followed the outline of her mouth with his fingers and slowly moved his fingers down her neck, his hands over her breasts. Her hands wandered down his back and up to his head. Wendy moaned. When the love making ended, Marty rolled onto his side and gave her a long passionate kiss.

They laid facing each other as Marty played with her hair.

"I hate to end this," Marty said, "but I continue to have early morning appointments, so I need to go, sorry. I know this happens too often, but it can't be helped. I don't always get the choice of times."

"I'm cool with it." Wendy responded as she put on her robe.

Wendy watched Marty dress. He always looked so perfect. He threw his tie around his neck as she walked him to the front door where they exchanged a quick kiss.

Marty made her life better as did her nursery. Now everything turned out the way she wanted it. She decided she didn't need any further sessions with Dr. Lewis.

CHAPTER 15

AS WENDY GOT OUT OF HER CAR THE NEXT DAY, she sauntered toward the nursery, but stopped and observed the outside…it still amazed her. The ivy and the name above it welcomed everyone. Once inside she checked around the nursery to be sure plants set down where they didn't belong were returned to their rightful places. People meant well, but in a hurry, those who carried a plant around and decided against buying it, often set it down wherever they happened to be. It elated Wendy there always seemed to be so many visitors.

Later in the day, Cindy called Wendy with very unexpected news.

"In two weeks, Brad is taking a weekend away from Hoffman's and he's singing in Palm Springs at the Desert Lake Inn…so outta sight. Do you want to go with me? We could share a room?"

"That's great. I want to go but what if Marty wants to come. I'll have to check. I think it will be really cool to see Brad perform somewhere else. Are you going with Brad?"

"Yeah, sure." Cindy kidded.

"You should."

"You're serious?"

"Of course."

"What if he says no, I'd feel uncomfortable being there. Maybe he's taking someone already."

"You won't know if you don't ask."

"Yeah, but I don't know…well, I'm going in any case, but let me know what you decide."

"As soon as I talk to Marty. What a great escape."

She called Marty at work. "Brad is playing at a hotel in Palm Springs in two weeks, Friday and Saturday, do you want to go?"

"I'm sorry. I wish I could but there are several meetings with some out of town brass in two weeks and I'm sure it will include the weekend. I must leave the dates open. If anything changes, I'd love to get away with you."

"I understand, I'll go with Cindy."

"Good. I'm really sorry, I'd change things if I could."

"I know. I'd better call her, talk to you later."

They hung up and Wendy called Cindy confirming she would be joining her.

"Outta sight! I decided not to ask Brad about going with me, I'm just not comfortable with asking."

"I get it."

As soon as Wendy arrived at work she talked to Carol.

"Listen, I need to ask a favor."

"Okay."

"In two weeks, I'm going to Palm Springs with Cindy to hear Brad sing and I wondered if you could run the nursery while I'm gone. It's Friday and Saturday and I'll return on Sunday."

"Sure, no problem. Is it okay if Brenda helps out?"

"I thought of asking Mary Ann, but Brenda's good."

Wendy met Brenda several times when she came to see Carol during the renovation and even helped once in a while.

"Great. I'll give her a quick call."

Two weeks later, on a Friday afternoon, Wendy and Cindy arrived at the Desert Lake Inn. Brad's performance was in the evening at eight and the same time again Saturday night. Both gigs were held in the hotel's lounge area.

They found their room on the third floor.

"This is one hell of a room," Cindy said.

Wendy went to check out the bathroom. "You're right…it's very nice."

"What should we do now?" Wendy asked after they were organized.

"Let's go explore."

The downstairs was huge. They saw a café and across the way a fancy restaurant. They found the gift shop, looked around inside, but didn't buy anything. They went outside behind the hotel where they discovered a mammoth sized pool designed to look like a lake. A waterfall and slide were at one end. There were loungers everywhere and an area with umbrella tables nearby. They turned to each other with a wow expression…an exceptional place.

They went back inside and out the front doors where they stood on the sidewalk. The hotel was located on the main drag. They looked up and down the street.

Cindy spotted a building across the street with a sign, Clothing Boutique. "Let's check it out."

They went in, strolled through, but quickly left.

"I couldn't believe those prices," Wendy spit out as they came outside.

"No kidding."

They walked a bit further and found a small eatery with a covered outside sitting area. They each ordered iced tea.

"I can't believe we're here," Wendy stated as they settled into chairs.

"Me neither, but what a great get away from LA."

Forty minutes later they headed back to the hotel.

Once in their room Cindy wondered. "Should I call Brad's room and let him know we're here."

"Hmmm…seems like a natural thing to do."

"What the hell," Cindy said as she reached the operator to have the call put through to Brad Hanson's room.

The phone rang twice, and he picked up.

"Hi, it's Cindy. I'm here with Wendy like I told you."

"Glad you came. I won't have time to spend with you. I hope you understand."

"Yes, of course". He ended the call by telling her he'd see her later.

"He was abrupt," she told Wendy as they hung up.

"He may be going to rehearse, who knows." Wendy lifted her hands, moving them about. "This is such a treat."

They watched some TV and took a short nap. At five they headed downstairs to have dinner in the café. Afterwards they returned to their room to shower and change for the evening. Both wore mini-skirts with blouses and high heeled shoes.

When they arrived in the lounge area, there were a number of people already seated with drinks in hand. Wendy and Cindy found a table with a good view just two rows from the small stage.

Fifteen minutes later Brad and a woman approached the area. Brad took two steps up to the stage. The woman lingered for a minute, said something to Brad, and sat at a table to his left. Wendy and Cindy's eyes darted at each other with astonishment when they recognized the dark-haired woman from the valley.

Cindy whispered to Wendy, "I'm glad I didn't ask about going with him. If he said no and I came and saw this, well, I would have been humiliated."

"Yeah." Wendy understood Cindy's response. "It's a shock to see her here, but he did talk to her often on his breaks."

"I remember," Cindy said sarcastically.

"I'm sorry, Cindy. Let's enjoy listening to him like we always do. This is still a great experience. Look around…if it weren't for Brad, we wouldn't be here in this paradise."

"I know, it's nice, but…this is aggravating, but to be honest, I guess I'm not too surprised. He's on vacation, sorta speak, and picked someone to be here during his down time. Just wish it had been me."

"I'm really sorry," Wendy repeated.

Brad started singing at eight. His strong voice caught everyone's eyes. The sexy, dark-haired woman sat fully immersed in watching Brad. Cindy glared at her with disdain.

Despite Cindy's frustration, Wendy loved the evening. She concentrated on Brad and his stupendous delivery of songs. She looked around and the people continued to watch him.

She stared at Cindy watching her rival. "I guess we both knew he wouldn't come alone," Wendy whispered.

"Yeah, no shit."

On Brad's first break he briefly talked to the dark-haired woman and walked around to visit with different people. His agent, Art Nash, who snuck in after Brad started to sing, stood at the back of the lounge. Brad talked to him. He eventually came over to Wendy and Cindy.

"Thanks for coming ladies."

"You sound great. This room has good acoustics," Cindy said as she hid her anguished voice.

"Thanks, have ta get back."

Wendy and Cindy stayed the rest of the evening. Brad spent most of his next break again visiting others, ending up at the table with the dark-haired woman, for whom they had no name.

On his last break he came back to Wendy and Cindy for a short stop. "Who's your friend?" Cindy didn't mince words.

"Her name is Karen. She's been to Hoffman's."

"We recognized her, but we didn't know her name," Wendy said.

"Now you do," he smiled and returned for the last set.

The audience's appreciation of his voice was obvious as they loudly applauded after each song. He was charismatic. He also made some funny comments as he often did at Hoffman's. And the audience appreciated those with laughter.

After Brad finished, Wendy and Cindy returned to their room before he and Karen left. They speculated about his relationship with her, but no way existed to know how special she might be to him, or if she was just one of his 'girls.'

"I sincerely doubt she's his favorite, but we'll have to wait and see what happens when we get back. She is stunning."

"True," Cindy admitted.

The next day they were in the café for lunch when Karen and Brad came in. He nodded to them as he passed by but didn't make any introductions. Wendy and Cindy watched as they settled at a table.

Wendy looked at Cindy and took hold of her hand, squeezing it. "She's not going to be his one and only. You know it, don't you?"

"Yeah, I do. It's just so damn hard to watch them together and wish it were me."

"I know," and Wendy did.

Wendy and Cindy relaxed by the pool for most of the day.

Cindy remained quiet and Wendy could imagine her disappointed thoughts and hurt feelings. Wendy also knew Cindy would learn to accept what happened because she couldn't change anything. Just to know he was still interested in her too should bring comfort. Maybe, at another time, he would ask Cindy to join him somewhere.

Saturday night was similar to Friday; however, the management added more tables to accommodate a bigger crowd. Word must have spread about Brad's great voice. Brad's agent sat at a back table. It intrigued Cindy and Wendy that Brad spent so little time with Karen between sets. He mostly visited audience members, offering him a good opportunity to tell people about his performing at Hoffman's. People from Palm Springs often visited LA.

Later, in their room, they replayed the two evenings with Brad… his wonderful performances, his voice, and Karen. They discussed it all. Once in bed Cindy tossed around a bit and finally nodded off, but Wendy lay in bed reliving the astonishing time. It wasn't just Brad's singing that excited Wendy but the chance to getaway, to walk around in a new place, look at different shops, plus stopping for tea in the outdoor eating area. What a relaxing time.

"A penny for your thoughts," Wendy said while they sat in silence eating breakfast the next morning.

"The realization of his being with another woman helps me accept my reality, in regards, to our relationship. Before, I always hoped I was more special than the others, but now I know the truth. I can handle it."

"I'm glad. I've been so worried."

"I know you were, and thanks. I'm okay." Cindy sipped her coffee and chomped on a slice of bacon.

"'Be calm and carry on,'" as the saying goes."

"Yeah."

After breakfast they returned to their room, packed, checked out and headed home.

During the drive, Wendy considered how much she wanted Brad to desire her. Wendy realized Cindy and other women at Hoffman's all wanted this talented and gorgeous man to find them special and for people to know such a great guy wanted them. To Wendy it had to do with ego because now that she looked sexy, she wanted Brad to acknowledge it by finally wanting her too. Maybe, for the first time in her life such an amazing man might find her desirable.

CHAPTER 16

SOON AFTER THE RETURN FROM PALM SPRINGS Marty suggested a trip to Santa Barbara. Another great getaway. Marty finally had some time off for them to spend together. They mellowed out as they drove north. They stayed over for two nights and visited different sites. They went to the Santa Barbara Mission, walked through a beautiful park and visited Lotus Land, an estate with thirty-seven acres of unique garden designs and unusual plant species. On their drive back to LA, they stopped at a coffee shop. They walked hand in hand as they strolled along the boardwalk near different beaches.

Once back at The Shade House, Wendy talked to Carol about what, if anything, transpired since Wendy's last call to Carol from Santa Barbara. Fortunately, nothing much was important and no bad news. In the office she checked the receipts. They continued to show a formable increase. The expenses were pretty much unchanged, a relief. Wendy called her accountant, Howard, and he confirmed everything was good. She ruminated about what a wonderful life she had.

Wendy and Marty sat on her back porch and watched colorful Fourth of July fireworks fly up from another street. They sat in silence as they appreciated more displays in the sky. They sipped wine and Wendy yelled out as one of the fireworks exploded high in the sky in miscellaneous colors.

Then, out of nowhere Marty announced: "Hilstrom wants to buy your nursery."

Wendy turned to him and barked. "What?"

"I know it's a shock, but they think your location is a terrific place for a restaurant."

Wendy stood up, stepped away and swung back to him. The news crashed down on her. "This is crazy." Her voice faltered. "How long have you known about this?"

He stood. "What difference does it make? They want to offer you $80,000! That's a fantastic price."

"I can't believe you're saying this."

"I'm sorry, I know you're upset, but they wanted me to approach you about selling. I think it's a great offer."

"I've been in business less than four months. Why did you think I'd be interested? You know how much the nursery means to me."

"I had to ask."

"No, you didn't. You could have told them I wouldn't be interested."

"I told them, but they still wanted me to ask. So, I need to give them an answer."

"What in the hell do you think mine is? Never mind. It's my heart and soul I put into the nursery. Shit Marty, it isn't the money."

"I'm their attorney."

"How long have you known they wanted this property?"

"Awhile."

"How long is awhile?"

"It doesn't matter."

Anger enveloped her face as she walked straight up to his. "It does, just answer me."

"Three weeks."

She turned away and back at him. "Why now? Is this what was discussed while you were in San Francisco?"

Marty hesitated. "Yes. The company rep. came down here and saw it, from the inside."

"You told them about this place, right?"

"They wanted a Santa Monica site, so I mentioned the entire Santa Monica area. They drove around and saw your great parking area. They walked into the place next door and came into the nursery liking it immediately, for its size."

"So, they want to buy both properties?"

He ignored the question. "I know you're angry but think how much money that is. You could open an even bigger nursery in a more prime location."

She turned away and then faced him. "This is a prime location! You don't even care how I feel about all the work I've put into the nursery or how much I love what I'm doing. You know what I think?" She moved closer and locked eyes with him. "I think you've been playing me for months. I think you knew they were interested in property in this area for a long time, but you didn't get the go ahead to convince me to sell it until recently. Boy, did I misjudge you."

"Honestly, I didn't want to hurt you."

"Right." She glared at him with her hands on her hips and pointed a finger at him. "They were going to give you a big fat commission if you made the sale, or a promotion. I trusted you and you betrayed me. Leave now," she snapped.

Marty stared and walked through the house, stopping at the front door. Wendy followed and waited near the entry with her arms folded. He turned and looked at her. She scowled. Without further comment he opened the door and left. She grabbed the door and slammed it shut. She turned into her living room and fell into a chair where she cried, mortified and stunned.

As soon as she opened the nursery the next day, she called Cindy. They decided to meet for dinner. Wendy spent the day with customers hoping to stop thinking about Marty, but she couldn't. She genuinely thought he cared a great deal for her. What a shrewd shit.

Wendy and Cindy met at Callender's.

Cindy commiserated with Wendy. "I'm really sorry. I feel awful. I thought you two were so right for each other."

"Me too, goes to show how easily I can be taken advantage of. I will never trust men again. I don't need a serious relationship. They're just not for me. I think I'll just have fun and enjoy the life I have."

"I can't argue that. So, you truly believe he told his company about your building?"

"I have absolutely no doubt at all. He admitted he told them about the area, and I'm sure he specifically told them about the area around my nursery. I find it loathsome. I can't believe he did this to me. I can't believe..." she struggled to find the right words. "I don't know what to say, it's so incredibly outrageous." Her illuminated mind brought reality. "I thought he loved me. I guess he loved his job or money more, not much different from Scott. Maybe I should go back to Dr. Lewis. She could help me deal with this."

"If you think it's what you need, I agree."

"Damn it, no, I can handle this, and anything else that comes my way. Scott and Marty are two shits. This reminds me, it's time to file for divorce, so Scott's gone too.

"You're sure?"

"Marty's behavior reminded me about how awful men have been to me. I don't know why I haven't filed sooner, but it's definitely time to get it over with."

"I haven't seen you this angry since the separation. You know what you need? You and I need to head to Hoffman's so we can both chill and you can get the assholes out of your mind."

"Totally agree."

They arrived in separate cars but walked in together. It wasn't too crowded…they slipped in between people to reach the piano bar. Brad acknowledged them with a nod. Cindy smiled back, but Wendy showed no expression. Seeing Brad and listening to his gorgeous voice wasn't helping. She considered leaving but instead looked at the people around her. She wondered what their lives were like. Had women here experienced anything similar to what men did to her? She erased the thoughts and turned back to Brad. She couldn't resist his expressive face and those sparkling eyes…oh so riveting.

A few minutes later Wendy looked around and noticed Mike, the head bartender. She talked to him briefly a few times. He was always so sincere and agreeable. She decided to talk to him about Marty because she needed a man's insight.

On one of Brad's breaks Wendy went to the bar and swirled into a seat. Mike headed toward her from the other end where he had just served a drink. He had a great full body with his height maybe five feet, ten inches, with black curly hair and big brown eyes.

"So, what will it be, Wendy?"

"Just water, I still have a screwdriver over there." She pointed backwards.

"Okay, one water coming right up."

As he set the drink down Wendy looked up with wet eyes. She tried to hold the tears in abeyance, but she couldn't.

"What's wrong?" Mike asked.

With the back of her hand, she wiped the tears away. "Well, just having a rough time right now. I just broke up with Marty."

"I'm sorry. Listen I need to get some liquor from the storage area. If you'd like to talk, you can stay after everyone leaves."

"You're so nice, but... are you sure?"

"Of course."

"I'd like too. Thanks, Mike."

She left the water and went back to the piano bar.

By one fifteen only five people remained, so Brad ended the evening and packed up his stuff. Wendy told Cindy she was staying to talk to Mike. Brad went to the door and Cindy followed him out, giving a wave to Wendy as she left.

Wendy was glad Mike was willing to talk to her. The few people who remained soon left, and the owner locked up as he exited.

"Care for a drink?" Mike asked.

"Thanks, I'll take a white wine."

Wendy rose when Mike came out from behind the bar with two drinks and led the way to a small table in the restaurant.

Once they were seated across from one another, Mike focused on Wendy. "Tell me what happened."

"I just found out Marty was using me so his company could buy my building in order to build a restaurant."

"Man, that's crappy. I'm really sorry."

"Yeah, me too. I liked him, and I believed him when he said he cared about me. He told me his company would offer me a lot of money if I'd sell, but he didn't seem to care about my feelings and all

I did to make The Shade House a success, or how much it meant to me. What a fool I've been. I'm sorry, I shouldn't go on like this but..."

"It's okay. I know when we talked before you were so happy with how everything turned out at the nursery. One thing you'll learn from this is you can't be thin skinned. You can't let someone else ruin your life. Try to forget what happened and keep on truckin'."

"I'm trying, but it really hurts. I know I'll get over it, but right now I feel like crap."

"I can understand completely."

"You're being very nice. Thank you."

"I like you, Wendy. I've watched you here for a long time and considered you a calming element in this crazy bar scene."

"Really. How could you tell?"

"Well, when you've been around this "scene" for as long as I've been, you notice things no one else does."

Wendy didn't know much about Mike. "How did you get interested in bartending?"

"I hung around bars and found most of the people were pretty laid back. I liked it. Some became like family."

"Family, huh? Do you have a family of your own?"

"Yeah, but the kids are older with lives of their own, and my wife has different interests. We slipped away from each other and recently separated."

"I'm sorry to hear it. I guess you can really understand how I feel."

"I wish I could be more helpful. The guy's obviously a money hungry bastard."

"You're so right. Thanks for listening, it's very much appreciated."

"Any time. This will be hard to deal with for a while, but it will be less bothersome soon."

"Thank you." Wendy looked at her watch. "I'm sorry. It's getting late I'd better split."

The drinks remained on the table. Wendy grabbed her purse.

"I'll lock up and walk you out."

"Thanks."

Wendy and Mike stopped next to her car and without warning he took her shoulders, leaned down and briefly kissed her lips and pulled back.

"You're one great chick. See ya later," he said, as he started toward his truck.

Wendy couldn't respond, too much in shock. She unlocked her car, got in, and sat a moment before she headed home.

CHAPTER 17

AT WORK ON MONDAY WENDY'S MIND WANDERED to Mike. She still wasn't sure if the kiss was out of friendship, or for another reason. She just wanted his friendship. She needed his insight and appreciated he seemed to really care about what she went through.

In the afternoon the unexpected happened. She couldn't believe after all these months Scott came to the nursery. What audacity to come here. What could he possibly want? She wanted him to disappear.

"Scott," Wendy said without any emotion.

"Hi."

Her face went blank. "What are you doing here?"

"I saw a flyer with your picture on it. I thought I'd stop by and say hi."

"Okay, hi."

"May I have a tour?"

She hesitated, reluctant to spend time with him, but said, "Okay, but I may be called to the front."

"It's fine."

As they toured the nursery Scott asked a lot of questions about the space and asked about a few plants. Very much surprised by his interest since he never showed any with her garden. They reached the pond area and stopped.

"You've done a great job here, Wendy."

"Thanks."

"I also stopped by to tell you I'm changing to a different import company because I don't want to travel so much."

She stared at him. This came out of left field. "Really? Let me know how that works out. Thanks for coming by." She wanted to end the conversation, so he would leave. She couldn't deal with him and Marty right now.

He hesitated before saying, "I'm very excited for you."

She smiled and watched as he went out the door. She needed to sit and think but a customer interrupted her.

"I'm interested in the Star Pine Tree you have, but I can't take it now."

"It's okay. I can set it aside until tomorrow."

"That'd be great thanks." They went to the counter where the woman paid and left.

Wendy put the pine on the hand truck and wheeled it near the potting area. Her busyness for the rest of the day gave her no time to be fixated on Scott's visit.

As soon as she got home, she called Cindy and told her about Scott showing up.

"What do you think he's up to?" Cindy inquired after Wendy explained their conversation.

"I don't know. I imagine he wanted to make sure I understood he wasn't going to be traveling as much. Maybe he's ready to change his priorities, by changing jobs."

"How are you going to handle this?"

"I have no idea. I won't believe anything until I see…I don't know…something to believe."

"All that aside, are you still in love with him?"

Wendy paused. One trait she admired in her friendship with Cindy, her honesty…no game playing.

"No, I'm still so angry at him. Right now, I'm going to grab a bite and head to Hoffman's."

"I have too much school work tonight so I'll have to skip Hoffman's."

Wendy walked straight to the piano bar where there were several vacant bar stools. She liked the fact that Brad now included her in hellos and waves goodbye. Once in a while he'd lean toward her, if she was seated, and make a random comment about nothing in particular. Brad smiled at her as she sat and he continued to sing, "Kentucky Rain," an Elvis song. Brad's voice gave a somber feel as he sang about a girl who left home and her boyfriend didn't know why, so he's walking in the Kentucky rain as he searches for her. The theme said so much about meaningful relationships.

When Brad finished his set, Wendy went to talk to Mike.

"Hey kiddo, how ya doin' tonight?"

"A little better, thanks for asking."

"That's good. I'm sure, with time, you'll move on from that fucker and find someone better. Hang on a minute," and Mike went to make a drink for a customer. "You look bitchin'," he said as he returned.

"Thanks, Mike." Brad started his next set. "Talking to you helped, thanks for caring." She returned to her seat.

Hoffman's brought Wendy the comfort she needed. She talked to women who came there. Some exchanged brief conversations with her, mainly about Hoffman's or Brad. They were part of Brad's groupies, but she didn't mind. Most of the time their smiles relaxed her. They shared different stories about men and their other interests.

At Brad's next break Wendy turned to Laura, the woman to her right.

"How are you doing Laura?"

"I'm having a ball. This place always cheers me up."

"Are you down?"

"Just a little, nothing major. You're here quite a bit. Are you seeing Brad?"

"No, I just enjoy the music and the fun atmosphere. Why did you ask?

"I'm not sure, really none of my business. I'd love to be with him."

"Well, it may happen, only time will tell."

"I know. It's just he's so bitchin'."

Wendy knew what Laura felt, but Wendy could never share those feelings with her, or anyone there. She finished her second screwdriver and tapped on the bar as Brad sang. He grinned at Wendy as he belted out John Denver's, "Rocky Mountain High." She picked up the maraca and softly began to play along. He followed "Rocky Mountain High" with "Cherish," a soft song made famous by The Association. She put the maraca down and listened. The song told about how much a woman cared about someone but hid her true feelings.

After the end of the set, Wendy said good-bye to Laura and waved good-bye to Brad as she got up and started toward the door. She glanced back toward Mike who waved.

As Wendy lay in bed her thoughts went to Scott. He obviously came by to tell her about the job change and his not having to travel so much. Her anger and disdain made it difficult for her to feel anything for him. She couldn't get her feelings for Brad out of her mind and now maybe Mike might enter her life. The images of these men consumed her. More than anything Wendy wanted to feel cared about and appreciated.

CHAPTER 18

THROUGHOUT AUGUST THE NURSERY BECAME impressively busy. Customers strolled around as they searched for a great find. Several couples came to Wendy about different plants they wanted on their patios, and she gave them suggestions about plants for morning sun as well as those for the shade. One couple wanted to know what plants might be good in the room where they were getting married. After they showed her a picture of the room Wendy took them around to see different plants she had in mind. The couple agreed with her choices.

At the counter Wendy wrote up the order and the delivery date they wanted. The gentleman wrote a check for the entire amount. Wendy liked the fact she could make a difference.

"Miss," a middle-aged woman said as she approached Wendy.

"Yes, may I help you?"

The woman set a pothos she carried onto the counter. "Are you by any chance the owner?"

"Yes, I am. I'm Wendy Murray."

"My name is Claudia Amber. I've come here quite often since you opened the nursery. You have made this place into a haven. It's an escape filled with beauty. And I appreciate new pots being available."

"Thank you so much for saying that." Wendy's face flushed.

"I'm not just saying it to be polite. Was the design idea yours?" she asked as she turned her head to look at the whole place.

"Yes. I wanted it to be a tropical paradise and a mountain retreat, so I made the far end a combination of forest and woodland-like with tropical plants mixed in and around the nursery."

"Well, you're very creative. Could you pot this pothos? I left the pot I chose on a shelf in the container area."

Wendy went with her to get the pale blue pot she decided on, and they moved to the potting area. The variegated plant looked very nice in the chosen pot. When finished, they went to the counter where Claudia made her purchase. She thanked Wendy, took a business card from the counter and left.

What the woman said overwhelmed Wendy and she left work that day with a renewed respect for her capabilities.

A week later Wendy received a call from Claudia. It turned out she owned a design studio called House Retreats and wanted to talk to Wendy about joining her to do some patio and indoor plant designs. Wendy's mouth dropped.

The two women met at a local restaurant. Claudia was a tall regal looking woman. As soon as the waiter left Claudia explained the proposition. "Much of my work is decorating indoor spaces and a great deal of time on patios. Gazebos are also in my domain. I cater to very important business people, celebrities, and corporations who want patio gardens in their buildings, sometimes in a courtyard.

However, the issue is, gardens and plants are not my specialty. I prefer creating the indoor spaces with arrangements of the furniture, buying new drapes, anything I know will bring satisfaction and at the same time keeping in mind the owners' desires."

Wendy hadn't begun her lunch, just listened intrigued by what she heard.

Claudia chewed a bite of her salad, put her fork down and continued. "For indoor plants and the patio, I've tried several landscapers, but they don't have the creativity and flare I'm looking for. I believe you do. If you're interested, I'd like you to be part of the business, at least, occasionally."

Wendy gasped.

"I realize you are very involved with your own business, but if you could find time to work with me you could do your own designs. There will, of course, be deadlines, but a good salary also."

Wendy's stomach fluttered. Awe transformed her face. "I don't know what to say."

"I realize this is a bit of a surprise."

'Get a grip on yourself,' Wendy told herself. "Yes, but an intriguing one. The thing is I'd love to be involved in what you are offering. I just don't know how I could find the time. And I'm one of those people where everything has to be just right."

"I saw that in your nursery, and I expect nothing less. I may be able to work my projects around your schedule if, occasionally, you are able to take some time off."

Wendy didn't hesitate. "I think so." She kept her excitement in abeyance.

Wendy ate as she listened to Claudia describe several projects she'd done in the past.

As they finished their lunches, Claudia said, "I'll tell you what, why don't you take a few days to mull it over and give me a call." Claudia pulled out her business card handing it to Wendy.

"Thank you so much for thinking of me. I'm very flattered and I will give your offer serious consideration."

Once she reached home the first thing she did was pour herself a glass of Chardonnay and sit in the comfy chair near the fireplace, resting her feet on the footstool. Can I really take this on? she questioned. She weighed the pros and cons. The challenge of the fun projects Claudia mentioned could keep her creativity flowing. Her heart quickened and she sat upright. "YES!" she yelled. "" I want to do this. I'll find the time."

She called Cindy and told her the good news.

"Wow! That's primo!"

"I'm heading to Hoffman's, want to join me?"

"Love to. See you in a while."

"Okay." Wendy put the unfinished glass of wine in the fridge and spruced herself up. She decided she wanted a picture of Brad...if he'd let her. She grabbed her camera off the dresser. With a picture she could see him all the time, sitting tall with his great smile.

At Hoffman's she went to Mike first.

"Hey, cool mama. How things goin'?"

"Everything is rad," Wendy answered, delirious with excitement as she contemplated what's to come.

"How's that?"

She blurted out, "I just got an offer from a design studio, called House Retreats."

"That's far out. What will you be doing?"

"I'm going to be planning all the plants inside houses and on patios."

"Super."

"Thanks, I'm really diggin' it.' She laughed at herself for all the trendy words now tripping out of her mouth. At the piano bar Brad started to set up.

"I'm really happy for you. If you want to stay after we could celebrate."

Wendy wasn't quite sure what celebrate meant, but she was willing to find out. "Sounds cool."

"See ya later."

She sat at a bar stool in front of Brad. Cindy still wasn't there.

"Hey, Wendy," Brad muttered as he got comfortable on his tall stool and set his music on the stand. He leaned toward her. "How you doin'?"

"Great, actually. I'm going to do some design work of indoor and patio plants for a company."

"Sounds great, have fun with it."

"I hope too. Would you mind if I took a picture of you while you play?" she asked hyped enough to ask the question.

"Sure. I'd like that…only if I get a copy, of course."

"Definitely and thanks."

"What can I play for you?"

That was the first time he ever asked her for a song request. "How about 'First Time Ever I Saw Your Face?" Wendy loved when he sang this great Roberta Flack song. She liked to think about the first time she saw his face when Cindy and she pushed their way through the crowd. She snapped the picture as he sang and tucked the camera back into her purse.

A few minutes later Cindy came up next to Wendy. "Have I missed anything exciting?"

"Nothing much. Oh, I told Brad about my new job and he's happy for me."

"Of course, he would be, always has kind words."

Wendy decided to keep the picture taking a secret for now.

Cindy and Wendy ordered wine when the waitress came to them.

"A toast," Cindy said when the drinks arrived. "To the new garden designer."

"Thanks," and she leaned toward Cindy to whisper, "I'm staying after tonight so Mike and I can celebrate."

"That's cool. Brad's coming over tonight, if it's an early close."

Wendy and Cindy exchanged approving looks and tipped their glasses for a toast to Wendy's new venture and their evening to come.

Cindy left early to get things ready in case Brad showed up. A slow evening on a Tuesday night was not unusual so Brad could leave and go with whomever he wanted. Tonight, Cindy, but Wendy wondered about the girl with the long brown hair who always stared with desirous eyes.

A little while later Wendy went to the bar where Mike finished wiping it clean. At twelve forty-five the place emptied.

She sat and watched as Mike finished and came around to her with two filled glasses. Wendy had no idea what drinks he carried. She followed him to the same table where they sat previously.

"Give this a try, it's a martini." Mike said.

Wendy slowly sipped her new drink not knowing what the taste would be. She pulled the drink from her. "Love this drink, thanks, love the mild apple flavor.

"I'm glad. I've wondered what makes you keep coming back to Hoffman's?"

"I like the atmosphere, the music, the camaraderie, the people. It's a great escape."

"How 'bout Brad?"

"What about him?"

"You have the hots for him like the others?"

"I find him a great entertainer with a magnificent voice." She didn't quite answer the question, but at least she didn't lie.

"You're really bitchin."

"Thanks. I like you too. You've been so kind and comforting to me. I appreciate our friendship."

"I thought I'd put on some orchestrated music so we could dance if you want."

Wendy hesitated for a second but nodded, "Okay."

The same music played during Brad's breaks.

The slow music soothed her. Mike wrapped his arms around her shoulders and held her tightly, then pulled back and kissed her. His kisses were ardent and arousing. She needed him more than she realized, his caring and kindness, so comforting. They only danced to that one song.

"You're such a treat for me. Listen, there's an office on the other side of the tables with a comfy sofa." He said as he pointed. "Interested?"

Without hesitation, "Sure."

Wendy followed him into the office. The office wasn't very big, but the brown suede sofa looked inviting.

This caring man, with a great personality, lived up to her expectations. His touches were ardent, in addition to great things he said to her, giving her an inner glow of being appreciated and desired. She ran her hands down his neck and back. Wendy moaned with every touch to her body. She cried out breathless in complete satisfaction.

When they sat up, she didn't know what to say.

"I see a fun relationship. What do you think?" Mike asked.

"I'd like it too."

She got home after two and crashed into bed sleepily thinking of what a great lover Mike was. She knew this relationship could be relaxing and fun, as he said, and yet his desire for her gave Wendy confidence. She didn't see it as anything serious.

"Hi Carol," Wendy said as she entered her nursery and went to the counter.

"Hi, it's so pretty out, I hope we have a great day."

"I do too, but I wanted to talk to you. I was wondering if you'd be interested in running the nursery by yourself on Mondays and again on one of the weekend days, for a while. You can ask one of your friends to help."

"Sure. You need more time off."

"I will, although not right away. I'll be doing special projects for a company called House Retreats. The company designs home interiors and patios. The woman who owns it, Claudia, asked me to pick the plants and place them on the inside and on patios or in gazebos of homes she works on. Also, I might be creating plant locations for businesses who want plants around to give more character and charm to their workspaces including interior patios. She doesn't like doing the plants, so she wants me to."

"Sounds super."

"I agree. Of course, you'll get a raise."

Carol beamed. "Thank you. When do you start with House Retreats?

"I have a meeting Sunday if you can cover that weekend day and I'll take Saturday."

"No problem. I'm very happy for you. Hope it's fun."

"Thanks. It will be a challenge, but I hope it will be fun too." What a pleasure to have someone trustworthy like Carol working for her. Now, Wendy could accept the job Claudia offered her.

It was such a thrill to have her nursery continue to do well. Word of mouth certainly helped. Several customers came in every week, some to check out anything new, or as two of them told her, "We just love to be here."

Wendy's creativity and devotion to the nursery brought her complete satisfaction but to design with others will be a thrill. As a youngster, she used to draw pictures of cats and color them in. Her mother encouraged her to draw other animals and trees in the yard.

But, watching her mother work in the garden, not only motivated Wendy to draw but to take part in the beauty in the garden. She and her mother spent hours planting all sorts of plant varieties, especially her mom's favorites: Oriental lilies, irises, and rose bushes. The varieties came in different colors, all of them lit up in late spring and summer. Wendy enjoyed being with her mother in such a special way.

CHAPTER 19

THE FOLLOWING WEEK WENDY CAME INTO HER house to the phone ringing.

"Hi, Jake," she said as soon as she recognized his voice.

"Hi, dear. I haven't talked to you in a while, and I wondered how the nursery is doing."

"It's great. I'm so thrilled with its success."

"I don't blame you."

"Why don't you come over and I'll make dinner so we can visit?" Wendy prompted.

"How about I meet you for lunch instead. There's something I'd like to talk to you about."

Her interest was piqued. "Sure. Why don't you pick the place?"

"I like La Italia's on Wilshire."

"Me too," Wendy responded. "I love their pizza and lasagna."

"Forty-five minutes, okay?"

"Sure, Jake.

"See you there."

La Italia became a popular restaurant in the West LA area. Parking was sometimes a challenge, but it rarely stopped people from appreciating the great food and the Italian style decor. Wendy always liked being there. As soon as you walked in, you see a large wrought iron chandelier hanging in the center of the main room. The tables had iron legs with thick wooden tops. On one wall was a shelf with a carved wooden mirror, and on each side of it were wooden candle holders with broad yellow candles. On other walls were pictures of windows with flowerpots painted on the bottom with blue shutters on the sides. A painted tile with a bowl filled with bright colored fruits stood out. Wendy could almost see herself in Italy.

Jake, already at a table when Wendy came in, waved her to him. She gave him a quick kiss and slipped into the chair across from him.

"It's so good to see you, Jake."

"I'm glad we have stayed in touch. I always enjoyed talking to you."

"Oh yeah, me, Miss Chatterbox."

"Not really, I've always enjoyed the times we've shared with each other.

"Thanks, me too.

The waiter came over, set down glasses of water, took their orders and left. Neither of them needed to look through a menu.

"So, what did you want to talk about?" Wendy asked anxiously.

"Well, I'm interested in purchasing a small diner in Malibu. It's set back a little across from Pacific Coast Highway and not far from the Malibu Pier."

Wendy's mouth fell open, "Wow, sounds great!"

"Like I said, the place isn't very big and only does snacks and finger foods and drinks, from three in the afternoon until eight at night. It's decorated beachy, which most places are in beach towns."

"Not full service, and this works for the place?"

"It surprised me too, but yes, it works. The owner, Jim, wants out of the business. He's a friend of mine and the bartender there is also someone I know. I want to buy it."

"What made you want to do this?"

"Actually, you did."

"Me?" she questioned as she sat back from the table.

"Yes. I saw how well you handled your nursery, and I've wanted to venture into something different for a long time but didn't know what until I talked to Jim. I've thought about my conversation with him for several weeks and I decided to give this a try."

She leaned forward. "I think it's a great opportunity. Business on PCH in Malibu has to be a hit."

"I'm glad you agree. I wonder," he hesitated and went poker-faced, "if I could interest you in partnering with me on this venture."

"You're kidding, I'm blown away. Why would you want me?"

"I like your good business sense and your ability to keep everything on track. Also, I think it'd be fun to work with you."

"Wow! You want me to put up half the money and a make me full partner, is that right?"

The waiter put their food down.

"Yes." He ran his hands through his hair. "I can't quite swing it without some financial assistance."

She focused on his endearing face and bit her bottom lip. "That's a wonderful offer, but I don't know if I can take it on. You see, I just agreed to collaborate at a place called House Retreats. The owner wants me to design patio gardens, including ones in office buildings."

"I can understand your hesitation, but my accountant, attorney, and I will handle the business aspects. You could be a partner in absentia if you prefer."

"Hmmm...can I go see it and take some time to think about it?"

"Certainly."

"I'll check it out tomorrow and give you a call, okay?"

"Definitely, and if you can't do it, it's alright, but I thought I'd ask you first."

"Thank you. I'll let you know as soon as I can."

"Great."

After they finished eating, they headed out and Wendy left with fond thoughts of her cousin. She wanted to be there for him, but she needed to think about this. The dividends from the stocks her folks left her to use anyway she wanted were there, but the issue…her time. She shook her head in disbelief, two wonderful offers in such a short span of time.

The following afternoon Wendy drove to the diner tucked against the Malibu Hills. Wendy saw little space between the back of the building and the hillside. The parking was to the right of the building. She walked into the diner, sat at a table and ordered an iced tea from a very pleasant waitress. Wendy glanced around the room, impressed with what she observed. It lacked any definitive décor, although there were a few buoys hanging on the wall. She did love the fact there was a fireplace with a foot-high hearth that could add warmth and atmosphere to the place during increment weather. After she finished her tea, she went to look at the fair size bar, maybe twelve feet long. She stood back, turned and looked at the opposite end where the fireplace stood.

"Excuse me," a waitress said, "did you need something?"

"No, I'm sorry. I was just admiring this place."

The waitress looked around as if seeing it for the first time. "It's nice. I like working here."

"My name's Wendy."

"I'm Amanda. Sorry, someone needs me," she said noticing a man waving at her."

As Amanda moved away, Wendy decided to go ahead with the partnership, if she could afford it. Malibu included very high-priced real estate and might be beyond her financial capabilities, but she'd see what the price was before she made the decision. She needed to consider the time involved in taking on another wonderful project, although it shouldn't be a problem since she wouldn't be involved in running the place.

CHAPTER 20

"How'd it look?" Carol inquired as soon as Wendy came to the counter.

"I like it a lot, but I have to talk to my cousin about the price, so we'll see."

Wendy strolled around her nursery as she dwelled on the diner. She came to a stop in the forest area where she noticed a man staring at something, but she couldn't see what so intrigued him. She stepped closer. Apparently, he saw her out of the corner of his eye and turned toward her.

"Hi. I'm sorry to interrupt, but I noticed you were looking at something, and I wondered what."

"The way the light from the small window above highlights the purple orchid."

Wendy stepped closer for a better look and, sure enough, the orchid had a shine to it. "I never noticed it before, very unusual for this plant. Amazing, I'm so glad you called my attention to it."

"My name is Elliott." He reached out and shook her hand.

"I'm Wendy, the owner of the nursery. You seem to have a connoisseur's eye."

"Yes, well, I'm a painter so I tend to notice little things. You have a great nursery here, where a calmness prevails," he complimented.

"Thank you. What kind of painting do you do?"

"Watercolors."

Wendy was intrigued. "Have you painted for long?"

"Since I was eight."

"Eight," she laughed. "Amazing, what did you paint then?"

"My attempts were different objects, like bicycles or horses. Now it's scenery." His voice surged with enthusiasm. "I'm about to have an art show at the Painter's Art Museum in Playa del Rey, near Marina del Rey."

"That's wonderful. Congratulations."

"Thank you."

Carol called for Wendy on the intercom. "Sorry, I have to go back to the front, but if you can wait, I'd like to hear more about the art show."

"Sorry, I can't stay but if you want to come to the opening, it's in two weeks. Food will be served outside at five-thirty and the museum opens at seven. I'll leave a business card on the counter as a reminder if that's okay?"

"Sure, thanks."

As she walked away, she thought how impressive Elliott looked with broad shoulders, quarterback body, deep brown eyes and the creative type like her.

Between work, the drive to Malibu and back to the nursery Wendy was exhausted. It had been a long day. After a calming rest and some dinner, she dragged herself to Hoffman's. As tired as she felt, she wanted to talk to Mike about coming to her house before work the next day. She ached for personal attention, thankful for this new relationship.

People filled the room when she arrived but not like a weekend. She went to the piano bar where Brad was singing, "If I Had a Hammer," a folk song written by Peter Seeger. Cindy came up to Wendy and sat next to her. They hadn't spoken for a few days. The song finished and Brad took his fifteen-minute break.

"What's the buzz?" Cindy asked.

"I tried to call but couldn't reach you. I wanted to tell you about a diner my cousin Jake wants to buy in Malibu, and he wants me to partner with him. It's so cool looking and even has a wood burning fireplace. Can you imagine how it will look on a cold, winter day, with a fire burning? I'm really jazzed."

"I can tell. You're going in half with him?"

"Yes, but he'll handle the business end. I'm going to be a partner in absentia, but I'll still have input."

"How 'bout entertainment?"

"Probably not, it's just a gathering place offering drinks, snacks, chicken wings, cocktail hotdogs and a few other assorted items."

"Sounds primo, can't wait to see it. I'm excited for you. How are you and Mike?"

"We're cool. He's fun. I'm going to see if he can come by my place tomorrow before work."

"Hope he can."

"Me too. I'm going to see him now and then leave. I'm exhausted."

"Gotcha."

"As Wendy reached Mike, he spoke first. "Hey, Wendy, what's the word?"

Standing next to the bar she leaned into him. "I wondered if you'd want to come over before you start tomorrow?"

"Sure. I start at five. I could come around three thirty."

"That'd be cool. Gotta go, see you then," and she left.

The following morning, Wendy stopped to pick up the picture she took of Brad. He looked amazing. She'd frame it and place it in her office for a constant reminder of someone special in her life.

She entered the nursery feeling light-hearted and ready for a great day. This September day turned out cooler than yesterday and the day before. The customers were in an enthusiastic mood, no doubt thrilled by the temperature drop. It had gone from ninety-eight degrees two days earlier to eighty degrees. She chatted with some customers. She liked when they shared about their gardens.

Carol came in at one. Wendy picked up her stuff in the office and looked forward to a captivating afternoon.

CHAPTER 21

WENDY MADE A QUICK STOP AT THE GROCERY store to pick up dip for the chips she bought earlier. At home, she poured the chips into a clear glass bowl and took the dip and placed it in a small green and yellow striped bowl, a cheerful addition. She stirred it, covered it, and put it in the fridge.

Next, she looked around her bedroom. A vase filled with short golden mums stood on the dresser. Wendy bought them yesterday and cut them down, so they weren't too high in the vase. She cleaned up, changed into a navy-blue mini skirt and a white crop top. After gazing at herself in the mirror, she told herself, 'Looking good.' Her weight was down. Her clothes fit smoothly, and her waist was twenty-four inches, one reason she now loved to wear all her new outfits.

Wendy put on her favorite instrumental record album, soft music for quiet times. The living room looked comfy as she designed it to be. The doorbell rang on time.

"Hi Mike, come on in. Like something to drink?" she asked as he closed the door.

"Beer, if you have?"

"Is Lucky Lager okay?" She went to the kitchen.

"Sure. Your place is like really awesome," he called out to her.

She came back into the living room as he finished his compliment. She handed Mike his beer and set her wine on the end table. "Thanks, I like it."

She sat next to him on the sofa while they sipped their drinks. She admired his muscular build. He was a happy guy and Wendy appreciated his company and his concern for her welfare. "Do you see your kids often?" she asked to calm herself.

"Pretty often. They're fun to be with since they're older. We can relate as adults."

"I bet. What made you..." before she could finish her sentence, Mike set his drink down on the coffee table and took hers and set it next to his. She didn't resist when he turned her toward him. With their arms wrapped around each other they shared a prolonged kiss.

As they pulled apart Mike asked, "Can we go to the bedroom?"

"Sounds like a plan." She stood, and he followed as Wendy led the way.

"Bitchin," he said surveying the room.

Wendy went to the bed where she threw back the chenille bedspread. They quickly undressed.

As they lay nestled together, they gazed into each other's eyes. The kiss they shared was resplendent. After a few seconds Mike pulled back and ran his hands over her shoulders and continued to move his hands down her body as he fondled all the places she loved. Their love making consumed every part of her. Mike was what she needed. She knew he cared about her, and he was kind. What more could she ask for?

They relaxed in bed for a short time.

"Would you mind if I smoked a reefer," he asked.

"No, go ahead."

"He took a ready-made joint and a lighter from the pocket of the jacket he threw over a chair, and lit up, "Want a hit?"

"I don't know…I've never tried it before."

"You don't do pot?"

"Never.

"It relaxes you a lot." He took a couple more hits while they talked.

Although Wendy was hesitant, she had heard so much about it being calming and since he already had one lit. "May I try it?"

"Sure, take a toke. You need to inhale it deeply."

Wendy tried but coughed as smoke poured out.

"Try it again, only inhale it slower."

Wendy did and it worked.

"Good, now give it some time and take another hit."

Wendy did as he said, and it wasn't long before she felt completely relaxed.

"Well, what do you say?"

"It is certainly making me feel funny."

"Funny, how?"

"I don't know how to describe it. I'm like in another world except I'm here."

"Okay, just wait awhile and the mood will go away." He took a drag on the weed and put it out.

As she came down from her high Mike asked, "Are you okay?"

"I'm good. Thanks for sharing the pot with me. Quite a different experience, but I liked it."

"Glad you enjoyed it. I'd better get going, so glad you invited me…a far out visit."

"Right on." She held him tightly as they kissed goodbye at the door.

She turned on the TV and watched the sitcom, *Bewitched*, it always made her laugh. After a while she switched to the news. She was stunned when the sport's commentator announced Billie Jean King beat Bobby Riggs in straight sets. What a great tennis win for women since a woman never beat a man at the high level of competition they just played. Women started to follow their dreams, many of which were crushed by the male dominated society.

As the announcer finished the news the phone rang.

As soon as she picked up, she heard Scott. "Hi, I hope you don't mind my calling."

"No, but I am surprised. Why are you calling?"

"Just wanted to see how things were."

"They're fine. And how's the new job?" She didn't know why she started a conversation, but she did.

"Good. Thanks for asking."

"Glad to hear that."

"Well, I just wanted to say hello. I'll let you go."

"Okay, thanks."

They hung up and Wendy didn't know what to think. An unsettling call, like he wanted to say something and didn't know how or couldn't. She still hadn't done anything about the divorce. Her mind concentrated on her nursery.

She headed for the kitchen when Jake called. He told her the price the owner quoted for the Malibu property. It sounded reasonable for the location. Wendy talked to her accountant who assured her it was a good investment, and she had the means to join with her uncle.

Wendy agreed to the partnership. She called Cindy to let her know and Cindy shouted with excitement, "Fantastic!"

Wendy admitted she was nervous but pleased the bartender remained someone who already knew the ropes. Another new challenge awaited her, but she was glad she didn't have to be involved in much except for the re-decorating of the diner…something she looked forward to. Since Jake admired Wendy's taste at her nursery, he wanted her to do something special with the diner, plus find a new name for it. The Beach House needed to change to something different. Everything around Malibu was beach themed. She went outside and walked around in her back garden, a few minutes later a theme came to her. She'd decorate it like a mountain cabin. Since there was a fireplace, she decided on the name Fireplace Grill. She called Jake, also enthusiastic about the plan and the name.

CHAPTER 22

TWO WEEKS PASSED BEFORE HER COUSIN AND
Wendy were given the keys to the diner. Escrow would close two
weeks later, but they were allowed to go in early and do whatever
they wanted. The owner was a nice guy, relieved to be rid of the
responsibility of maintaining and running the place.

Wendy spent some of those two weeks working at the Fireplace
Grill. Her friends from the gardening club she attended when she
could, joined her. Mary Ann and Judy willingly worked on the bathroom and the kitchen. Afterwards, they hung pictures of deer and
moose around the dining area. The ambience was calming and cozy
like Wendy pictured.

Her cousin hired two waitresses and an additional bartender to
work with Stan, a strong looking six-footer with curly black hair who
smiled a lot.

Wendy stood near the entry as she focused on the end results.
Fortunately, the previous owner had left everything in pretty good
shape. Wendy placed short squat candles on each table. To give a
natural look Wendy brought four hanging plants. She hoped this

site in Malibu, along Pacific Coast Highway and not far from the pier, would bring foot traffic from the beach across the way, as well as people who drove by.

"What do you think?" she asked her cousin as Jake made his first appearance at the finished Fireplace Grill. He came by once to see how things were but decided not to return until it was completed.

"I think you did a magnificent job with everything, but I knew how good you were at creating your nursery. I like this new mood it establishes."

"Thanks."

They moved around as they discussed all the little additions Wendy made. On the mantel were a wooden moose and a deer with pinecones interspersed among them.

"I love those mountain inspired signs. I can actually imagine being at a cabin in the woods."

"Great."

On one side of the hearth was a wrought iron holder with a stack of wood. On the other side was a three-foot high wooden bear holding a welcome sign.

Wendy and Jake sat at a table and discussed the opening and other details. Instrumental music was played early, but soft pop music started around five.

Stan came by while they were there. "Hi, just wanted to tell you two I think the place looks fantastic and I look forward to working for you."

Wendy appreciated the compliment. "Thanks, Stan. You've been working here for three years, right?"

"Yup."

"You must like your work."

"I do, the people are cool and love being so close to the beach. After work I can just jump right into the ocean."

Wendy and Jake laughed.

"Gotta go."

"Thanks for being here for us," Jake said.

"Sure thing."

As he walked away, Wendy turned to her cousin, "I think he'll be great to work with, plus he knows what's happening."

"I think you're right. We're lucky he agreed to stay on."

Wendy and her cousin talked about the completed diner. It was now ready for the opening.

On her drive home, along PCH, she admired the beautiful pink sunset as it glowed onto the water, like out of a movie, beautiful to see. She looked forward to seeing it more often with her rides to and from Malibu.

At home she poured a glass of wine and turned on the boob tube. Wendy watched the ugly pictures on the TV. She hated hate, and all she saw were pictures of war-torn areas and people who scrambled to find safety. I need to get out of here, she thought, as she shut off the television. She grabbed her purse placing the picture of Brad in it.

At Hoffman's she dropped down onto a bar stool…Mike stood nearby preparing a drink.

"Hi. I got the impression you weren't coming tonight."

"I wasn't, but with the ugly news and all the violence…I needed to get out of the house."

"Pretty shitty, huh?"

"I will never understand hate. Why don't people just do their own thing and leave others to do theirs?"

"A screwdriver?" Mike asked ignoring her question.

"Yeah, thanks. I'm sorry." While he fixed the drink, she turned around toward the piano bar then back at Mike as he set the drink down. "Thanks."

"You'd better grab the last bar stool before it's gone."

"Good idea."

As she sat a woman asked Brad to sing, "The First Time Ever I Saw Your Face," the song Wendy adored.

"Thanks, Patty," Brad said as she put $1.00 into his tip jar.

Patty's face flushed.

While Brad was on his break, Patty turned to Wendy and said, "Hi."

"Hi, I'm Wendy."

"I've seen you here a few times. Are you one of Brad's gals?"

Wow, quite a question, but not totally unexpected when you consider she was there a lot. "I just enjoy his voice. It's bitchin'."

"Yeah, it's great."

Patty went to the restroom. Wendy pulled out the picture of Brad and reached around his music stand, placing the picture of him there.

When Brad sat down to start the next set, he looked at the picture and smiled up at Wendy.

Wendy left after the fifth song finished. "I have to leave, see ya again," she said to Patty. She stopped by the bar to say goodnight to Mike.

The busier than usual nursery surprised her. Dozens of people came in and strolled around. Claudia stopped by to talk to Wendy about meeting her on Monday and taking Wendy to a home she was designing. While at the nursery Claudia bought a prayer plant for her office.

When Claudia left, Wendy went to her office to check her calendar for all the events next week. She stared at Wednesday where she wrote in Elliott's art show. On the calendar she had paper clipped the card he left with all the details. She looked forward to seeing his work. When Wendy talked to him at the nursery, he sparked a spirit in her unexperienced in a very long time. His creative mind intriguing her. He was so different from Brad, Mike, and Scott.

On Sunday, October 1ˢᵗ, The Fireplace Grill opened. Judy and Mary Ann came and brought people with them who Wendy didn't know. Paid for snacks were placed on the tables. The increasingly large crowd was impressive.

Wendy introduced herself to some patrons and moved around pleased people complimented her on the food and the décor. They may have been surprised by the mountain décor since the place faced the ocean, but no one said anything negative about it.

As Wendy stood near the entrance two women on their way out stopped to talk to her.

"We wanted to tell you, or whoever owns this place, that it's a great escape like being in a mountain cabin. We'll definitely be back."

"Thank you so much. I'm one of the owners and it's great to hear positive feedback."

"Glad we could give it to you," and they left.

Once a week she drove to the Grill to make sure everything continued to run smoothly. Jake said he'd go by regularly as he handled the business end just like he said. Stan would make the deposits at the bank and her cousin, and his accountant would keep on top of things. Stan was a godsend. Ralph, the other bartender, also handled the bar well.

CHAPTER 23

MONDAY'S MEETING WITH CLAUDIA WAS AT TEN in Holmby Hills, a very exclusive section of Los Angeles. The homeowner wouldn't be there, so Wendy could share her ideas with Claudia without someone listening in. Wendy met her in front of the house.

Once inside the living room it impressed Wendy with the magnificence of the space. The living room and dining room were finished off white with gold inlay on the drawers of the cabinets. The drapes were a shimmering soft gold, a wonderful softness prevailed.

"Beautifully decorated. You did all this?" Wendy asked as she turned around to face Claudia.

"Yes, I did."

Claudia opened the sliding door and showed Wendy the patio just next to the living room.

Wendy stepped outside. "I love this patio and especially with the semi-covered overhead. Plenty of light for the plants but only touches of sun came through. I can already picture a camellia bush," Wendy commented as she looked around the area. "Some fantastic possibilities."

"I thought you'd like it. Go ahead and draw it. I measured the area as 14'x18'. Claudia headed back inside, and Wendy stood on the patio making a quick sketch. Wendy wrote down the size so she could put it to scale at home.

Pulling her tape measure out of her purse Wendy marked the width of the living room door opening. She also measured the distance from the door opening on one side and did the same on the other side of the opening. This would help her decide what size plants to place outside the living room wall.

After agreeing to connect with Claudia in a few days, Wendy drove home. In her study she took her architectural ruler and started the sketch. It looked so different when she saw it to scale. Now, she could better visualize how it might appear and the possible placement of some furniture and plants.

At five-thirty, Wendy started to get dressed for the art museum. It was a warm October, so she wore a lightweight pair of purple hip huggers with white dots. The scoop neck top matched the bottoms. The fluffy shoulder sleeves straightened out at the elbow. She looked in the mirror and realized how much she liked the additional makeup she now used. The dark eyeliner with black mascara made her hazel eyes pop out, big and brilliant. With the exercises she did and by maintaining a reasonable diet, she finally had confidence as a desirable, sexy woman. She never thought she would be able to say that about herself.

Wendy drove to the Painter's Art Museum on Pacific Avenue in Playa del Rey. Thank goodness for valet parking because the street parking was full. There were many small shops along Pacific Avenue and crowds of people walking about.

Wendy approached the concrete walkway leading to the art museum. On the left was a large patio area with tall tables set up with snacks and wine. Wendy bypassed the patio and walked toward the entrance and took the two steps up. The inside was crowded. Wendy looked around but didn't see Elliott. She moved toward the back of the room and found a large room to the right, separated into small spaces to display different types of art. Elliott stood nearby, talking to someone. He looked incredible in blue jeans and a floral shirt, open necked, and a black vest over the shirt. His wavy brown hair fell just below his neck. She figured he must be about five foot nine or ten.

"Hi Wendy," he said as he came toward her. "So glad you came."

"Thanks. I'm impressed," she said as she viewed the different paintings on the two walls near her.

"My work is in the next space over. Do you want to see it now?"

"Love to." She followed Elliott to where he pointed out his two watercolors.

She was locked in a moment of silence. "Elliott, these are extraordinary. You have tremendous talent."

"Thanks. Nice of you to say that."

"No, I mean it. These are wonderful."

A river ran in the middle of the picture. The soft blue color gave the appearance of a moving river, so very real. The stately trees with low bushes and rocks along the shores were so very real looking. She looked closer and the details astounded her. The second painting, a mountain scene with snow-capped trees and hills, also impressed Wendy. The ground was covered in snow, but the stream below still seemed to flow.

"How did you get the ripples in the water to look so real?"

"It's a matter of the right stroke, kinda hard to explain."

"Wow! I can see myself in both of those places. Your work stirs my imagination."

He blushed and Wendy hoped she didn't embarrass him with her overly enthusiastic response.

"Hi Carl," Elliott said as a man came to him."

"Hi."

"Wendy, this is a friend of mine, Carl. Those paintings next to mine are his."

"Hi, nice to meet you. She turned to see his work. "Beautiful use of color."

"Thank you."

"Care to see some of the other art?" Elliott asked Wendy.

"Sure."

See you in a bit," Elliott said to Carl. Wendy and Elliott strolled to another small area filled with all kinds of paintings.

"Elliott, these artists are so talented. I'm sure all the paintings took a great deal of time to do with all the detail. How long did it take for you to paint each of yours?"

"It's pretty hard to measure the time. I stop and start a lot, but… maybe two months." He smiled down at her. "There's going to be a party here at nine when the art show closes. Would you like to stay for it?"

Wendy smiled. "Thank you. Sounds like fun." Her eyes glowed at the unexpected invitation.

"Good. Listen, I was going to take a break and grab something to eat first. I'll ask Carl to answer any questions people might have while I'm gone. I've worked on shows with him for years. He knows my work. Want to join me and then we'll come back for the party."

"I'd like to. I'm a bit hungry myself."

They walked down the block to a fish restaurant and were seated within minutes. The waiter set the water down and they perused the menus.

"Wendy, tell me about yourself. I'm sorry I don't mean about your personal history I mean about your nursery. How did you come up with the design?"

He sounded a little nervous to Wendy, but so was she.

"I jotted down what I saw in my head. I just visualized it and then created it."

"What made you want to open a nursery?"

"I love plants and nature as a whole, like your paintings. You seem to like nature too."

"I do. A long time ago I used to backpack. Beautiful scenery wherever I went. One time I went with the Sierra Club to Ojai. I never realized such beauty existed there. We walked paths where the same stream followed us, or we followed it, totally breathtaking. I backpacked at Sequoia National Park and walked around the Hoh Rain Forest in Olympia National Park in Washington State. They were all inspiring...I was drawn to the idea of making scenery look alive, as real as I could."

Such soothing speech, just like he described the scenery. He wanted his paintings as real as Wendy wanted some of the nursery to look like forest scenes she saw in the books she studied. "Sounds like beautiful trips."

"They were. I will always remember them in my head, but I also took some pictures that I put into an album."

They ordered and talked about their interest in the creative arts.

Wendy couldn't stop staring at Elliott. He not only looked great, but as he spoke, she savored his wonderful enthusiasm. They ate and headed back to the art museum. Outside the high tables and food were gone. Once inside Wendy and Elliott mingled with artists he knew.

"Wendy, this is Tom Schneider, a portrait painter."

"Hi, Tom. Elliott showed me some of your work upstairs. Your portraits are so real. You capture facial expressions wonderfully."

"Well, thank you. I'm glad you appreciated them."

They moved to another group where they visited with other artists whose work was also on display. The different approaches the artists used and how they decided what they wanted to paint intrigued Wendy. Not much different from when she decided where to place the different plants. She pictured where they would look their best.

As the evening wound down Elliott asked, "Would you like to come by my place, I'd love for you to see some other paintings I have there, if you aren't too tired?"

Wendy's mind said, 'Don't unravel,' but out loud, "I'd love to see them."

Wendy got into her car and followed Elliott to his apartment, just ten minutes away.

"Sorry, the place is a bit messy," he said as he picked up newspapers lying on the floor.

"It's fine," she uttered as she looked around at the nicely decorated living room.

"Want a drink?"

"White wine if you have some."

"No problem." He went into the kitchen and returned with two glasses. They sat next to each other on his loveseat and sipped the wine.

Wendy looked at the walls. "So, all these paintings on the walls are ones you did?"

"They are, but over a period of years."

"You're very prolific." She stood up with her wine and stepped to the wall in front of her. She saw such depth in each of them.

He joined her. "It's kind of hard to appreciate them with so many crowded together. I wanted to show more at the museum, but two were the maximum this time. I showed three paintings there in the past and sold all of them."

"How wonderful. Maybe someone will buy the two there now."

"Maybe."

They carried their drinks back to the loveseat.

As they sat down Elliott surprised her. "You're a very kind person."

That compliment took Wendy off guard, her face paled. "So nice of you to say." She humbly asked, "What makes you say it?"

"You have a sweet disposition and the way you share your impressions of the art is very moving to me as an artist. I think we appreciate each other's talents."

Wendy realized how right he was, and how much she appreciated, not only his words, but him. She knew from his art, his backpacking adventures, and their conversations that he showed a refreshing attitude and kindness.

They sipped and continued to talk until he held her hand in his.

Although stunned Wendy focused on their hands together. He put their glasses down, turned her to him pulling her closer. Clasping her tightly, Wendy relished the electrifying kiss they shared. As their lips parted, Elliott pulled away and rose as he took Wendy's hand and moved to his bedroom. It took little time getting undressed and crawling onto the bed. The lovemaking was slow, but replete.

When they separated Wendy pushed strands of his hair behind his ear. In bed, they talked about how similar they were with their need to create, to express their inner thoughts and feelings.

As Wendy put her clothes back on, they talked about getting together again. Elliott put his arms around her shoulder and gave her a quick kiss. "Your hazel eyes are beautiful."

She blushed, "Thank you so much."

Elliott smiled at her and stroked her cheek.

When ready, Elliott walked her to the door, opened it where they kissed goodnight.

As she drove home, the world swirled around her. She recognized how proud she was of herself that such a talented and amazing man found her interesting. So wonderful that he liked nature as much as she did. She hoped he'd be the someone she could really connect with and develop a meaningful relationship.

CHAPTER 24

WENDY DRESSED FOR THE COLD NOVEMBER weather. A beige turtleneck sweater and her dark brown slacks were under her long, black wool coat. She preferred the cold to the heat. In the cold you could cover up with sweaters, jackets, or coats, but you could only take off so much when the heat hit. The LA area never got extremely cold, but for the natives, even the fifties were cold.

When she arrived at Claudia's Wilshire Blvd. office Wendy showed her the scaled sketch and a list of plants. Claudia studied it briefly. "I truly think the five plants for the inside will look wonderful. The patio plants look like they will be used to their best advantage. Great job."

"Thank you. When can I take the plants and set them up? Also, do you select the outdoor furniture or do I?"

"I'll take care of the furniture. It will be a wrought iron table painted white with four matching wrought iron chairs. Two for each side. The cushions will be covered with a yellow and peach floral pattern."

"Sounds distinctive," Wendy said as she took notes.

"You can have the plants delivered next week, but I'll call the owner first to see when she wants us there. Claudia handed Wendy a key to the back door of the Holmby Hills' house in case the woman was away at the time Wendy brought the plants.

"Thanks. I'll wait for your call."

"Good."

Two days later Claudia called and said Wednesday was the best day and the owner wouldn't be there. On Wednesday Wendy and the driver, Charlie, drove over with the plants. Charlie carried the plants to the back and set pots on the patio where Wendy indicated. A schefflera and a palm were placed inside the living room near the sliding doors. She set a croton next to a window. Outside she placed six smaller potted plants on a four-foot-wide wrought iron plant stand she brought. On the table Wendy set a pink impatient.

She looked at Charlie. "What do you think?"

"Looks great to me."

"Good and thanks."

Wendy admired the picturesque scene she created. This successful challenge validated her and compelled her to keep focused on her skills. She left the key under the pink impatient.

They returned to The Shade House. Charlie went on to other deliveries.

Wendy called Claudia to let her know she finished the job, also telling her where she left the key. Wendy liked the work she did with Claudia and hoped she could do it again.

As soon as she got home Scott called.

"How are you?'

Wendy still wasn't sure why he continued to stay in touch with her but because of her pride and excitement over the job she just finished she wanted him to know about the achievement.

"Fine. I just got in the door. I just finished a patio decorating project."

"So happy for you."

Wendy heard something out of him she remembered a long time ago…kindness. "Thanks. Listen I really need to get going."

"No problem, I understand."

They hung up. He impressed her with his attitude and his contacting her again. But she didn't have time for him in her life. Too many good things in her head.

The weeks passed quickly with Christmas just around the corner. Wendy and Mike met regularly at the bar and her place. In between she and Elliott spent times together. They went to movies, ate out, or enjoyed other activities. Wendy's life excited her more than she ever imagined. She appreciated the changes she had made in herself that made her so desired, not just by one man, but two men who cared about being with her. The swinging seventies were for her.

The Fireplace Grill started to turn a profit after three months and Wendy and Jake couldn't be happier. They appreciated all the people who drove along PCH, and enjoyed the walk out to the pier, or standing on the beach and watching the waves as they hit the sand. Pacific Coast Highway stretched for hundreds of miles, always packed with traffic. Fireplace Grill was one of only three food stops leading from Pacific Palisades to the center of Malibu, so cars stopped often.

At the nursery the holidays brought in many more customers than Wendy dreamed of. Plants made wonderful holiday gifts. For customers she suggested decorating them with red ribbons or anything festive to add to their cheerfulness. Businesses liked to decorate their offices and she received calls for plants from several of them. A local hospital requested two dozen six-inch plants.

People still complimented her about the nursery and the calming environment it gave, especially with the hustle and bustle of the holiday season. It offered a respite from all the activity.

Carol managed the nursery with precision and thoughtfulness.

Wendy and Carol stood behind the counter. Wendy opened with, "I appreciate all that you do here. I think it's time for a raise."

Carol turned to her. "Thank you. That's very nice of you."

"It will be a six per cent increase."

"Thanks, that's so generous."

"You deserve it."

When at the Fireplace Grill, or when Wendy saw her guys, Carol was always there for her. Carol's friend, Brenda, helped whenever necessary and Wendy appreciated having her on the team.

Cindy continued to see Brad, but not as much as earlier in their relationship. Cindy met a man from her building, Kenny, and they dated.

"Kenny is so cool," she told Wendy. "He makes me laugh all the time."

"I'm so happy for you."

"Thanks, and I'm glad you have found two good guys for you."

"Me too."

Wendy sat at Cindy's pool, watching some macho guys brave the water. The women watched them, in or out of the water.

"Hey, Wendy, do you see the guy in the gold bikini trunks? He raised his eyebrows and smiled at you."

"I saw it too. Makes me feel good." The wind whipped her hair, and she brushed it away from her face.

"Your makeover is fantastic especially with the weight loss. Your long, straight auburn hair is pretty sexy looking, not to mention your greater use of makeup. No wonder guys now stare at you. You look so different from when we started going to Hoffman's…great changes.

"Thanks, you're really sweet." Wendy appreciated the attention she now received. "So, how are things with you and Brad?"

"They're good and he's hot. Still wish we could get together more often."

"Just be grateful you're still one of his interests. I mean there are a lot of gals who wait for the opportunity."

"Yeah, I'm sure he gets it on with Patty and the blond girl. I think her name is Jean. And, of course, Karen, the Palm Springs date."

"Is she still buggin' you?"

"It will always bother me, but I accept what is. Be calm and carry on, right?"

"If it really bugs you, you could always leave and forget him and the place." Wendy giggled and squeezed Cindy's arm." But, of course, you'd miss the good times."

"Yeah, we're movin' and groovin'. I love being part of the scene. I know I belong there. Besides, I now have Kenny in my life and he's great to be crazy with."

"And I have Mike. He's really a good person and fun too."

"How about Elliott. How's that going?"

"I think he's truly awesome. At least with him we can go out… lunch, dinner, a movie. He treats me so well."

"Don't you and Mike ever go out?"

"No."

"Why not?"

"He's really busy with work."

"Sorry to hear that. I'm hungry, you want to go to lunch?"

"Sure."

In the evening they went to Hoffman's. During one of his breaks Brad and Cindy talked. When she came back to her seat she leaned into Wendy and whispered, "Brad's leaving here."

"What?" Wendy asked too loudly.

"Sshhh," Cindy looked around to see if anyone reacted to Wendy. "He and one of his friends bought a bar/restaurant not far from here and he will play there. He'll be his own boss. Can you imagine what that will be like?"

"I'm shocked. I never thought about him ever leaving here. When is he leaving? What's the place called?"

"Not sure of the exact date, but soon, I think. He can't make an announcement here, so it will be word of mouth. It's called Pirate's Cove."

"Wow, I went there with Marty. It's pretty cool."

After two more songs Wendy decided to leave. She went to see Mike first.

"Busy night," she remarked.

"Yeah, haven't had a free minute."

Wendy and Mike talked about Brad and his friend buying Pirate's Cove. Of course, Mike already knew. She imagined anyone working there knew.

"For sure." He leaned into her. "It will be quite an adventure." He paused, "Can ya dig it?"

"Right on, but it surprised me."

"Brad's pretty wired. He's been here close to three years. He's ready for a change."

"Then I'm glad he got it. Gotta go, be cool."

It pleased Wendy that Brad decided to try something new. She made good decisions with her two businesses, so there was no reason to doubt these men couldn't do the same with Pirate's Cove. She looked forward to more adventures at the new place.

CHAPTER 25

WENDY'S RELATIONSHIPS WITH BOTH MIKE AND
Elliott continued to thrive. She enjoyed their differences. Mike, the
laid back and casual one who seemed to live in the moment. He never
discussed his wife, or their separation, and Wendy never asked. She
just enjoyed the time they spent together.

Wendy smiled thinking about Elliott and his more sophisticated
look than Mike. Elliott always dressed impeccably, whether dressy
or casual. Wendy liked the times they went somewhere special, and
she could dress up. The conversations with Elliott were more philosophical than hers with Mike. How lucky to have two men she liked
and who desired her.

Both of her businesses prospered, and she occasionally did work
with Claudia. There were challenges with a lot of hard work, but they
satisfied her desire to continue to be creative. She savored everything in
her life. Of course, her biggest desire was not yet met…Brad. His looks,
so enticing, and his fun personality and talent continued to entrance her.
She also admired how kind he was whenever he interacted with people.
Wendy just knew he would be a caring partner if they ever got together.

Cindy and Wendy approached the outside of Pirate's Cove where a billboard stood and a picture of Brad as he sat with his guitar, and his name in big print: Coming Attraction, Brad Hanson. They both stared at it and grinned. The open door in the center of the restaurant welcomed them. As they walked in Wendy noticed more detail this time and remembered its immediate appeal with rattan and bamboo walls behind the piano bar. She remembered the big picture behind the piano bar of a pirate holding a flag with pirates on it. The bar was straight ahead when she came in, and the kitchen off to the left of the bar. To the right of the entrance were those tables and chairs with the two steps up and the railing all around the edge…the dance floor nearby.

"What do you think?" Cindy boomed over the noise of the workers.

Wendy yelled back, "Really awesome. It's so very different. I never noticed most of this when I was here before."

A man came toward them as they moved further into the room.

"Hi ladies, may I help you?"

"Hi. I'm Cindy and this is Wendy, we're here to help out."

"Oh, yeah, Brad mentioned you'd be by. I'm Rusty, Brad's buddy and the other owner."

"This place is groovy," Cindy shouted over the continuing noise.

Rusty yelled back, "It will be when we're finished. Thanks for the offer to help out."

The noise ended.

"We're glad to," Wendy interjected before Cindy could say anything.

"First, would you two mind helping to get the kitchen organized?"

"Sure, no problem. Okay Wendy?"

"Lead the way."

They followed Rusty into the kitchen.

The kitchen wasn't unpleasant, but Cindy and Wendy recognized the need for some elbow grease and the pots needed to be rearranged. The utensils hung down onto hooks over the two stoves. They were in disarray. A stench of some sort existed. They needed to find it and extricate it.

Through a door next to the kitchen, they heard Brad's voice. He and another man came out.

"Hi Cindy, Wendy. This is my friend, John. He's an assistant here. I see you met Rusty."

"Yes, nice to meet you, John," Cindy said, and Wendy shook his hand.

"Sorry guys, but I need to grab some food before my four o'clock gig." Brad left.

As Wendy watched him leave, she admired his body in the tight denims and the satin shirt with the brown fringed vest.

Rusty went into the bar and Cindy and Wendy worked on the kitchen. They spent two hours there. Thoroughly exhausted Wendy left a few minutes later, but Cindy stayed behind to do more work.

Other times Wendy stopped to help out. Once she helped with the tables on the landing, above the rail. They needed to be re-arranged and new tablecloths needed to be picked out. There were lots of decisions to make. Brad let Rusty and John make most of them. When Wendy or Cindy made suggestions, the men accepted some of their ideas. They started to feel like they were part of the Cove.

Although busy with different activities Wendy knew her relationship with Elliott was steadfast. Their lives together were exactly what she looked for in a relationship. They continued to go to movies, for drives, to eat out, fun activities. Many holidays also brought more fun opportunities, like a party a friend of Elliot's gave.

As soon as they arrived Elliott introduced Wendy to his close friend, Will.

"So glad Elliott brought you. I've been wanting to meet you since you two got together."

"Thank you, very nice of you to say."

"Elliott, has been a trouper, helping me out with work issues."

"Hey Will, you know I'm right here, right?"

"Yeah, sorry, just wanted to brag about your kindness."

"I know his kindness too," Wendy interjected, and Elliott glared at her. "Elliott you don't have to feel funny. We're just two people who feel the same way about you." She grabbed hold of his upper arm and squeezed it to her. He patted her hand.

"Thank you both, but could we discuss something else? How about we go get a drink?"

Wendy and Elliott grinned at each other as they joined Will at a small bar.

The rest of the evening involved meeting other new people and a lot of laughing.

As the crowd began to disperse Wendy and Elliott thanked Will and they said good-bye. On the drive home they discussed how much fun they had. It was nice to get to know each other's friends and maybe get together at other times for parties or dinners. Wendy felt she fit right in with his friends.

On New Year's Eve Elliott and Wendy went to a movie and ate a late dinner.

"Such a fun movie," Wendy said as they drove to the Orange Grove Restaurant in West Los Angeles.

"Yeah, lots of laughs."

The restaurant astounded Wendy. The room looked like a garden with many plants and flowers. Some hanging and many others were spread around the room.

"Love the décor."

"Thought you might. That's why I picked this place, a friend told me about it."

"Your friend has good taste. Thanks. You're always so thoughtful," she said looking up at him as she clenched his arm.

"And so are you."

They ate and talked. Wendy told Elliott about Pirate's Cove, describing it in detail. In return, Elliott told Wendy about a show he may enter. They both had a lot going on and they discussed the excitement in both their lives.

Pirate's Cove finally opened on a sunny Friday in January, two weeks after the New Year,1974. With the holidays behind them people relaxed. Pirate's Cove became a new destination and hopefully, an escape for people.

On opening day, a large crowd gathered by five o'clock. Wendy didn't recognize most of the people. She assumed there was publicity somewhere for the opening, or the partners spread the word. Three waitresses were hired and moved around from table to table, plus they served the people who sat at the piano bar, including Wendy. The bartender looked somber. He was Rusty's friend.

Brad welcomed everyone and started to sing to a very enthusiastic audience. People were friendly, and Brad joked around more than at Hoffman's. Well, why not? Wendy thought. He was co-owner. Lots of dancing and laughter around as everyone seemed to enjoy the evening. A great opening with people hearing the compelling voice of Brad Hanson.

Wendy's weekend continued to be outstanding. She did call Mike about getting together, but he made excuses for any time she mentioned. Finally, she asked the question.

"Are you upset with me?"

"No. I'm sorry, but we'll have to end our friendship. I'm going to try to make things right with my wife. We want to make it work." Mike's voice was determined.

Although surprised, Wendy fully understood. "I'm glad to hear it. I hope it does work out. We've had a good ride. Good luck."

They said their good-byes and Wendy hung up. Her eyes drooped. She'd miss Mike...such a good guy.

She went to the den with a glass of wine to watch *"The Waltons."* She was fond of this large, caring family who lived in Virginia's Blue Ridge Mountains during the depression. There were good times and rough times, but they were always there for each other, and any neighbor who needed help. They cared about others, so important.

As soon as the morning traffic thinned out Wendy headed for Fireplace Grill to meet with the bartender. Stan said everything there was going well. Many guests were now regulars.

"They like the food, but they particularly like the cozy atmosphere. At least it's what some of them told me."

"That's great."

She liked to spend time there and mingle with many of the people who were all nice and loved to chat. Wendy always left feeling reassured about this new business venture and its continuing success. She thought the different atmosphere was a reason people came and returned.

Carol was with a customer when Wendy arrived at the nursery, so she headed for the office and checked her week's schedule.

Carol came to see Wendy after she finished with the customer.

"What's up, Carol?"

"Things are good, but..."

"Uh, oh, something about 'buts'..."

"I need a stronger person to help here. I'm sorry, but can you consider hiring a man, or a stronger woman than us. They could carry large plants to peoples' cars and move some of the bigger boxes."

"I'm sorry. I should have thought of this at the beginning. With all you and Brenda do, I didn't realize how much a man could make things easier for everyone. Of course, I'll put an ad in the paper."

"Great, thanks."

"You're the one who has been great. I'm lucky to have you. Until I hire a man I'll try to be here more often."

"Perfect."

Saturday morning a journalist from the Los Angeles Sun newspaper came to the nursery. He wanted to interview Wendy for a write up in the paper. Excitement filled Wendy's face…she was so proud they chose her place. They talked while Wendy walked with the reporter, Bill Taylor. She received first rate compliments. She gave him the history of the nursery, her thoughts about the place, and about the atmosphere where people liked to linger on a bench or in the gazebo. The article would appear the following Friday.

In the evening Wendy and Elliott went to see *The Way We Were*, starring Barbra Streisand and Robert Redford. The movie came out the end of December to rave reviews and many customers mentioned how great they liked it. They hadn't had time to go see it, but they found an art movie house still showing the movie on the weekends.

"What a fabulous movie," Wendy said as they left the theatre."

"A wonderful surprise…great acting."

"For sure, although the ending wasn't what I was hoping for."

Elliott put his arm around her shoulder as they walked to his car.

"Want something to drink?" Wendy asked as soon as they came into her house.

"How about some coffee?"

"Coming right up." Wendy started the coffeemaker and went back to Elliott where they cuddled. They talked, drank the coffee and finally retreated to the bedroom.

CHAPTER 26

IT WAS FEBRUARY WHEN WENDY AND CINDY drove to the Westwood Banquet Center for an evening of fun sponsored by the faculty and staff at Cindy's junior high school. Wendy wished Elliott could be there, but he flew to San Francisco to see an art show a friend of his entered.

Wendy and Cindy looked sporty in their wide legged hip huggers and printed tops. They were ready to indulge in a kick back evening.

As soon as they entered a teacher friend of Cindy's walked over to them to say hi. A musical combo sat in a corner…one guy on the guitar and the other on the piano accompanied by a woman singer. Although a crowded room Wendy and Cindy found two seats at a small table. Each table had a bowl of popcorn. Wendy watched as a young woman with long, brown hair, in a stunning black sheath dress, added more popcorn to bowls. Wendy wasn't hungry, but Cindy crunched away.

Several minutes later a woman screamed. She stood next to a wall and attempted to climb it. The music stopped when someone else screamed. Without warning, Cindy slipped from her seat down onto the concrete floor. Wendy kneeled next to her as Cindy yelled, "Get the ants off me."

Wendy told her there were no ants on her, but Cindy screamed and cried, "There are, there are."

The room spiraled into chaos. She stood Cindy up, holding onto her as she collected their belongings. Unstrung and scared Wendy rushed Cindy out of the building and drove to the local hospital. When they got to the emergency room there were already many people from the party screaming and crying.

A nurse placed Cindy onto a bed in an ER alcove, and she gave her something to calm her. Wendy shook. She asked the nurse what happened, she told Wendy they weren't sure yet. Wendy sat on a chair near Cindy. Twenty minutes later Cindy awoke groggy and remained silent. Wendy stood next to her.

"How are you?"

Before Cindy could answer the nurse came back to check on her. She reported all these people were experiencing the results of taking ecstasy. It was a hallucinogen that had been sprinkled on the popcorn often in liquid form.

"Oh, shit!" Wendy exploded.

"The test results were positive," the nurse said.

"From where?" Cindy mumbled.

"We don't know for sure. It was in powder form so probably in something you ate."

Wendy remembered the woman in the black sheath adding popcorn to the bowls. She knew the drugs were in them since Cindy didn't eat anything else. "How awful," Wendy scowled. She realized how lucky she was not to have eaten any of them. "All those people, what a horrid thing to do."

Cindy became more awake. "It was so terrible I can't even tell you. Ants were climbing up my arms and I kept swatting them away."

"I know. I told you there weren't any, but you didn't believe me. I'm so sorry. How do you feel now?"

"I wanna go home."

Wendy went to find a nurse but returned with a doctor who checked Cindy out and gave her the okay to leave. Wendy helped her down from the bed.

Wendy drove to Cindy's in silence where she spent the night, just to be sure Cindy remained okay.

The next morning, they discussed the evening. Wendy told Cindy about the sexy woman in the black sheath.

"I don't remember seeing her. Everything is such a blur."

"You should take it easy today. I need to go."

Wendy changed out of the nightgown Cindy loaned her and back into her own clothes. "I'll call you later."

"Okay, and thanks."

At the nursery Wendy told Carol what happened. "I'm horrified."

"I know, me too."

Wendy felt some relief from the anguish since The Shade House smelled so fresh, more so than usual. At that moment Wendy appreciated the lushness and the serenity it gave her. After a short stroll Wendy returned to her office and turned on the radio. The news of the party came out. She turned off the radio. She didn't need any reminders.

After dinner Wendy headed for Pirate's Cove and sat at the piano bar. Cindy wasn't there, but she told Wendy she would be coming. Brad sang Johnny Nash's, "I Can See Clearly Now," as he looked at Wendy with some concern. The song dealt with having a bright day. Wendy shook her head. Brad saw it and held a quizzical expression.

When he finished the song, it ended the set. Wendy briefly explained about Cindy. At the end of his break Cindy appeared and stood next to Wendy. She hooked eyes with Brad, who nodded at her with a contemplative stare, saying I know, and I hope you're okay.

At Brad's next break, Cindy joined him in a corner.

Wendy waited, curious about what he said.

"He's coming over tomorrow," Cindy smiled. "He's very interested in hearing all the details. He really cares about me, he's such a great guy." Cindy's eyes sparkled.

Soon after, Wendy left.

CHAPTER 27

SEVERAL DAYS LATER WENDY ENTERED PIRATE'S Cove and saw Cindy and Rusty in deep conversation. As soon as they finished Cindy fast walked to Wendy.

"You won't believe what Rusty wanted."

"You look in shock."

"I just accepted a part time job here. I'm going to prepare small appetizers. Serving time will be between five and six. I can get here around four. One of the waitresses is already doing it, so I won't have to handle it alone. He also, are you ready for this? He asked me to put the house music on and off when Brad is on break. I couldn't believe he asked me. He could have asked anyone, but he picked me."

Wendy gulped some air. "He knew you were trustworthy. I'm so happy for you."

"Maybe Brad and I will become closer, maybe I can be with him more often. I can't believe this."

It wasn't that Wendy wasn't happy for her, she was…but wasn't prepared for the jealousy to be so strong. Oh, how Wendy wanted to be in Cindy's shoes.

Not long after Cindy started to help, Wendy saw behavioral changes in her friend. She acted like a "big shit" with a new-found self-confidence. Sometimes when Wendy listened to her talk to people, she heard arrogance in Cindy's tone…at least, it was Wendy's take and she knew Cindy well. It's silly, Wendy lamented, but she knew she'd adjust to Cindy's being more in the loop. Besides, she had Elliott who always made her feel special like going to San Diego next weekend for a mini vacation.

The news article about the nursery appeared on Friday as expected. The writer gave the nursery high praise. Wendy wondered how it would affect business if at all. She drove to Fireplace Grill to see how things were going there. A nice lunch crowd gathered. Wendy played hostess, welcoming people as they entered, and seating them.

Wendy talked to Stan. "Business has been good, it picks up the most around four-thirty, or five for cocktails and snacks," he told her.

"Good to hear, thanks." Wendy felt relief that everything was going her way.

As she walked out, she knew it wasn't just her businesses that she appreciated but also the changes she made to herself, giving her confidence she never experienced before, especially when she saw good looking men stare at her.

The following Saturday Wendy and Elliott arrived in San Diego around eleven. A beautiful day greeted them with clear blue skies. They checked into a motel on the Motel Circle. After eating lunch nearby, they headed for Sea World. They explored the grounds and stopped at most of the exhibits. They watched the dolphins as they flipped in and out of the water and they looked at the fish tanks with many colorful fish and very large crabs. Wendy loved the beautiful white jellyfish, in their own small aquarium. They were so dainty in their slow upward and downward movements…spectacular to watch.

"All these sea creatures are exceptional, don't you think?"

"They truly are." Elliott turned around and looked at a display. "This is the first time I've seen such large crabs. They look gross."

"Maybe it's why I don't like shellfish," Wendy laughed.

Elliott laughed with her.

At the gift shop Elliott bought Wendy a black tee shirt with a dolphin on it. She loved it. They stopped to buy ice cream cones and brought them to a bench near the starfish pool where they watched children touching them, followed by squeals of excitement.

They dined at an elegant restaurant with the booths separated by gold and silver cloth. They sat next to each other instead of across. They cozied together as they talked about their day and their immediate plans. As soon as dinner ended, they were back in their room, the evening ending with Wendy's unrelenting passion.

On Sunday they went to the San Diego Zoo. The animals were so close. Wendy and Elliott laughed at the antics of the monkeys and strolled to the elephants. Wendy hadn't laughed this much in a very long time. She stared at the elephants and for the first time realized how big they were and was impressed at how regal they looked. Baby elephants stood next to their mothers who flopped their ears back and forth.

Another wonderful day sped by and before they knew it, they headed home. During the long drive, they talked incessantly about their time together and how similar their interests were. Their shared need for creativity locked them together. In addition, he was nurturing and supportive of what she believed in.

After a discussion about women's rights Wendy added, "I'm so happy you're good with equal rights for women. In the late sixties it was Gloria Steinem and Betty Friedan who first made me aware of the importance of women and equal rights. These women led the women's liberation movement, or women's lib, as it's known. The overwhelming support helped push the Supreme Court to approve Roe vs Wade which allowed for abortion."

"I knew about some of the action, but never looked into the movement. It amazed me how gutsy and supportive activities increased over time. I remember the marches and women standing outside the Supreme Court with signs. Women finally standing up for their rights, it must have been invigorating."

"It was…a whole new world opening up for women."

They stopped in San Juan Capistrano for lunch. As they continued their trip north, Wendy realized how much she truly liked everything about Elliott. He always asked about her businesses and was supported of both.

Once at Wendy's, Elliott walked her into the house, but he couldn't stay. They were both exhausted and he needed to stop by his office.

The next day Wendy pulled into her parking spot at The Shade House just as Carol was unlocking the door.

As she approached, Carol greeted her. "Hi, how'd San Diego go?"

"Fantastic, and the weather turned out perfect. How are things here?" Wendy asked as they walked in.

"Good. The news article made a huge difference. People came and went, many of them mentioning the article."

"Terrific. So, the weekend was better than usual."

"Go check out the receipts…you'll be surprised. By the way, I need a couple of days off. My sister is coming in from Seattle. Brenda said she'd help out again until I get back if it's ok with you?"

"Sure, no problem. I can't wait to see the continued effect the publicity has on business. Word of mouth always helps too."

They went to stack pots the new hire, Jim, unboxed the night before. He was a great asset, able to do things the women couldn't, like fix the low flow that developed in the waterfall.

Brenda came in the next day. Carol stayed a while to explain some items and business, then said good-bye to Wendy and took off.

The week did see more customers than usual. Brenda showed wonderful energy as she helped out and she listened with interest as Wendy explained different plant options to people. The two were by the counter when a man came to them to ask about a plant. Wendy followed him, and Brenda tagged along wanting to learn more.

"It's this one," the man said as he pointed.

"It's a diffenbachia. It needs bright shade and likes to dry out a bit between waterings."

"How tall will it get?"

"It's slow growing, but after a few years it can get to six feet."

"I'd like something shorter at least a foot shorter, if you have it."

"Come this way, please." He followed Wendy to a plant sitting on a tree trunk.

Brenda slipped away when she heard the bell ring at the counter.

"This is a dwarf cordyline. Its maximum height is about three feet."

"I like it, and I'll take it."

Wendy carried the plant up to the counter where Brenda finished the sale and Wendy retreated to her office for down time.

She ruminated about the constant calmness the nursery gave her. She enjoyed talking to customers who depended on her to explain the plants and their care. What a grcat way of life.

CHAPTER 28

IN MARCH, WENDY RECEIVED A CALL FROM JAKE with not good news. The income from Fireplace Grill and the costs did not match up. Stan was out when the merchant called so Jake talked to him to confirm the regular order of four cases of wine for three hundred and fifty dollars. Jake looked at the invoice but saw two cases. The merchant insisted it was always four cases. Jake decided to meet with his accountant and get back to the merchant as soon as possible.

Jake called Wendy. Puzzled, she leaned back in her office chair, turned slightly and stared at the wall across from her. 'That can't be right,' she muttered. She stood up, went to the window, and stared into empty space.

After Jake met with the accountant, he called the merchant. The accountant said the last receipt was for four cases. Stan put the amount on the spreadsheet for two cases of wine for two hundred seventy-five and apparently took the others and sold them. He also altered the invoice.

Fine lines creased Wendy's forehead. How many other ways did Stan cheat them? Wendy and Jake thought Stan could be trusted.

He handled the books for many years before Jake and Wendy bought the Grill. What might happen next, she didn't know. Wendy was livid. She wanted to call Elliott, but she remembered he was at a meeting about an art project. She needed to get away. She headed for Pirate's Cove.

Cindy moved around serving cocktail hot dogs. Wendy walked straight to her and said, "Let me know when you have a minute, I need to tell you something." Cindy nodded and moved on.

Wendy found a seat at the piano bar. Brad smiled at her as she sat, but she didn't return the smile, just nodded. Brad didn't react.

Cindy came over to her. "Sorry, I only have a sec."

"There's a situation at the Fireplace Grill......"

Cindy saw a customer waving her over. Wendy saw it also. "Talk later, okay?"

"Sure, no problem."

Brad took a break and Cindy put the house music on and took some empty plates into the kitchen.

Rusty came over to Wendy. "Hi."

"Hi. The place is really buzzing."

"People lined up earlier to get in. That's a good sign. We owe most of it to Brad. People drink, talk, dance, and of course, listen to his voice."

"Yeah, his talent is great, but we both know it, and now so do a lot of other people. Great vibes. Brad seems happy, I think happier than at Hoffman's." Wendy could tell because he seemed more relaxed. This informal setting may have been the factor to motivate him and/or because he was his own boss.

"So true," Rusty acknowledged. "I need to talk with the bartender. Good chatting."

"Thanks."

She stayed until ten thirty and left, without a chance to talk to Cindy. Wendy now knew her relationship with Cindy was changing, but she understood Cindy's schedule must be exhausting, teaching all day, and working at the Cove late afternoon until nine.

As soon as she got home, she turned the TV on and watched the news. She shut the depressing news off. Her life was at a standstill. How would the Grill be handled? Could they get money back?

Elliott came to The Shade House the next day and took Wendy to lunch. She told him about the thievery. They discussed it for a while, but there wasn't much to say until the accountant finished with all the receipts. Elliott shared his news too. He and a business acquaintance were headed for New York for a week to work on a design project for the front of an art museum.

"How exciting."

"It is. Maybe we can go there together sometime." He put his arms around her shoulders, and leaned over and kissed her.

The way he looked at Wendy made her sure of his devotion and love for her.

"I'd love it since I've never been."

"The city that never sleeps," he said.

They smiled at each other. They returned to the nursery and stood by his car.

"You goin' to the Cove later?" Elliott asked.

"I think so, why?"

"Maybe I'll stop by."

Wendy bubbled with excitement. "I'd like that."

He gave her a quick kiss. "Good, see you later."

Wendy stared as she watched him leave. His strong build with broad shoulders were a constant turn on. She considered how great it was that he stopped by to take her to lunch. She recognized he was truly a good person, and it gave her incredible excitement to know he wanted her in his life, just as she wanted him in hers.

Carol and Wendy discussed ordering new plants. Wendy wanted more variety of plants than the nursery already carried. They went through two new catalogues. They both offered many new varieties.

"This is great," Wendy said as she read the plant descriptions out loud.

Carol added, "The regular customers will be so surprised to see so many different plants."

Together they marked the ones they liked best. Wendy went into the office, filled out the request form from each catalogue and prepped it for the mail. It made her so happy that house plants remained so popular.

Pirate's Cove was quiet when she arrived that night. Sixteen people filled the four tables above the steps, and a few sat at the bar. She sat at the piano bar next to a woman she recognized from Hoffman's. Wendy introduced herself and Stacey responded. They chatted a few minutes about how different this place looked compared to Hoffman's. Wendy looked around, but Brad wasn't there yet. Elliott arrived a few minutes later and sat on the other side of her. Wendy introduced him to Stacey.

Elliott said hi and turned to Wendy. "You look groovy in this outfit," he said, looking her up and down.

"Glad you like it."

Wendy wore a new pair of navy blue, hip hugger bell bottoms. Her top, a light green and powder blue paisley design, just hitting at her waist.

Brad came behind the piano bar, shook Elliott's hand and said, "Hey," to Wendy.

Cindy came over to say hello and being in a punky mood stayed and chatted with them. She babbled about how much she liked working there.

Wendy told Cindy how happy she was for her…and she was.

Brad sat on his tall stool and started to sing as Cindy went into the kitchen to prepare the treats.

The waitress took their drink orders, and Wendy and Elliott spent a perfect evening with food, entertainment, and watching people dance. They left after eleven and visited in the parking lot for a short time. The good night kiss was long and intense. They held onto each other for a while, before pulling apart and leaving.

CHAPTER 29

IT WAS EARLY APRIL WHEN SCOTT CALLED. HE was polite and nice, but Wendy just didn't know what to make of him. She didn't want to share anything going on with her. It had been a while since he contacted her. They talked briefly about inane subjects and he finally, maybe realizing the discomfort in the conversation, ended it politely. She couldn't understand why he kept contacting her, but she did know something was different about him and his attitude.

At the nursery Wendy picked dead leaves off plants and turned some around where the sun had pulled them one direction and the other side looked empty. Later she stood behind the counter and smiled when she noticed the sun highlighting a tall cane begonia leaf.

She talked to customers about plants they were interested in and potted several for people. Around eleven Wendy noticed many people wandering around the nursery…a good sign.

She left work at noon to get lunch and run an errand. Afterwards she headed for her accountant, Howard Wrightman. She couldn't believe two weeks passed since Stan's Fireplace Grill scam had been discovered. She sat on a bench in the outer office while Howard finished with clients. Two gentlemen came out and shook hands with Howard and left. Wendy stood.

Howard shook her hand as he guided her into his office.

"Good to see you, Wendy."

"Good to see you too, just not for the reason I'm here."

He indicated a chair across from his desk as he sat.

"Along with Jake's accountant I agree. Your bartender did steal money, in this situation, cases of wine. The sum comes to approximately five thousand dollars."

"Oh, my God. He did it in four months."

"I'm afraid so."

She had trouble wrapping her mind around the news. She stood and paced, then turned back to Howard. "What do I do now?"

"First, you talk to your cousin, I'm sure he has hired an attorney. You could fire the bastard and take him to court."

She sat back down. "Is that your suggestion?"

"Actually, no."

She leaned forward. "Why not?"

"Mostly because if you take him to court it could be costly and now you're going to have trouble covering some of the outstanding business expenses."

Wendy took a deep breath, "What if I use some money from The Shade House account?"

"It could put you in jeopardy of not being able to pay for what you need at the nursery. Remember, you have insurance, utilities, salaries to pay and other expenses on a regular basis."

"I can't leave Stan there to do more damage."

"No," He stood up and went around to Wendy. "I'm thinking something else."

"What?"

"If I were you, I'd sell Fireplace Grill."

Wendy jumped from her chair. "Sell it! Oh, shit." Her voice shook as her anger exploded. "We just got it. My cousin loves it and I really like it and it's doing so well." She calmed herself. "Well, it was. Maybe I could find someone trustworthy to run it."

"That's entirely up to you."

"Thanks, Howard," I'll talk to Jake then we'll check with the attorney."

Howard came around to her, took her hand in his and said somberly, "I'm really sorry. I know it's a tough deal."

She inhaled and exhaled, "Thanks."

She arrived home and fell onto the bed. She didn't know how to handle this. She wanted to talk to Cindy, but they didn't seem to be communicating much. Besides, with her being so busy Wendy didn't want to burden Cindy with her issue. No, this decision she'd have to make with Jake. But what was the best way to handle it? Too tired to think she instead got herself a glass of wine and watched the news. Deep trouble for Nixon and it looked like impeachment was imminent. She set her wine down, turned off the TV and went to her office.

At her desk she wrote down what she discussed with Howard… to fire Stan and find someone to replace him, thereby maybe saving the Grill, or to simply sell the Grill. She knew to cover the mounting bills Stan only made minimum payments. They owed money to several different sources. If they sold the Grill, they'd be able to pay the debts, but probably not make much of a profit. The ideas of firing Stan and replacing him or selling raced through her mind. There didn't seem to be much choice.

She met Jake the next day at his attorney's office. Jake's eyes focused on Wendy. "I know we could make a go of it by borrowing money, but to be honest Wendy it is a lot of work to keep the diner going. I'm ready to let it go."

"I'm sorry, Jake. I know how much you wanted the place."

"It's okay. I tried it and now I'm ready to retire. I'd like to travel."

"What a wonderful idea." She went to him and gave him a big hug.

"Thanks, meanwhile, we need to find when to close the Grill and let the patrons know. We also need to know when to stop deliveries. I'll talk to Ben and let you know.

Elliott and Wendy sat together on her sofa, he held her hands as tears trickled down her cheeks.

Using his fingers Elliott wiped away the tears. "I'm really sorry about this whole mess. I know how hard you worked to make the Grill good."

"Thanks. I never, ever thought something like this could happen to me. I mean, I knew about situations like this from people and the news. I just never expected to have the same problem."

"You're lucky he got caught before you lost everything."

"I can't wait to fire the bastard myself. Will you come with me?"

"Sure, when?"

"How about tomorrow?"

"You can't do it then. Jake should be there."

"I don't know why I said that. I wouldn't do anything without Jake. You're right," she said with regret and exasperation.

"You couldn't anyway because the business is still open, and you need him."

"Oh shit. I can't think straight. All right, I'll talk to Jake about posting a sign when the Grill will be permanently closed. What do you think?"

"I'd imagine your cousin and his attorney will be on top of that.

She kissed his cheek. "Thanks for helping me grapple with this. When we fire Stan, we'll still need to find someone to run it until it closes. I guess the other bartender, Ralph, could run it."

"You may not want him there."

Wendy looked at Elliott with questioning eyes.

"You don't know if maybe he was entwined in the scheme, but I think I know someone you can trust."

"Even if it's short term?"

"Yep. He's on the lazy side so he'll like a short-term job, plus he worked at a hotel in San Francisco for years, which is where I first met him, and he moved down here and helped at a couple of art show parties. He's learned all about booze, as well as other useful things involved in the bar business."

"I'll have to check with Jake." Needing reassurance she asked, "You're sure we can trust him?" She nestled next to his legs like a cat cowering in a corner.

"Definitely, don't worry. Listen, why don't we get out of here and do something fun?"

Wendy sat up and her anger lessened. "Okay, I guess I can't do anything more right now."

"There's a place in Hollywood called Chip's Jazz Club. I've been wanting to try it. Does that interest you?"

Wendy stood next to him as he rose. "Yeah, jazz is groovy. Thanks again for being here for me."

"Of course. This is difficult and I feel your anger. I'm really sorry."

"I'm so lucky to have you," she squeezed his arm and stood on her toes to give him a kiss.

He stroked her hair. "And I'm lucky to have you too."

Forty minutes later they arrived at Chip's and were seated a short time later. Chip's was a popular restaurant and entertainment spot. The duet, singing at one end of the room, was a man and a woman. Their music was light jazz. The waiters and waitresses were in constant motion as they tried to serve and take orders as quickly as possible. The audience consisted of mixed ages, and all seemed in high spirits as they swayed to the beat of the song.

Behind the duet stood a grey concrete wall. Water cascaded down it into a trough and went back to the top. Wendy's eyes were riveted on the movement. The clapping of the audience, as the duo sang, brought her back to the here and now and the beat generated a thrilling sensation of liberation.

Wendy and Elliott sipped their drinks.

"What do you think of this place?" Elliott asked over the cacophony around him.

"I think it's outta sight. It's so different from other places we've been. I thought it might be sedate, but people seem thrilled to be part of this. Good choice."

Along with the music the surroundings proved inviting. The large room had a dance floor next to the entertainers. There seemed to be a lot of regular attendees, as she watched several people mingle, moving around to visit other tables. Smiles were everywhere. Wendy's anger vanished.

They enjoyed all the music and the high spirits for two hours, but finally headed to Wendy's.

They relaxed on the sofa where they reviewed the night with anticipation of returning.

"How 'bout we get comfortable?" Wendy asked.

"Thought you'd never ask."

On the bed they were cocooned together, and Wendy's heart raced. His gentle touches stirred her on. Their lovemaking was intense. Wendy needed the evening…a sterling distraction from her agonizing day.

Elliott stayed the night. He showered in the morning with Wendy.

They stood in the bedroom as they dressed.

"Your bellbottoms and psychedelic blue and red shirt look very sixties. I like them."

"I found them in a used clothing store, lots of clothes from the sixties. Those were days of wild happenings. Remember how the 1969 Woodstock Music Festival woke people up to the importance of peace, love and the ideals of kindness. Thank goodness it's still happening today."

"Those sure were wild times, and you're right, they certainly opened peoples' eyes," Elliot added.

"I think it's when our generation realized the importance of caring for others, a subject not much discussed in the open until the 60's".

"Exactly."

Wendy loved these shared values. They finished dressing and Elliott left.

CHAPTER 30

THE DECISION ABOUT FIREPLACE GRILL WAS difficult. Wendy liked the place and the people she got to know. So many were regulars who hung out. It wouldn't be easy to tell them.

She met with Jake and his attorney to discuss the closure, but no final decision about the date was made. They would speak again in a few days, more paperwork needed to be finished. Wendy needed to process what was about to happen. To stop her thoughts for a while she headed to the Cove.

Upon her arrival Wendy watched Cindy as she continued to move around to different tables. Wendy didn't understand how she could have so much time and energy for the Cove, but it was her life and she seemed to love it. Wendy understood the job made her feel important and she needed to feel wanted just as Wendy did. Wendy remembered it had been several years since Cindy felt cared about the way Brad made her feel cared about. Cindy shared many of their private times together and the smiles and comments he made to her while he was on break. Wendy knew many of Cindy's prior relationships came and went like passing trains, but not Brad.

An empty stool by the piano bar at five thirty was unusual, and Wendy headed straight for it. The waitress, Julie, came right to her as she sat.

"Your usual, Wendy?"

"I thought I'd try something new, like a Pink Squirrel."

"Coming right up," Julie announced as she set off to the bar.

Wendy smiled up at Brad.

"Welcome to the five o'clock hour."

Wendy put a dollar in his tip jar and requested, *First Time I Ever Saw Your Face.*

As she looked at him, her mind flashed back to the first time she walked into Hoffman's and saw Brad's face. She loved his quips, his smile, his gorgeous voice, and his impressive body. Oh, how she wanted to be with him. She did love him, but in a different way than she loved Elliott. She really couldn't explain it. She worked so hard to make herself look appealing. Elliott found her desirable so why not Brad? She changed so much since those early days at Hoffman's. She lost a lot of weight, she wore all new clothes styles, very contemporary, and her hair hung long down her back. She liked how she looked. Apparently, it wasn't enough, but again, she'd never do anything to hurt Cindy, so it was a moot point.

She erased the thought as Julie set her drink down. Wendy took a quick sip and realized how much she liked the taste. She took a longer drink.

On Brad's break he came around and talked to her. She was totally taken aback. He rarely talked to her on breaks.

"I was thinking of coming by your nursery tomorrow. I want to get a plant for my sister's birthday."

"No problem. I'll be there from ten to five."

"Good, thanks," and off he went to mingle.

Wow. She never even knew he had a sister, but again she knew little about him. She never saw him away from a bar, except Palm Springs, of course. She was anxious to see and interact with him in a different setting.

She stopped her thoughts when Cindy came over and visited. She whispered about her last time with Brad. Cindy finally didn't care about the other women he saw as long as he still wanted to see her. She shook her head at Wendy. "I'm sorry we haven't had time for each other."

Wendy didn't know how to respond. She put her hand on Cindy's arm to let her know she stood with her. "It's okay. I understand." Wendy still needed to tell her about Stan's theft, but this wasn't the right time.

At the end of the second set Wendy left. She was in the house for a few minutes when Elliott called. He wanted to make her dinner the next night. Wendy grabbed at that like a toddler after a toy. Elliott made her happy. He represented everything she wanted in a man. He didn't seem to have any interests, except for his art and her, of course. She wanted to talk to him about what else he might want to do, or participate in, more of what they could do together. Tomorrow's dinner might be a good time to explore other possibilities.

She went to her bedroom, took a brown bag from a bottom drawer and pulled out a lid of weed and wrappings. After Wendy's pot experience with Mike, and knowing how much she enjoyed the reaction, she recently purchased some pot from Mary Ann, her gardening friend.

She got into her nightgown and sat on a chair near her bed. She set the items on the table next to her. She took the paper out, removed some small, crushed leaves, set them on the paper and rolled it, wetting the edges to make it stick together. She knew it wasn't a great job, but it would do. She lit up. After a few hits, she sat back and tried to relax. In a short time, euphoria, total joy, an idyllic state, a place of freedom from thought, made her laugh at nothing in particular.

CHAPTER 31

AT ELEVEN THE NEXT MORNING BRAD CAME INTO The Shade House. Although nervous about being with him she decided to be business-like, hopefully, that would keep her relaxed as usual customers did.

"Hi," Wendy said as he approached.

"Hi yourself." He did a quick look around. "I never realized how enormous your nursery was…I mean, I guess we never discussed it, it's very nice."

He obviously didn't realize they never discussed anything having to do with her. "Thanks." She looked into those engaging blue eyes. "So, what kind of plant do you want?"

"I have no idea. I thought I'd leave it up to you, you're the pro."

"Thanks. Do you want a plant for a table, to hang, or for a patio?"

"I think a hanging one might be nice."

They walked part way down the nursery and stopped. Wendy leaned down and picked up a Creeping Charlie plant as it hung down over a stump. "What do you think of this one?" she asked as she held it up.

He looked at it for only a second. "It's pretty. I think my sister will like it."

As he followed Wendy toward the front, she stopped and said, "I could plant it into a nicer container. We pot for free."

"Sure, why not."

Wendy showed him the pots and he selected a black one with a macramé hangar already attached. He watched as Wendy repotted the 'Charlie.'

"This really is a very nice nursery, Wendy. You designed this place, right?"

"Thanks, yes, I did." She struggled not to say too much, she didn't want to ramble. "There it is. Is it okay?" she asked wiping the sides.

He picked up the plant from the top of the hanger. "The container makes a huge difference. I like it."

"Good." He followed her to the counter where he paid, at a discount. As a businesswoman she wanted him to know they were friends, so a discount was a nice gesture to let him know. She placed the plant in a cardboard box.

"Thanks for this," he said as he picked up the box. "Again, this is a great nursery. See ya at the Cove."

"Thanks. See ya later."

As he left the tightness in her chest relaxed. Brad admired her business. Talking to him in a different setting and listening to his words confirmed what she always thought. He wasn't just talented, smart, and handsome, but truly kind. She basked in the thrill of Brad's visit.

She barely recovered from Brad when Scott dropped in. As he approached, she noticed his demeanor somehow looked calmer. He usually looked uptight with a blank look on his face or a scowl. His pace toward her was slow and deliberate and his face was calm. Wendy didn't move but let him come to her.

"Hi."

"Hi, Scott. What brings you here?"

"I just wanted to see you and know how your business is doing. Looks busy."

"Business is good."

Scott stared at her attire, looked at her up and down and back to her face. "You look sensational."

Wendy controlled her shock at his compliment and for a second didn't know what to say, "Thanks," popped out. She wore wide legged pants and a pink and white striped shirt. She clenched her hands together, "Time for a change. Glad you like it."

"How could I not, very sexy."

Wendy was overcome and proud. She never expected him to use the word sexy on her, he never had before except when they dated and the early part of their marriage. "Thanks." She wondered if what he said was just an act.

He looked around.

By coming to the nursery, he showed a renewed interest in her… but she didn't understand why.

"This place really shows the beauty of nature and great taste in the design."

His compliments sounded real, although so many at once worried her. "I did some advertising and it proved profitable."

"I'm glad for you. Listen, it's lunch time, can I treat you?"

Wendy was taken aback, but she decided what the hell. "Okay, but I have to be back in an hour, so it'll have to be fast food."

"That's fine."

Wendy let Carol know she would be gone for a while and followed Scott to his car. As she scooted into it, she became aware she no longer felt anger toward him, but still felt resentment and confusion. She appreciated his attempts to show a consideration for her, something rare in the time leading up to the separation. Now, she wanted to hear his story about what he'd been up to. She wondered, if he could possibly have changed.

McDonald's was close by. They ordered and found a table.

Wendy didn't beat around the bush. "So, what have you been up to?"

"For starters, I'm no longer traveling for imports or exports. I'm the director, in charge of managing the imports and exports."

Although stunned, Wendy remained calm. "Well, that's different. How did it happen?"

"I applied for it. I was tired of the constant travel and this position became available."

Their number was called, and Scott got the food.

As he sat, he continued with his news. "I do travel, but not often, and not out of the states, only to New York or San Francisco."

Wendy didn't want to show her shock, so she replied, "That's nice." She took a bite of her burger and drank some Pepsi. "What's interesting about this job?"

"The people I work with. They're accomplished and committed to their work." Scott took a quick sip of his drink.

"So were you, all the time," she said rather nastily as she leaned back against the chair.

"I know, I'm truly sorry. I was out of control."

"Yeah, you think?"

She didn't want to pursue a topic that would become unpleasant. She wanted to know more about the new job and was also curious about his down time. "What do you do when you're not at work?

"I play golf and..."

Wendy interrupted. "You finally found time to golf?"

"You bet, wish I had done it sooner, it's fun."

She paused before she said, "Glad you finally found time for the game."

"I've learned to slow down and enjoy life more."

His words were perplexing. Were they the truth? "That's good to hear."

They talked about the nursery for the rest of lunch. When they finished Scott drove her back to work.

"Thanks for lunch, Scott."

"You're welcome and good to see you. Maybe we can get together again?" Wendy hesitated, not sure what to think about these changes she saw and heard, or what to say about another get together.

"Maybe, I really have to go in. Thanks again."

She walked into the nursery letting Carol know she was back and immediately headed for her office. "Damn," she exclaimed as she fell into the chair. He sounded very nice, seemed calm for a change, and wasn't doing any major traveling. She just couldn't tell if he was for real. He sounded so truthful, and now golfing so she knew he opened up to new things, something he wasn't interested in for a very long time. She needed time to explore her scrambled thoughts toward him.

Wendy and Carol closed the nursery at five and Wendy headed home to clean up, and then over to Elliott's. She wondered what he was preparing for dinner.

The minute he opened the door, and she went in, the waft of something delicious hit her. "What do I smell?"

"It's stroganoff. We also have chicken marsala."

"Wow! It smells great. I never thought about you as a gourmet cook."

"I don't think you can call me a gourmet, but I do like to cook. Want some wine?"

"Love some." She sat down on the sofa when Elliott handed her the drink.

"A toast," he said as he sat next to her.

"Okay, to what?"

"How 'bout to our loving relationship?"

"I'll drink to that." They clinked glasses and drank.

Elliott finished up in the kitchen while Wendy set the table. A vase of daisies rested in the center. She considered how thoughtful he was…he always was.

At the dining room table, they sat kiddy corner from each other and relaxed in the luxury of being in this moment.

"You seem to really enjoy cooking."

"I do. My dad liked to cook so I learned from him and my mom. I like to create meals that are not only delicious, as I hope they are, but look good to the eye."

"It's wonderful. Love the food and the presentation." She learned something new about him…she didn't know he cooked so well.

They ended the evening cuddled together under a comforter.

After breakfast Elliott went to his art studio in West LA, and Wendy home to clean up and change clothes.

At the nursery she talked to a few familiar customers before going to the office. She perused the calendar. The stalling about closing the Grill was over. Jake and Wendy needed to decide on the closing date and when to fire Stan. Wendy ruminated for a while before calling Jake to see what he thought. They decided to meet at a local restaurant.

"How are you taking this?" Jake asked after the waitress left.

"I'm still grappling with it, but I'll be relieved once it's done, and I can move on."

"I know the feeling. So, how 'bout we fire Stan next week."

"Sounds great to me."

"I'll have my attorney, Ben, with us and Elliott's friend, Adam, the temporary bartender, so he can take over right then."

"How do you think Stan will react?"

"Well, Wendy, I imagine he will be furious, mostly at being found out and probably thinking of the money he'll no longer have access to."

"Agree."

"And we can smile as he walks out."

"Can't wait for that moment."

The relief of this nightmare coming to an end made her decide to go for a drive to relax, to get away. She steered toward Malibu. She bypassed the Grill and listened to a radio station she liked playing Barry Manilow's, *Looks Like I Made It*. A soothing song that helped Wendy realize she was about to be free of Stan.

Once in Malibu she pulled into a beach parking lot and stopped the car. She watched the seagulls as they dove for fish. Her mind returned to the two businesses, in addition, to the periodic assistance she gave to Claudia with her House Retreats. Wendy knew she was involved in too much and she acknowledged the complications involved in over-reaching.

She also knew she had so much to be grateful for. She was financially secure, she owned her house, thanks to her parents, and of course, there was Elliott. A man so supportive in everything she endeavored to do. She felt needed, loved, and cared for. So, why was she thinking about all that? Something was eating at her, depressing her but she couldn't define it. She realized she needed to go back to Dr. Lewis to talk to someone neutral. Maybe the sadness over the Grill plagued her. But she also considered Scott's changes and a possible changing relationship with him. She just knew Dr. Lewis could help her.

Her thoughts stopped when the wind whipped up and debris hit her windshield. She drove out of the parking lot, heading home. She needed peace and quiet and time to unclutter her mind.

As soon as she got home, she called and made the appointment with Dr. Lewis. Afterwards she got herself a glass of wine and sat on the living room chair concentrating on the unlit fireplace. She began to put her thoughts in order when the phone rang.

She set her glass down. "Hi Elliott."

"How was your day?"

"Busy, but I took a break and drove to Malibu to let myself mellow."

"Did it work?"

"Not entirely."

"How 'bout dinner and you can further mellow?"

Wendy laughed, "Sounds like a plan."

"Okay. I'll pick you up at six."

With dinner two nights in a row and with all the attention he paid her…she knew he really loved her. He was expressive and smart. She helped him by listening and being there for him whenever he needed her. Still, something was bothering her, but what?

She got up, went to her study and pulled out some weed. She rolled a reefer and sat back in her swivel chair. She took a hit, and another. She inhaled deeply, letting the smoke out in one long exhale, as she enjoyed the almost instant relaxation.

From her bedroom window, she could see birds flying high above against the fluffy white clouds. She collapsed on the bed without any care whatsoever. She loved the blue ceiling, only it appeared more vivid than usual. She closed her eyes until it was time to shower.

CHAPTER 32

BEFORE SHE GOT DRESSED FOR DINNER, WENDY took a few hits on a joint and put it out. She wore her favorite buff colored mini skirt with a navy short sleeved overtop. Leaning into the mirror she noticed that her eyes didn't look quite normal, kind of reddish. Probably not enough sleep, she figured. She put on lipstick. The comb easily flowed down her silky hair. She looked forward to a night of warmth and tranquility.

As soon as Elliott arrived, she completely relaxed. He guided her down the steps of her porch and to his car. Still a bit high, Wendy snickered when she slid into the seat.

Elliott leaned down. "What was that about?"

"Don't know…just feel fantastic."

"Ok. That's cool," he said.

They entered the restaurant, Cat and Mouse, to a beautiful wood paneled entry. They followed the host through the lobby and into the restaurant. As they went through the lobby, they passed the bar and a dance floor. Wendy liked the place already.

The host seated them at a small round table.

"What are you looking at?" Elliott asked as he noticed an empty gaze in her eyes.

Wendy shrugged, waved her hand in the air, "Just the tables."

"Why?"

"I honestly don't know," and without further comment she looked at the menu.

"You seem weird tonight."

"Just in a good mood."

Elliott looked at his menu. "This scampi looks good," he announced.

"Okay and I think I'll have the cobb salad."

The waiter appeared and took their orders.

Wendy looked around. She had calmed down. "I really dig this place…it's rad. Did you see the dance floor, as we passed through the lobby?"

"Yeah, looks nice," Elliott answered with little enthusiasm.

"Can we stay and dance after we eat?"

"I'm not much of a dancer, you know that."

Wendy ignored his comment. "I wonder what their entertainment is like."

"We'll find out later."

They ate and talked about their day's activities and after dinner they moved into the bar area. They sat at the piano bar and listened to Matt, the piano playing singer. He was a thin and nice-looking guy with short, curly blond hair. She leaned into Elliott. "What do you think?"

"I'll let you know after I hear him."

His first song was "Both Sides Now," a hit written and sung by Judy Collins. Normally, Wendy liked this song, but as she listened to the lyrics, she found them reinforcing the confusion about her life.

The song is about love and how you can't see its true meaning. The song ended, and Wendy sat solemn.

Elliott looked at her and asked, "Anything wrong?"

"No, the song just makes me think about life."

Matt started another song.

"So, what was your thought?"

"Just how life brings change, some good, some bad, some confusing."

Elliott bent toward her and asked, "In those changes, where are we?"

Wendy eyes latched onto his. "We're good, very good. I just don't know where I'm heading."

"I had no idea..."

Wendy stopped him before the conversation went any further. "Can we talk later? I'd like to just enjoy the music."

His intent look showed bewilderment, "Of course."

They listened and drank.

After Matt's set, they left. As they drove into the night neither spoke. Elliott glanced at her when stopped at a signal, but he didn't say anything.

Once in the quiet of Wendy's living room, Elliott asked, "What are your thoughts regarding your life? What is it you're bothered about?"

"I wish I knew, but I don't. There is so much going on and I can't seem to think clearly about anything, my mind is jumbled. I'm sorry, let's not talk about it."

"We need to. I'm here to help whenever I can."

"I appreciate you so much, but I'm just not sure how you can help."

"So, what do you see as the problem?"

"Things like what happened at the Fireplace Grill and my wanting to work more with Claudia on House Retreats. I really like working with her. She lets me create what I want, and she appreciates it. I need to give the nursery the attention it needs, and then there's..."

"When did all this start? I mean your confusion."

"I'm not sure, maybe a couple of weeks ago. Excuse me a minute." Wendy got up and returned with her box of pot and set it on the coffee table. "This is the one thing to calm me, well, besides you." She smiled at him, pulled out the pot, matches, and wrappers and set them down.

Elliott gawked at Wendy as she manipulated the materials. "When did this happen?"

"Do you object?"

"I guess not. Why didn't you tell me about the pot?"

"I was waiting for the right time. I wasn't sure how'd you feel about it, but I wanted to be honest, so now I'm letting you know."

"Did this happen at the same time your confusion started?" Elliott quizzed.

Wendy thought for a moment. "Yeah, come to think about it, I guess so. It's helped me relax." Wendy lit up and took a drag and offered it to Elliott.

"I'm not into drugs."

"This isn't any biggy. People everywhere smoke pot."

Elliott watched Wendy take some hits. "What do you feel?"

"Calm and happy. It makes me a bit impervious to my...whatever it is."

Elliott stared at her but didn't seem to know what to say. He watched as she continued to deeply inhale the joint. "This doesn't make you wild?"

"Not too much. She looked up at Elliott and decided to snuff the unfinished weed out and set the box with the remains on the carpet. She moved closer to him and wrapped her arms around his shoulders as she closed her eyes and they kissed. "That kiss was scrumptious," she said leaning her head against his shoulder.

"How scrumptious?"

She sat up. "If you're asking if I'm hungry for you, the answer is yes."

At that they walked to the bedroom, arms around each other.

CHAPTER 33

IN THE MORNING THEY ATE, CLEANED UP, AND
each headed for different destinations, Wendy to the nursery. It was
only eight-thirty, but the nursery now opened at nine instead of ten
because of the increased patronage.

Wendy moved along the paths, something she hadn't done in
a long time. She saw things she wanted to change, especially locations of plants which outgrew their original spots, and some needed
transplanting into larger containers. As always, she picked old
yellow leaves off plants and placed them in a brown paper bag she
held. She stopped beside the gazebo, leaned against it and looked
around the nursery. 'I love this place,' she said out loud. 'So, what's
buggin' me?'

She plopped down inside the gazebo. She put so much love and
caring into everything in her life-the nursery, Elliott, Cindy's friendship, and Jake. And she loved her times at Pirate's Cove. She seemed
to have it all, but she knew it wasn't enough, something was missing.
Could Scott be part of what's bothering me? Bewildered, she stood
and walked away shaking her head.

At the stream she turned and looked again at the length and breadth of her creation. Wendy needed to change the watering schedule. She needed to trim some of the shrubs and discuss the repotting of plants with Carol.

As she finished her thoughts Carol came in. "Hey," Wendy greeted.

"How the hell are you?"

"I'm good," Wendy answered. "I think some of the plants need transplanting. If you'll check around and see if there is more that needs to be done, I'd appreciate it. I think we have to adjust water schedules."

"And I need to mark prices on the new plants but before I do that I wondered if we should raise the prices on some of them."

Wendy stared at her quizzically. "What makes you say that?"

"I visited an outdoor nursery with an indoor section and their four-inch plants were a dollar more than we charge, so I thought maybe we should try it."

Wendy looked at Carol bewildered. "So, you want to raise them to four dollars from three and what about the six-inch pots?"

"Mark them five dollars."

Wendy didn't hesitate for a second, "Not sure I like this idea. The word is already out we charge less than other nurseries. We will continue to get more of their customers, and the business will be better if we leave the prices as is. Besides, our regular customers know our prices. If we raise them, they may as well go elsewhere, although they won't have the atmosphere they have here."

"You're right."

"I think I'll run an ad to remind people of our prices on the four- and six-inch plants, they'll be able to make comparisons with other plant businesses. Hopefully, it will bring more people in."

Carol's eyes gleamed, "It will be interesting to see what happens."

"I'll go write up the ad and send it out today."

While Carol swept a customer asked for assistance with a plant she held up. Carol went with her to the counter where the woman set a hanging Boston fern on it.

"Please, tell me about this plant," asked a tall, stately looking woman.

Carol explained its growth habits, its care, the need for shade, and watering needs.

The woman grinned and said, "Great, I'll take it."

In the afternoon Wendy did move five plants into larger containers and cleaned up the mess she made around the planter box. Her next step was to find new places for three of the plants that needed more room. She wandered around for a bit but eventually found good spots for all of them. She completed all she wanted to do and left feeling invigorated.

Three days later she met with Dr. Lewis.

"I haven't seen you in a long time. How are things?" Dr. Lewis asked as she headed toward the coffee carafe. "Coffee?"

"No, thanks."

Dr. Lewis put the coffee pot down and took her seat across from Wendy.

"Tell me, what's on your mind?"

"A lot and it has me confused. First, I've been seeing a great guy, Elliott. He is so good and caring. I think he's wonderful and..." Wendy paused.

"Go on."

"I love him. He is supportive of everything I want and do whether it's the nursery, weekend trips, whatever, he's okay with it."

"So, what's the problem?"

"I'm not sure. I think he's Mr. Right. It's just my life has changed so much since I last saw you and I've had trouble figuring things out."

"Explain, what things?"

"Well, I went into a diner business with my cousin, and it turned out the bartender scammed us, and we need to sell to make ends meet. I know it wasn't my fault, but it angers me it happened."

"I'm sure it does. I'm sorry. Time will ease the anger and the frustration you're obviously undergoing."

"I know. Also, I've worked periodically with a woman who designs house interiors and patios. She liked my nursery and hired me to help with patio and indoor plants. I love the challenge, but it put a lot of pressure on me with my business and hers." Wendy ran right on. "And now there's Scott. He's re-entered my life. He seems different, more open now. He even has a new job where he doesn't travel much and he's playing golf, something he always wanted to do but never took the time. And, for the first time in, I don't know how long, he complimented me, said I was sexy."

The doctor's eye lit up. "Well, there is a lot going on. I can understand your confusion. Let's take one thing at a time."

"First, I have to tell you two more things."

Dr. Lewis put her pad of paper on the table next to her. "Go ahead."

"I still want Brad. I've made many changes in my appearance as you've seen. I wanted to look good for Brad, Elliott and me. I want men to admire how sexy I look. I've never felt this way and I'm loving it. The second thing is I started to smoke pot. It helps me to relax."

Dr. Lewis saw Wendy's need to let go of intense emotions. "Would you like some water?"

"Yes, please."

Dr. Lewis went to a counter, put a glass under the cooler where the water dripped down from the spigot and handed it to Wendy who took a sip.

"Let's start with Scott. You're having trouble deciding whether you trust him because you see changes you like but you're fearful he hasn't really changed. Right?"

"Yes."

"I think to know the truth, you need to go out with him."

"I know. I'm just scared of being hurt again."

Dr. Lewis' eyes were intense. "Do you still love him?"

"Wendy sat straight with a somber expression. "I still like things about him, and he has changed," she sat back, "but I don't know if I can trust him so to say I love him is premature."

"I know this is hard for you, but there's only one way to find out."

Fine lines creased Wendy's forehead. "I know."

"Let's talk about Elliott. You think you love him, but you're not sure. What's holding you back?"

Frustrated, Wendy stood and paced a little. Dr Lewis' eyes followed her every step, but she remained silent. Wendy sat back down and struggled to explain, "I don't know."

"Wendy, just a thought, but maybe you're holding back because you want things to work out with Scott. You're torn."

Wendy frowned. "I think you're right. Elliott is so good. I can't believe I have these mixed thoughts. What do I do?"

"I can only tell you that you should start by making contact with Scott to see what your feelings are for him and his changes. They must have been very strong at one time if you're denying yourself Elliott."

"We dated for two years before we got married and in all that time Scott was always kind and caring, but his changes a few months into our marriage were abrupt and disturbing. I'm just not sure I can trust these new changes. But you're right about my need to go out with him."

"If Scott's not what you think he is this second time around you'll know if you should continue with him or not. As far as the marijuana issue, you'll have to decide whether it's making you feel better about yourself or if it's an escape from dealing with the issues you've mentioned. Running away will never help. If you're happy helping with the interior design and you can find the time, keep doing it."

"I know, I know. Thank you. I needed to hear all of this."

Wendy stood. Dr. Lewis put her arm around Wendy's shoulders as they moved to the door.

"Thank you for being here for me."

"Glad I could help you look at everything."

In May Wendy and Jake, his attorney, Ben, and Adam, the new bartender Elliott found for her, headed for Fireplace Grill. It was seven-thirty and the Grill closed at eight.

The waitress, Erin, came toward Wendy with a smile, "Good to see you."

"Thanks, Erin. These are my friends Ben and Adam."

Erin said hello to them and Jake.

Stan waved at Wendy from the bar. With no expression on her face, Wendy nodded back.

"Nice to meet all of you, like a booth?"

"Yes, thanks, Erin," Wendy replied.

They sat at a booth where they all asked for coffee.

Wendy was fraught with apprehension. "Ben, how do you want to do this?"

"Well, you, Jake, and I will take Stan into the office. Adam, why don't you wait near the bar in case someone wants a drink. It's almost time to close so maybe no new customers will come in, but just in case you'll be there."

They waited until there were only a few people left.

"Wendy, you ready?"

"Ready and very willing," Wendy answered anticipating closure.

Wendy approached Stan. "Stan, I'd like to talk to you in the office."

"Sure."

Stan gave a mystified glance back as the three of them followed him into the office. Adam slipped around the corner and behind the bar.

Erin looked over at Adam with a curious expression. She obviously had no idea what was about to happen. She went to Adam.

"Are you making the drinks?"

"Yes, what would you like?"

"A glass of Chablis and a Harvey Wallbanger."

"Coming right up."

"What's going on?" Erin asked.

"Wendy will explain when she comes out," he assured her.

"Okay," Erin answered with a curious expression, as she left with the drinks.

No one sat in the office. Ben and Jake leaned against the desk with Wendy standing nearby. Stan looked across at them. Ben introduced himself and started right in.

"Stan, we discovered you've been cheating on the wine orders. What do you have to say?"

"What, really. Do you have proof?"

"Ben handed Stan the one-page written explanation of all they knew.

Stan looked at the three of them when he finished reading the proof. "Well, what can I say." He tossed the paper on the desk.

Wendy spoke up, "I'll say it, you're fired."

Ben gave some detail. You won't be prosecuted, but if you ever come here again, action will be taken."

Stan walked out the office door toward the diner's entrance The three followed and watched as he stormed out.

"How'd it go?" Adam asked.

"We gave him the paper with the evidence and explained what we knew, and he was told never return or we will pursue the case."

Adam pushed his long, sandy hair back. "Seems like he comes out the winner. He has all the money," Adam stated.

Wendy snickered, "Apparently not, in his research Ben found out Stan bets on the horses and he's in debt. He not only went through the money he stole from us, but he owes others even more, so taking him to court would prove fruitless."

"Karma," Adam laughed.

Wendy eyes sparkled, "You bet."

"Glad this shit is over," her cousin said.

"Me too."

Adam stayed to run the Grill.

Ben, Jake, and Wendy headed back to Ben's office where Wendy picked up her car. She knew this incident would haunt her, even though she had no control over what happened.

CHAPTER 34

AFTER GETTING INTO HER CAR, SHE IMMEDIATELY
headed for the Cove, where Elliott was to meet her. She smiled
knowing the whole horrid diner affair ended.

Rusty stood near the doorway as Wendy entered. "Hey, Wendy,
how are things goin'?"

"Today, good. I fired my cheating bartender. Now, it's time to
celebrate."

"Sorry about that. Let me buy you a drink."

"That's really sweet, thanks."

Wendy sat at the far right of the piano bar where she could enjoy
Brad's cute profile.

Rusty returned with her screwdriver.

"Thanks again."

"You're very welcome."

"Is Cindy around?"

"I believe she's in the back fixing snacks. Go on back if you want."

"Thanks, I think I'll wait."

"No problem," and away he went.

Trudy, one of the waitresses, came over to Wendy. "Hi," she greeted. "Let me know if I can get you anything."

"I will, thank you." Trudy headed back to the bar. She was always nice to Wendy, and she appreciated it.

Brad came in from the kitchen. He set his guitar against the wall behind the piano bar. "Hey there, Wendy."

"Hi Brad, I'm looking forward to your soothing voice." She felt more relaxed speaking to him after he came to the nursery to buy his sister a plant. Wendy fit into the scene, more than at Hoffman's, perfectly comfortable at the Cove.

"Bad day?" he asked as he set his music on the stand.

"Actually, good but exhausting."

Brad nodded, "Glad some of it was good." He took out his guitar, adjusted himself on the stool and strummed a few notes, checking to make sure the guitar was in tune. He began to sing, "The Diary," an old song, written and originally sung by Neil Sedaka. The song moved Wendy when she thought about its message of making your dreams come true and how much a man means to you.

Wendy was in a better mood and glad she could see his profile and he couldn't see her as she gazed at him. Her imagination got the better of her and she pictured herself lying beside him.

"So, how'd today go?" Elliott asked as he came up next to her, shocking her out of her dream state. He sat and gave her a quick kiss. Wendy wondered if Brad saw it out of the corner of his eye. She shook her head. Why did it matter?

"It went well."

"Good."

Trudy came over and took Elliott's order.

"Stan was humiliated and embarrassed, and very outraged. I don't think his anger was at us as much as at himself for being found out."

Trudy set the drink down just as Cindy came into sight and offered them chicken wings.

Elliott took two wings and a napkin.

"How are you two doin'?"

"We're good, how are things with you?" Wendy really wanted to know about Brad but knew Cindy couldn't share anything about him here.

"Things are moving along."

Wendy took a chicken wing and nibbled on it as Cindy left.

Elliott and Wendy looked at each other and clicked their glasses in a toast to Wendy's day. They listened to Brad for the rest of the set and afterwards they decided to go get dinner. Wendy slung her purse over her shoulder, grabbed her sweater, and waved good-bye to Brad. Elliott gave a wave as he turned to leave.

After dinner they headed to Wendy's.

Wendy went to her study for the box of weed. Elliott went to the kitchen to make coffee. He was completely at home in her house.

Elliott came into the living room as Wendy returned from her study. She set the box on the end table. He looked at it. Elliott sat on the sofa, Wendy on the upholstered, floral chair kiddy corner to Elliott.

"I thought you were okay tonight?" he said as he indicated the box.

"I am."

"Why do you need weed?"

"I like the high it gives me."

"What about just going with the high I give you?"

Wendy stopped what she was doing. "I always love the high you give me."

"I have to be honest I don't like your use of pot."

Wendy flinched, "You said you were okay with it."

"I think the weed is turning you into someone else. Also, weed can lead to other drugs and they can cause a lot of problems."

"So, you're afraid I'll start to use hard drugs?"

"Yes, and I don't understand why you need any drugs at all."

"I just enjoy the weed, that's it. I just like the high I get, also it makes me passionate. Let me show you." She moved to sit on his lap, but he stood before she could reach him.

"The weed is a crutch. You need to find your answers with a straight head. I'm going to head home. I'll call you tomorrow and we will talk more." Be sure to turn the coffee off." He grabbed his jacket and headed for the door.

Wendy was rattled as she watched him walk away. Obviously, he wanted her to stop using the pot. Did she have to pick one over the other? His words hurt, and she realized it was the first big disagreement in all the months they were together. She wasn't sure what she wanted to do. What bothered Wendy was he pretty much gave her an ultimatum. But she really cared about Elliott.

Wendy took the box back to her study and left it on the floor.

After shutting off the coffee she crashed on the bed. She turned on her side and looked at nothing. Elliott was right about one thing, she didn't know why the pot became so important to her, but it did.

Something she couldn't identify distressed her. Once, Dr. Lewis suggested Wendy write down what her issues were and try to look at them with less emotion, think it through. She needed to do that.

She went to the window facing her backyard. She pushed the drapes aside and opened the window. The smell of jasmine drifted in from her treasured garden and she wondered if her life was crumbling before her. Things had been so good since she left Scott. She loved her new life and her changes. She was conflicted about Scott and

Elliott. She hated what happened at the Grill. She clasped her arms around her shoulders. The tears dribbled down her cheeks. She fell to the floor where she sat until her anguish subsided. She crawled into bed fully clothed.

CHAPTER 35

IN THE MORNING WENDY THREW HER ROBE ON and went to the kitchen where she reheated the coffee they never drank. She sat at the kitchen table mulling over what happened the night before. She didn't know what to expect when Elliott called. With a swift move, she sat upright. An idea hit her, she wouldn't use the weed around Elliott, a compromise. Yes, she'd talk to him about it when he called.

Although she planned to go to the Cove that night she decided to return to Cat and Mouse, where no one knew her. She arrived at five.

As she entered the bar area Matt was singing, "Smile." Charlie Chaplin composed the music and Nat King Cole wrote the lyrics. Wendy loved his voice. The message is about even if you're sad, you should smile, since life moves on. Matt played the piano softly as he sang in his sweet baritone voice.

Wendy sat at a small table across from the piano bar. The waitress came over and Wendy ordered a screwdriver. She looked around. She imagined the almost full room had to do with people coming from work.

It didn't take long for Wendy to mellow. She became enamored with Matt. He displayed a mild demeanor whether at the piano or when he walked around. She scanned the room again. It gratified her to be in such a calming and isolated space. It was clear to Wendy she would enjoy her new go to place, her escape from everything upsetting her. For the first time in days her eyes twinkled.

Wendy checked her watch. The time slipped away, it was six-thirty and she needed to leave. As she stood and walked past the piano bar Matt smiled at her and nodded his head like he knew her. Wendy smiled back.

She grabbed a TV dinner from the freezer and watched the news. She flipped the channel from the ugliness of the news and found *Mash*. Now, this show made her laugh a lot. The characters, Hawkeye and Trapper, were so clever with their pranks, especially against Charles, the doctor with no sense of humor. The show also became serious as it demonstrated the ugliness of the Korean War... of war in general.

Elliott called a little before seven-thirty.

"Before you say anything about last night let me ask you about an idea, more like a compromise."

"Okay, go ahead." His voice was solemn.

"What if I don't smoke weed when we're together?"

Elliott cleared his throat. "I'm worried about your need for it."

"I understand, but it isn't addicting, and my use will just disappear over time like peoples' idiosyncrasies do."

A second of silence followed. Wendy held her breath..

"All right, but I don't want to smell it on you."

"It's a deal. So, how was your day, Ellie?"

"Where did that come from?" he asked sounding shocked.

"I thought it would be my private name for you, if it's okay?"

"I'll have to get used to it, but I guess so."

"Great."

She decided not to say anything about her time at Cat and Mouse. "I had a good day, how 'bout you?"

"I've been busy working on a new painting of a young couple as they watch the sunset on the top of a mountain. I haven't seen a view like this before in quite the way I'm expressing it. There are a lot of paintings at the beach, but on a mountain top, not so many."

Wendy lowered her voice, "Sounds very romantic. I'm sure I'll love it. In her regular voice she asked, "Do you think it will take a long time to finish?"

"As I said, no way to know. I like the process and how this painting is slowly evolving."

"Sounds a lot like how I visualized the nursery before I put it together…it's all about the creative process."

"It is, and you and I share that love. Listen, I hate to interrupt but I haven't eaten yet and I'm exhausted. Want to go to the Cove tomorrow night? I can pick you up at five and we can grab a bite first."

"Sure, thanks. Have a good dinner," Wendy added.

She was pleased he went for the compromise. She wanted Elliott in her life, and yet he couldn't be there all the time, but the weed was, and it gave her comfort when no one was around. She knew he must really care about her to go along with the compromise.

The next day Claudia called. "Twelve other companies are putting together a design show at the Convention Center in downtown LA. I thought you might help with the patio design and the floral displays for the two rooms after I design the living room and dining room. What do you say?"

Wendy's quick response, "I'd love to be involved. Thank you."

"I shared some of your photos with other companies and they were impressed. No telling where it can lead."

"Very nice of you. I appreciate it."

"No problem, besides, we need expertise and talent to make our interiors and patios look great, so thanks for the yes. When can you come by and see my designs?"

"Hang on and I'll get my calendar." Wendy went to her office, grabbed the calendar and scurried back to the phone in the kitchen. "I can get away on Wednesday."

"Okay, how 'bout eleven?"

"I'll be there, and thanks again."

They hung up and Wendy whirled around with a huge grin. This was the type of creativeness she loved, and to do displays at the Convention Center, extraordinary. Instead of worrying about Elliott or Scott, or the Fireplace Grill, she could focus her attention on something completely different…the artistic challenge.

When Wendy arrived at the nursery, Carol stood at the counter writing up a sale. They exchanged quick greetings and Wendy waited anxiously while Carol finished the order.

"Thank you for visiting us," Carol said as the customer turned to leave. "Please come back."

"Oh, I will. I love to spend time here," said the woman as she ambled away.

"Carol, you aren't going to believe what I'm doing for Claudia, you know the woman who owns House Retreats."

"I know you loved working with her."

Wendy told her the story.

Carol's whole face lit up. "This should help with your frustration of not being able to do more here."

"I think it might. I'll meet with Claudia on Wednesday and see her designs and I can figure where I want things to go. This is so awesome."

"It's groovy."

CHAPTER 36

ELLIOTT PICKED WENDY UP AT FIVE AND THE minute she opened the door she bombarded him with, "You won't believe this, but I'm doing a Design Showcase at the Convention Center."

"That's quite a greeting and I'm very happy for you. I don't know what it is, so let's talk about it over dinner."

They went to Hamburger Hamlet. As soon as they were seated Wendy wasted no time as she began to explain the event to Elliott. She momentarily stopped when the waitress came over to take their dinner orders, then continued to rattle on.

"That's terrific. A great opportunity to do more creative stuff."

"Thanks, I'm stoked."

They continued talking about art and being creative.

Their dinners arrived. They ate and chatted. Elliott explained the enchantment with the mountain he was painting, and of course, Wendy went on about her new challenge.

As they entered Pirate's Cove, they were surprised by the extremely large crowd. There were no seats at the piano bar. She looked toward the tables. Just then Trudy, the very nice waitress, came over and reported she was about to clear a table if they wanted it. It was on the floor in the center of the table and chair area a bit back from the piano bar. A frontal view, at this distance, was new to Wendy.

Cindy came over and sat in a third chair. "Hey, guys, how's it goin'? Sorry I've been out of touch Wendy, really been crazy, with work here and my regular job. What's new?"

"A lot but it's too hard to talk here. Call me and I'll tell you about my new involvement in a Design Showcase event at the Convention Center."

"Outta sight, I'll call ya," Cindy said and off she went.

It surprised Wendy she even asked about her, or them. Maybe she finally recognized how much she missed their friendship.

As they waited for their drinks Brad sang Jim Croce's, *Bad, Bad Leroy Brown*, a great recent hit.

"Let's dance," Wendy begged, as she watched three couples dancing at full velocity.

"I keep telling you, I really don't dance, sorry. I never got the hang of it."

Although mildly irritated, she said, "I understand." She wanted to dance because she had so much energy she could explode. Elliott joined Wendy as she started to clap to the rhythm of the song, and others joined in. Wendy turned away from the dance floor and toward Brad. She wanted to touch him, to kiss him, to feel his body next to hers. She shook her head. What terrible thoughts to have as she sat next to Elliott.

After her mother died and her dad was demeaning and hurtful toward her, Wendy escaped into the world of make believe. She lived at the movies, every Saturday. She watched Gregory Peck, Cary Grant, and Clark Gable and their infinite manliness. She wanted a man who looked and acted like any of them…so good, and great actors and so loving and caring to the women with them. They were in movies, but Brad was real. He was the epitome of what she dreamt of. Elliott also possessed those characteristics, so why wasn't she dreaming of him the same way she did Brad?

Elliott and Wendy stayed for two sets. They waved good-bye to Rusty as they passed him and headed for Wendy's.

They visited for a few minutes in the car, then kissed goodnight. Wendy walked up her front porch, opened the door and turned the porch light on so Elliott knew she arrived safely inside. As he drove away Wendy realized how much she truly cared about him. For a reason she couldn't explain, she didn't have the same kind of love for him as she did for Brad.

Cindy called Saturday morning and they decided to meet at the local deli for lunch. The gesture surprised Wendy.

"It's good to see ya, Wendy. I know I've been in my own world for a long time and I'm sorry. Full-time teaching and work at Pirate's Cove part time, just too much pressure."

"I actually thought you were mad at me until you sat down the other night and talked to me."

"I wasn't mad, I was just selfish, and it's taken me awhile to figure it out. I'm very sorry. I started to believe in myself as someone special because I felt so needed at the Cove. I now know I wasn't any more special than any other woman there."

"You're still special and needed there," Wendy said with encouragement.

Cindy's voice cracked and her face flushed. "I'm not."

Wendy stared puzzled.

"They decided to add more hours and I can't do them with my teaching job and that comes first."

"Couldn't you still work weekends?"

"Nope, they want to give the new person they hire full time work." Cindy's face contorted. "To be perfectly honest Brad and I had an argument and I think this is why the change." Tears formed in her eyes. "I had to quit."

Wendy's mouth fell open, "Oh no, I'm really sorry."

"Thanks." Cindy dabbed at her tears.

Wendy hurt for Cindy. "Incredible," was all she could say.

"I don't mind leaving too much…two jobs exhausted and stressed me out. Plus, he's seeing at least three different girls. They even tell me about some of their times with him, maybe not aware that I may be one of them too, or they just wanted to gloat. I see the way he looks at them, and how they look at him, not to mention the cute asides he makes to them."

"Do you think he's dumping you?"

"I think he made that clear by increasing the hours plus not talking to me much. I mean what can I do, confront him? You don't do that to him. You get my drift?"

Wendy reached across the table and put her hand on Cindy's arm. "Unfortunately, I do. I'm terribly sorry."

"Thanks. I'm not sure I'll even go around there anymore."

Wendy pulled back. "I can't believe you said that you like being there."

"I don't care anymore. I don't want to go back to a place that has caused me such pain. There are other hunks out there I can dig and maybe will appreciate me more. Once in a while I still see Kenny. At least I'll have more time for him and maybe someone else will come into my life."

Wendy hurt for Cindy. "I'm glad you have a positive attitude about this."

"It's taken me awhile to face the reality. I will dream on and keep on truckin'."

Wendy held her hands in Cindy's. "Good for you."

"Thanks for being here for me after I ignored you for so long."

"It's okay. I understand."

They finished lunch and agreed to get together later in the week.

What will happen next at the Cove? Wendy pondered. She also wondered what would happen to Cindy and Brad's relationship. If he's hardly speaking to her, is that the indication it has ended?

Jake called to inform her the realtor he hired had found a buyer for Fireplace Grill. In three weeks, it would close temporarily while the new owner made changes.

The next day they met in the parking lot of the Grill. Her cousin held a bag with the sign about the closure, and its reopening under new management. He handed the bag to Wendy. They drove there to notify Adam and display the sign.

They walked into a lively group of about a dozen people. Two people waved at Wendy when they saw her near the entrance. She waved back. Her concern was their reaction when she told them they were selling the place.

They headed to the bar.

"Hi there," Adam said as they approached.

"Hi Adam." Wendy leaned over the bar and said quietly, "Three weeks before it closes. We hope you'll have time to find something else."

Adam's response, "Don't worry about me."

Wendy remembered he didn't like long term jobs.

Wendy pulled the sign out of the bag. "I'm going to post this." She held it up under new management effective…and it gave the date.

"That's clear," Adam stated. "You want a drink, Jake?"

"Sure, thanks."

With the scotch tape she brought she taped the sign inside of the front window. She walked over to the people she waved at. They chit-chatted and Wendy informed them what was about to happen.

"Oh, no," Bonnie said. "But why? This place is rad."

"Thanks. It may still be rad. My partner and I can't give it the attention it needs but maybe the new owner will. Stop by the nursery and say hi anytime." Most regulars knew about the nursery.

Their disappointment with the closure made Wendy sad. She moved away. She looked around and relived the entire Stan ordeal. Her mood went sour.

She went and sat with Jake for a while as she sipped iced tea and visited with Adam.

The minute she got home she went straight for the weed, lit a ready-made joint, and sank into a living room chair. Her thoughts concentrated on how she failed with the business venture. There were such high hopes for it. To be scammed not only embarrassed her, but stole her confidence, although she didn't have control over what had happened. She took a couple of hits of her joint, grabbed a quick bite and watched, *Three's Company*. That show usually made her laugh… only tonight it didn't.

The phone rang part way through *Three's Company*, but she had no desire to talk to anyone. She wanted to be alone.

CHAPTER 37

THE NEXT NIGHT WENDY WENT TO LISTEN TO MATT.
This June evening needed to be focused on fun.

Cat and Mouse was comfortably crowded as Wendy stood at the entrance to the bar area. A man left a piano bar seat a few minutes later and Wendy quickly moved to it before anyone else could.

Matt looked at Wendy and they exchanged smiles. She ordered a glass of Chablis and listened as he played and sang, "Somewhere," from *The Westside Story.* He seemed to sing a lot of Broadway tunes and Wendy loved them all.

The woman next to her was Alice. Wendy remembered hearing her name last time she came. Alice turned to Wendy and asked if she came often and when Wendy said this was her third time. "You should come more often. This place is super cool."

"I think most bars are."

"This one is special."

"What makes you say that?"

"I've been coming here for months and there's always a good time, if you catch my drift?" Alice giggled and placed a finger on her lips.

Wendy had no idea what Alice was hinting at. She supposed it had to do with the men who came in, or the affairs people were having, or something directly related to Matt.

Alice emphasized, "Oh, you know, the guys, the great drug parties, and just stuff."

Wendy figured she was on something. Wendy only wanted quiet here and a chance to unwind. She nodded her head to the beat of the music.

At the end of the set, "Goin' to the bathroom," Alice announced to Wendy.

Matt moved around visiting with different people and came over to Wendy. "So, I've seen you here a few times now. What's your name?"

"It's Wendy."

He smiled. "Well, glad you came back."

"Thank you. I have to say your voice, your piano playing, and song choices are all great."

"That's bitchin', which reminds me I'd better go back and demonstrate those qualities. Do you have a particular song choice?" he asked as he went around to the piano.

"I like Johnny Mathis', "Wonderful! Wonderful."

"A favorite of mine too."

By the third note Wendy's admiring eyes widened. What a beautiful rendition. She enjoyed it almost as much as Mathis' version. She sat back in her seat as Alice returned to hers. Alice started to speak but Wendy put her finger to her lips and nodded toward Matt. Alice smiled in agreement.

Cat and Mouse, her secret escape from everyone and everything.

After his first set Wendy and Alice visited some more. Wendy thought she seemed a nice woman, although she couldn't see them as friends. As soon as the conversation ended Alice went to the bathroom again. Wendy believed it was in the bathroom she dabbled in whatever drug she used.

Matt waved to Wendy as she put on her sweater. He mouthed thank you, and she took off. Although she had no romantic interest in him, he did make her tranquil. She drove home in an upbeat mood.

The next afternoon Wendy kept busy helping customers and transplanting plants. She still loved to work with the customers and help them find the best ceramic container for their particular plant.

At closing time Scott came in. Wendy wasn't surprised to see him.

"Hi, Scott," she greeted.

"Hi to you. How've you been?"

"Not too bad, but busy."

"If you have time for dinner, I'd like to hear about it."

Wendy didn't know why but without hesitation she said, "I have time." She wanted another opportunity to get to know him, to see if he was different, not so bossy, not critical of her. At least he wasn't traveling like he used to. "Let me close up. I'll take my car. Where should I meet you?"

"Is Russell's okay?"

"Sure. See you there shortly."

"Okay."

After Scott left Wendy turned off the fan in the office and all the switches as she exited.

Scott waited for her inside the entrance to Russell's.

"So, why have you been so busy?" Scott asked as soon as they were seated.

The waitress came over and they ordered drinks and they each knew what they wanted for dinner. I'm busy at the nursery. It looks the way I visualized, so I'm happy. The woman working with me,

Carol, is a great gal. And soon I'll be displaying plants for a design company project at the Convention Center."

"That's wonderful. For what it's worth, I'm really proud of you."

Wendy's face went blank. "You've never shared anything like that with me. Thank you, I appreciate it."

"I wasn't very good at saying those kinds of things. But I started to listen better to people at my jobs and learned more about myself."

"Like what?"

"How others' opinions are sometimes better than mine. I always thought mine were best."

Wendy focused on his eyes. "I always thought you loved your old job."

"I did for a long time, but things changed, and it started to bore me and became too competitive. The CEO never seemed to appreciate my work, so I quit."

"Why didn't you ever say anything?"

"I don't know. I wanted you to think I was macho," he confessed.

"You didn't need to prove anything to me."

"I know that now. I was much different then, than I am now."

"How?"

"I accept things with less tension, and I don't get upset so much about things I can't control."

Wendy studied him for a moment. "Those are nice changes."

"Thanks, I think so too."

Their drinks arrived and they sipped the Chablis they both ordered.

Wendy realized this conversation was the first time since the beginning of their marriage he shared this kind of information with her. She certainly saw a change in him. The question was, would he stay this way, or change again in a negative way. For that matter, was what he said real? She struggled with her emotions.

The waitress brought their dinners.

"You sound like someone I used to know."

"What do you mean?" Scott asked as he took a swallow of the wine.

"You shared things with me when we dated and when we were first married, but suddenly everything changed. You didn't share much, never had time for us. We started to argue about almost everything and you constantly criticized me."

Scott leaned into her. "I'm so sorry. I don't know what happened to me except I became selfish. I hope I've changed."

"It's hard to tell right now."

He reinforced his positive outlook, "I hope you will see the changes."

She didn't know what to say except, "Maybe."

They ate silently for a few minutes until Wendy broke the tension. She told him how she was scammed at the Fireplace Grill.

"How terrible. You must have felt awful, and the financial loss must have hurt."

"It did…it still does, but I'm handling it."

He took her hand in his. "Good for you. I know it must have been tough."

She casually pulled her hand back to pick up her fork. "It was."

The discussions slowed as they finished their dinners.

When they left Scott saw Wendy to her car where they said their good-byes. There was no kiss, and she was relieved. She wasn't ready for kisses to be part of what might be a new and improved relationship.

At home she watched the news, smoked part of a joint and floated off to sleep.

In the morning Wendy made a concerted effort to get going. She couldn't explain her mood. When she left Scott, she never thought they could get back together. After last night his transformation made her think there was a chance. He admitted to being selfish, but he emphasized he'd changed. She needed to hear that. A chance to be a couple and share their thoughts and feelings was how their marriage began. She didn't want to dwell on their horrible arguments about his absence, or his criticism, or his inability to share what he thought or felt. His openness and interest in her gave her encouragement. She needed to watch her criticism of others too. They needed to spend time together to be sure he was a transformed person.

Wendy threw on her grungy jeans and old sweatshirt and went to the backyard. She needed this down time. Her life needed to ebb and flow like gentle tides, smooth and less tense. Working in her garden would work. She dug up a small azalea and transplanted it to an area closer to her bedroom window so she could look out and see its precious pink flowers. After a little weeding she sat back on her heels, looked around her yard and reminded herself she was good at what she did. She wanted to continue to channel her abilities in areas where she could excel. She hoped the Convention Center project offered her another opportunity to do just that.

She brushed her gloves together to get the soil off, pulled them from her fingers and tossed them on the patio table as she went inside. It was near the end of June, and Wendy stopped major garden work except for upkeep. Plants didn't like to be planted or transplanted when it was hot. It could put them into shock.

Wendy showered, dressed and read the paper as she ate dinner. She thought about Elliott and called him to see if he wanted to join her at the Cove, but he couldn't. She forgot he was teaching an art class at Santa Monica College.

As she drove toward the Cove, she couldn't remember the last time she sat at the piano bar near Brad. She looked forward to it tonight.

As she entered, Rusty greeted her. She flashed a smile and walked past him as he gave her a light touch on the shoulder.

Thankfully, the bar stool in front of Brad was open, she slung her purse on the back of it as she sat. A waitress, she didn't know, immediately came over for Wendy's drink order. She returned with the drink just as Brad came to set up his music, and ready himself for the night's performance.

Wendy exchanged small talk with him before he took his seat. His first set was filled with all the songs she liked. People around her were in good spirit although they talked as he sang. He was used to it, but she preferred not to talk while he sang. She imagined how great it could be to see him perform in concert. He certainly deserved one.

Brad came around to visit with her at the start of his first break.

"So, what have you been up to Wendy? Haven't seen you in a few days."

She couldn't believe he even cared. He rarely asked her anything personal. "The nursery keeps me busy and somehow I find time for other activities, thanks for asking."

He was about to say something more when a woman, with a pixie haircut, broke into their conversation, Brad nodded to Wendy as he turned to the woman. They moved away and visited. The woman laughed out loud.

After Brad's second set, Wendy took a small metal case out of her purse and went to the restroom, just like Alice at Cat and Mouse. She stood in a stall and pulled a joint out of the container and lit up.

She leaned against the metal wall and blew the smoke straight up. After four hits she snuffed it out against the stall divider and put the remainder back in the container and walked out.

As Wendy stood near the main bar, Rusty came to her.

"A woman who came out of the restroom said she smelled pot in there. By any chance would that be you?"

"Caught me, just a few hits."

"Not sure you should do it here in case someone reports it."

"You're right, won't happen again."

"You know, Sunday night a friend of mine is having a weed party. Want to come?"

Wendy face brightened by the invitation, and she didn't hesitate, "Sounds bitchin', should be fun. Thanks.".

Wendy returned to her seat with a confident swing to her walk. Two women dreamily stared at Brad, just as she did.

CHAPTER 38

IT WAS A STAR LIT JUNE EVENING WHEN ELLIOTT and Wendy drove to Hollywood for dinner and a movie. Afterwards they walked the short distance to Whisky A Go Go, a popular nightclub on the Sunset Strip. It became popular in the sixties and continued to be. The Doors and Janis Joplin had performed there as did many other stars. Before they entered a billboard announced tonight's new entertainer, Mandy Silver. She sang as they entered.

Wendy liked the place immediately even though it was packed to the hilt. The lights were low. The huge area had a balcony for Go Go Dancers who were dressed in fringed dresses with white boots. Wendy and Elliott moved around the floor and squeezed around people until they found a space to stand. The crowd danced and clapped while they moved to the beat of the music.

"What do you think?" Elliott shouted.

Her head started to move to the beat of the music. "Such a groovy place."

"She's good," Elliott said of the singer.

"She is," Wendy confirmed as she continued to clap and shake her head to the music.

A waiter came by, and they ordered drinks. As the waiter moved away a small round table opened up, and they grabbed it.

"Wish you danced."

"We aren't going through that again, are we? I come with you to places because I enjoy you, the atmosphere and the music."

"Sorry, I won't mention it ever again. It truly is a groovy place, isn't it?"

He nodded. The singer took a break. Wendy and Elliott chatted but stopped and watched people around them. It appeared to like other entertainment spots where people enjoyed themselves and escaped into a different world than their own.

Elliott took a small swallow of the wine he ordered. Wendy guzzled her screwdriver. In a short time, half the glass was empty, and she was ready to dance.

The singer returned and began another set. "I really wanna dance." She looked at some women who just started to dance together. "Look at those women," she said as she pointed at them.

"Go ahead, I'll watch." He encouraged her.

"Thanks."

Wendy joined in with the group. They welcomed her as they continued shaking their bootie, swinging around, and bobbing their heads to the fast beat. They laughed, and at times, sang loudly with the music.

Elliott shook his head as he watched Wendy.

The song ended, and Wendy collapsed into her chair and took a couple of long swig of her drink.

"What ya thinking, Ellie?"

"I thought you were completely absorbed in the music. You really like wild dancing?"

"Sure, why not? That's my jam."

"Your silliness surprised me."

"I didn't think it was silly. I thought…terrific fun. You need to loosen up." Wendy took more sips of her drink as her head moved to the music.

"And, I think you've had too much to drink. Maybe you should slow down."

"No, I want to get down. This place is outta sight." Wendy was impervious to Elliott's disgust.

He scowled. "Did you have a joint before I picked you up?"

"Just a few drags."

"How are you feeling right now?"

"I feel great and still wanna dance."

She stood to return to the dance floor, but Elliott grabbed her arm and held her back. "Wendy, you're smashed and stoned. I'm taking you home."

He took her purse and swung it over his shoulder. Wendy tried to pull away, but quickly capitulated. She was in no shape to fight him.

Wendy fell asleep on the way back to Mar Vista. He woke her when they arrived at her house, and she staggered out of the car. Elliott guided her to the front door. He propped her against the wall as he struggled to find the keys in her purse. Once inside he walked her straight to her bedroom where she sat on the bed.

"Hey," she mumbled.

"How do you feel?"

"Crappy."

He helped her out of her clothes. She collapsed onto the pillow.

"We'll talk tomorrow. I'll see…" She was out cold before he finished his sentence. He shook his head and left.

In the morning Wendy squinted into the bathroom mirror and cringed. She turned on the faucet, wet and wrung out the washcloth, covering her face with it. As she dried her face she sighed. She again looked in the mirror. "God, I look like shit," she said aloud. She swallowed two aspirin.

After her shower she felt alert and ready for a new day. She ate breakfast and afterwards headed for the nursery.

"You look awful," was Carol's greeting. "What happened?"

"Thanks loads," Wendy said sarcastically as she threw her purse and a plaid, flannel shirt on the counter.

"Well, what happened?"

"Too much partying. Anything happen here I should know about?"

"Not really."

"Okay." Wendy went into the office and tossed her stuff on the chair. She went back into the nursery and stood against the counter, looking out at The Shade House.

Wendy worked her way around the nursery and sat on one of the benches near the forest area. She tried to remember exactly what happened the night before. She remembered she danced with some women and Elliott took her home, but her mind blanked out with whatever else happened. Wendy stood and strolled around the main path and went back to the office. After moving her stuff, she fell onto the chair, sitting forward as she perused the calendar. She checked to see her schedule for the week. She leaned back against the chair. "I've gotta get outta here," she said disheartened.

She took her purse and shirt and walked out and around the counter. Not seeing Carol anywhere, she yelled, "Carol."

Carol came out of the container area. "You called?"

"I don't feel well, I'm heading home."

"Sure, go veg out. Hope you feel like your old self soon."

"Thanks," and Wendy left.

When she got home, Wendy threw her stuff down and headed for the kitchen. She nibbled on part of a peanut butter sandwich she didn't finish a couple of days ago. Afterwards she went into her backyard and worked in the greenhouse for a while.

She returned to the house and headed to her study when the phone stopped her.

"Hi Elliott," she answered him. "I'm sorry about last night, thanks for helping me."

"We need to talk about it. May I come over?"

"Now?"

"Yes."

"Okay."

Wendy didn't like the sound of his voice. She did a little fussing with her makeup and gave a quick comb through her hair.

As soon as he arrived, they sat on the sofa facing each other.

Elliott began. "I think we are drifting in different directions."

Wendy gasped, taken aback by his comment. "What do you mean?"

"Your behavior lately has changed. You've changed."

Wendy peered at him. "How do you mean?"

"For one thing, the pot smoking is bothersome to me even when you're alone. And, last night, your drunken and stoned behavior embarrassed me. You've changed in a way I'm not comfortable with."

Wendy winced. "I'm sorry. You seemed okay with my pot when I said I'd use it when you weren't around, a compromise."

"I know what I said then, but that, in addition to the intoxication, is making me see things differently now. I do care about you, but I need to let go."

Wendy's face flushed and she stiffened. "Won't you even give me a chance…I can change?"

"You can't change who you are, Wendy. This is hard for me too, but we need to face reality."

Wendy couldn't come up with a response. His mind was made up.

Elliott stood up and Wendy silently followed him to the door.

"I wish you the best," he said as he opened the door.

She didn't say anything, just stared, dumbstruck.

She watched as he closed the door behind him. She shuddered. Wendy didn't know if she was angry at him, or herself. He was so indignant, not even offering her a second chance. In her bewildered mind, she realized that maybe he was right, they were too different. She liked her change. She looked out the living room window. Maybe his conservative outlook confused her about whether she loved him or not.

CHAPTER 39

BRAD WAS IN THE MIDDLE OF A SET WHEN WENDY arrived at the Cove. There were no seats available, and as she stood off to the side of the piano bar, she recognized how much she liked the sound of the guitar. At that moment she decided to learn guitar. She pulled out of her vision when a woman she didn't know stood next to her. Wendy and the woman exchanged smiles.

During his break Wendy spent the entire time talking to the woman next to her named Sue. Sue's speech was sophisticated, and her clothes elegant. She wore a beautiful cut crystal necklace with matching earrings. She reeked of wealth. They visited on Brad's next break too and they seemed to have some similar beliefs about politics and the movies out. Sue invited Wendy to join her for dinner the next night. Pleasantly surprised Wendy agreed. She welcomed what could be a new friendship. At Brad's next break Wendy excused herself from Sue. She was anxious to tell Brad about her decision about guitar lessons.

She waited for him to finish a conversation then asked if she could talk to him. They stepped away from the crowd.

"What's up?"

"I just wanted to tell you I'm going to take guitar lessons."

Brad sounded surprised. "Really?"

"Yeah, I thought it might be fun and a challenge. Do you have any advice for me?"

"Just that it will take a lot of practicing."

"I'll keep it in mind."

"But have fun with it," he emphasized as he went back for his next set.

Wendy mentioned her idea of guitar lessons to Sue. Sue nodded but didn't have time to say anything as two bar stools opened up and they moved to them as Brad began his next set.

Halfway through the set Wendy left in an upbeat mood. For the first time in a long time Wendy made a new friend and looked forward to dinner with Sue.

The women met at Francisco's, an Italian restaurant. Red velvet fabric acted as dividers between the booths. Black candle holders with red candles stood out on the red and black plaid tablecloths. They were escorted to a corner booth, great for quiet conversations.

Wendy read through the menu. Sue seemed to already know what she wanted. The prices were exorbitant, which wasn't a surprise to Wendy. They ordered their drinks and dinners.

"I like this place," Wendy said as she admired the restaurant from her corner of the booth.

"Yeah, I like it a lot. So, how long have you known Brad?"

"It's been..." Wendy had to think back, "almost two years. I first heard him when my friend and I went to Hoffman's at the Goodman Canal in Venice."

"I heard he was there a long time."

"Three years, I believe."

"You two seeing each other?"

Not a question Wendy hadn't heard before. She laughed. "No, I just enjoy his music."

"He does have a lot of women hanging around him, at least from my perspective."

"You're right." Wendy wasn't sure how to handle this. "However, some women just come to hear him sing and to meet up with friends." She was curious if Sue's dinner plan was really to build a friendship or for her to learn about Brad and his women. Wendy looked down admiring her artistically folded napkin.

"Can't blame them."

To stop further discussion of Brad she asked, "So, what do you do, Sue?"

Sue took a sip of her water. "I work for my grandfather who owns McPhe Studios."

"Wow! They make some great movies."

"Yes, we do."

"What do you do there?"

"I'm in charge of movie distribution."

Sue's answer showed an air of arrogance. But Wendy didn't want to pass judgment right away.

"Not sure I know what it means."

Their drinks were served. Wendy decided to take it easy. She didn't want to drink too much and lose this new and perhaps very interesting friend. Sue explained about her job, and Wendy listened without interruption. It impressed Wendy that Sue had such a huge responsibility in distribution. But to work for her grandfather she must be diligent.

When the bill came Wendy started to pay her share, but Sue treated.

"Thank you, that's very nice."

"No problem."

Next time, if a next time happened, Wendy would treat.

They walked out together and agreed to see each other the next night at the Cove. Sue could bring new excitement into Wendy's life.

The next evening Wendy looked up guitars in the Yellow Pages and found a store that not only sold guitars but gave lessons. She'd check it out later but couldn't wait to learn to play. As she put the phone book down Scott called. He just wanted to know how she was. They had a short conversation where she shared about taking guitar lessons.

"That sounds fun. Never knew you to be musical."

"I wasn't but I thought I'd give it a try."

"Happy for you. Well, I won't keep you."

"Thanks, bye."

Well, what to think about his call…she had no idea. He continued to sound so different, so nice.

After dinner Wendy got dressed and headed for the Cove.

As soon as she arrived Rusty took her aside. "Are you still interested in the private party I told you about?"

"Sure."

"Ok, it's Sunday night. I'll give you the address before you leave."

"Outta sight, thanks. You'll be there?" she asked as she started to turn away.

"Not to be missed," he said winking. She nodded back and headed for the piano bar. Sue held a seat for her.

They both watched as Brad poured out his exquisite voice. Sue whispered to Wendy several times about Brad's showmanship and his personality. They chatted during his breaks. She enjoyed that they could share Brad in their conversations. At his next break Sue went to talk to him. They visited for almost his whole break.

When Sue returned, she didn't say anything about their conversation. Wendy considered their relationship was already moving forward, or this evening would be the start. Wendy decided to leave. She told Sue. On her way out she stopped to see Rusty.

He handed her the address, "Be there or be square," he yelled over the clatter.

She chuckled and put the address in her jacket pocket as she left.

As Wendy drove home, she thought about Sue and what her relationship with Brad was. Wendy wrinkled her nose as she thought about Sue being obsessed with him, Wendy understood and didn't care if they had a thing going. She'd be delighted to hear anything Sue might be willing to share.

On Friday she stood at the forest end. The sun beat into the nursery, casting shadows from the lattice below the glass roof. Wendy pushed the button to open the glass about eight feet. The electrifying glow from the crimson sun fascinated her. As she looked down, she stared at the little window Elliott pointed out to her when the orchid looked so shiny. She shook her head and moved away.

CHAPTER 40

TWO DAYS LATER WENDY WENT TO HER GUITAR lesson. She started to get the hang of it. She took her sheet music home and practiced the song, "Close to You." She had difficulty trying to learn to coordinate the strings on her right hand with the left hand, but she was determined to make it happen. One problem she encountered, she didn't know how to tune the guitar, even though the teacher showed her. She needed the teacher to explain again, but Wendy's sense of tone was not good. She'd learn it eventually, she told herself.

Wendy groped and gawked at the different clothes she moved back and forth in her closet. What to wear to the Weed Party? She pulled out two pair of pants and several tops and laid them on the bed. She loved the denim, hip hugger bell bottom pants and decided to wear them with a blue and white colored tie dye top.

She put on black eyeliner and mascara. She brushed and combed her long, thick, auburn hair so it would be tangle free and shiny. Looking in the mirror, she blew herself a kiss.

Wendy grabbed her purse, jacket and car keys and checked the address. After looking it up on a map she knew right where it was.

She drove east on Santa Monica Boulevard turning north onto Westwood Blvd. The house was on Wilkins Avenue. A porch light lit it up. Wendy parked and walked to the front door and knocked. A sexy, long haired blond woman opened the door.

"Come get down," she greeted.

Wendy went in and immediately looked around for Rusty. She passed the dining room table loaded with all kinds of snack foods, beer and wine. She wandered down a hallway where she spotted Rusty leaning against a door.

"Glad to see you made it."

She followed him into an unfurnished room and sat on the floor along with everyone else. The guitarist, Cary, was quoting poetry. There were twelve other people there. He started to play "Mr. Bojangles," an unhappy song, about a man who dances in worn out shoes, a ragged shirt, and baggy pants.

Several joints were being passed around, so you could take a toke, pass it on, and a minute later have another hit. Everyone mellowed and their eyes were glued to Cary. Wendy took her second hit, and then another. Rusty grinned and she momentarily put her head against his shoulder. Wendy was somewhere else, wandering around in her head.

The music stopped and everyone got up to leave, except Wendy. Rusty saw her glassy eyes and helped her up as Cary walked toward her and said, "You owe me an apology."

Wendy couldn't focus. "I do, why?"

"You know."

She looked at him like he was an illusion. "I don't know."

Cary left. Some guy following him out the door said to Wendy, "Don't worry about it."

Wendy looked at Rusty confused. Her head wasn't clear, and she was bewildered.

"Let's go see what's happenin' in the living room," Rusty said as he steered her there.

There were two bridge chairs open for them. The group talked about Nixon's precarious position in the Watergate Scandal. Impeachment was close.

Wendy didn't care, she just wanted Rusty to tell her what made Cary mad at her.

Wendy leaned into Rusty. "Please, tell me what happened with Cary."

"In a while, this conversation interests me."

Not to Wendy…she sulked with frustration. She tried so hard to remember the events in the bedroom. Cary read anti-war poetry. A conversation followed as they discussed the importance of caring about others. He sang a couple of songs. The next thing she knew everyone stood up. She remembered she couldn't quite get her balance and Rusty steadied her. It was then Cary came over and hit her with the need to apologize.

Rusty shook her arm to get her out of the trance like state. "Are you okay to drive?"

"Yeah, I'm okay."

Are you ready to go?"

"Definitely."

As soon as they stood by her car, she pleaded with him. "Rusty, please tell me what happened."

"Okay. First, you have to understand you were totally stoned. I looked at your face a couple of times and your eyes were glazed over like you were somewhere else. I think the weed was a very strong variety."

"But, I talked, right?"

"Yes, a couple of times, but you were gone, metaphorically speaking."

"Oh, great. So, I said, or did what?"

"You told Cary his voice was strident, and you couldn't follow the song."

She shuddered. "Oh, fuck. What did he say?"

"Nothing, but if looks could kill..."

"Shit. I did owe him an apology."

"Yes and no. You couldn't apologize when you didn't know what you said, besides he should have known you were out of it, and completely unaware of your words."

"I feel like...I don't even know. It's time to quit weed. I used to get a good high off of it, but now..."

Rusty interrupted. "You don't have to quit. Just be aware drugs you don't know could have more impact with their potency. Are you okay now?"

"Yeah, I'm fine." She stopped for a second. "Thanks, Rusty."

He bent down to her, lifted her chin and gave her a kiss that lingered a bit too long for a friendship. "Good night, sleep tight." He walked away.

The kiss stunned her. She got into her car and drove home. Once inside the house, she closed the door and leaned against it, still dazed by the ardent kiss.

CHAPTER 41

SEVERAL EVENINGS LATER WENDY WENT TO THE
Cove. Sue and Wendy talked between breaks. During one of them,
Brad and Sue talked quietly in a corner. When they were done Sue
came back, got her stuff, and without speaking to Wendy she left.
Wendy didn't understand. She'd call Sue tomorrow to see why the
abrupt departure.

During another break Rusty came over to Wendy and asked to
talk to her. They went into the kitchen.

Wendy stood next to him outside the office wall. He looked to
be contemplating what to say.

Finally, "Can I interest you in coming to my place for a drink
tomorrow night?" It was his night off.

Wendy thought for a moment. "I don't know if that's a good idea."

"Why not? I find you a very special lady."

"You are so nice, but if we got something going, and later split,
it'd be very awkward for us here."

He held her shoulders. "Why, I wouldn't say anything."

"I'm sorry, I'm just not comfortable with it. I mean if we broke up…can you see it from my viewpoint? I know it's negative thought, but we have to be realistic."

He raised his eyebrows. "I see your point."

"I do think you're a great guy. I'd love to have you as a friend, someone I could trust and share things with. Is this something you can go with?"

"Yeah. I like it too."

"Friends forever, okay?"

Rusty's happy expression said it all. "Right on," and they held their arms up and slapped each other's hand.

They both grinned, and Wendy went back to her seat as Brad started another set.

She called Sue the next day. She said Brad and she were in a discussion about something important.

"That's cool. You left without saying good-bye, so I thought you were hurting."

"Sorry, I just needed to get home, I was very tired."

"Okay." That didn't sound right to Wendy. Sue could have said good-bye. Wendy sat right next to her when she gathered her stuff. Something must have happened during her talk with Brad.

"Say, I'd like to borrow your guitar. Would it be okay?"

"Sure. I don't have another lesson until next week. Are you taking up the guitar?"

"I don't know yet. I'll know after I try yours. Can I come by and get it?"

"Of course." Wendy thought she could duet with Sue if she decided to take lessons. What a blast.

"I'll call before I come."

Wendy got off the phone and went to practice. She almost mastered the one song, "Close to You." She felt good about it. Her next song attempt was Carole King's, "You've Got a Friend." This song became more difficult. After three stanzas she stopped. The problem was she couldn't work the fret movements with the strings. She kept after it for almost an hour before her fingers tired. She put the guitar in the study and picked up the picture of Brad, smiling at it.

Sue called on Thursday and came to get the guitar. They didn't chat very long as Sue was on her way to an appointment. Wendy wanted to ask again why she left Pirate's Cove so fast but decided to keep out of it. She knew Sue wasn't telling the true reason.

The time of the Showcase Design was close, so Wendy headed to Claudia's office to talk, in more detail, about the displays for the Convention Center. Claudia was eager to get the drawings finalized. Wendy admired the detail of the living room layout Claudia showed her. Wendy placed x's on the places in the living room where she wanted to put the plants as well as floral arrangements.

"I like the idea of the rubber tree plant right here," Wendy stated as she pointed to the spot.

"I think it's a perfect spot."

Claudia brought out the patio drawing showing where the white wrought iron table would be set, with four matching chairs, two for each side with cushions.

"Looks good, Claudia."

"Thanks, I'm going to check the final details for the living room on the other drawing. You go ahead and indicate where you want to put whatever you have decided on or put a question mark if you aren't sure." She handed Wendy the sketch. "Go ahead and draw on it if you want. You can take it home."

"Thanks. Do you know when our display will be set up at the Convention Center?"

"I think Tuesday. I'll let you know for sure in a few days."

"Good. I'm anxious to see the setup."

"I don't blame you."

Wendy sat at a table in Claudia's office, looked over the sketches and tentatively placed the names of a few plants in the patio area. She finished and showed it to Claudia.

"What do you think of these plant locations?"

Claudia took a minute to study the plan. "Looks good. I'll know for sure when we put everything in place. But I don't foresee any changes unless you make them."

"Thank you. I don't think there is anything else I can do right now. I'll still need to think about which plants I want for other positions."

"I understand perfectly."

"Thanks, I'm going to take off."

Wendy's enthusiasm increased now that the Convention Center show approached. What a great opportunity to share her designs and intermingle with other designers. Wendy put the plans into a folder, then into her briefcase. She drove to the nursery.

The man Wendy hired, Jim, was busy when Wendy arrived. He made a great addition…extremely helpful with many things neither Carol nor Wendy could do like lifting heavy items.

The next day Claudia called and told her the set up would be on Tuesday. Wendy met with Claudia on Friday to finalize the plans.

"What do you think, Wendy? Are you ready for this?"

"I am. I have the plants and containers. When do we take everything to the Convention Center?"

"The truck will pick up everything at my warehouse, if you will get your stuff there on Monday, they will deliver it that day and we'll set up on Tuesday."

"No problem. I'll meet you at the Convention Center on Tuesday. What time?"

"Ten."

They discussed more details about the set up and Wendy left for the Cove. She was stoked and hungered for a rapturous good time.

It was only four forty-five when she arrived, so she had no problem about getting a seat at the piano bar. Brad started to set up. The waitress brought Wendy her screwdriver.

"Hi what's up?" Brad asked.

"Well, I'm getting ready for the Design Showcase at the Convention Center.

"That's outta sight."

"Yeah, I'm pretty jazzed about it."

He smiled at her and sat down on his stool, tuned his guitar, and began to strum it. For a moment Wendy reveled in the solitude of no one on either side of her…she had Brad to herself. He began to sing James Taylor's, "Something in the Way She Moves." He followed it with "Blowin' in the Wind," a popular song written by Bob Dylan.

Wendy sipped her drink. She half expected Sue to show up since it had been a couple of days since she'd been there. Wendy decided she wouldn't call her although curious to know why she wasn't coming. She figured something else caught her interest. Totally elated Wendy moved her shoulders to the beat of the music.

Sue didn't show for the following two nights either.

The next day Wendy spent part of the day at her nursery office as she worked on the final set up for the Design Showcase. Claudia gave her all completeded plans and Wendy smiled since Claudia liked the ideas of where all the plants and flowers would go, although the flowers were just for the show. Wendy didn't carry them at the nursery.

Finally, Wendy could call Sue because it was time to get her guitar back. At seven she made the call.

"Hi, it's Wendy," she said when Sue picked up.

"Hi."

"I've miss you at the Cove."

"Yeah, I've found better things to do."

"Really, care to share?"

"Not really."

"Okay." Wendy could tell she needed to mind her own business but didn't know why Sue said that. Wendy didn't say anything more except, "Listen, can I come get my guitar tomorrow?"

"I'm keeping it."

Wendy eyes popped wide. "What?"

"You heard, I want it."

"I don't understand. Can't you buy yourself one?"

"No, I want yours," she blurted out and hung up.

Wendy pulled the phone away from her ear and stared at it. 'Shit,' she said aloud. Stunned, Wendy set the phone down in its cradle. She had no idea why Sue behaved the way she did. Wendy sat back in the chair and relived Sue's last time at Pirate's Cove. She talked to Brad, and suddenly left. Wendy thought maybe it was to get ready for Brad, but no. Something must have happened between Brad and Sue, and it angered Sue, but what? Whatever it was, Sue harbored feelings of anger at Brad out on Wendy. It didn't make sense. Nothing like this ever happened to Wendy. Sue wanted to learn about Brad from Wendy and since she knew Wendy was a friend to Brad her way at getting back at him seemed to be to hurt Wendy, but how did that get back at Brad? Wendy accepted the fact that she mistook Sue's earlier kindness, instead she saw Sue as a strange and mean-spirited person.

While Brad set up the next night, Wendy told him what happened.

"Gee, I'm sorry, Wendy. I have no idea why she'd do that."

He sat down and started to play. Wendy knew he was lying, and she knew it definitely had to do with something between him and Sue. However, she didn't really expect Brad to tell her. Wendy misjudged Sue. First time Wendy experienced hurt like that from a woman. She'd be more careful picking new friends.

TUESDAY MORNING WENDY GAVE HER NAME AT the side entrance to the Convention Center and immediately went to find Claudia in Section Eighteen. Men were setting everything up with Claudia's directions. Wendy's plants and flowers were set aside in a mixed group.

She joined Claudia and a woman standing next to her. "Wow, it already looks impressive."

"Yes, it does. Oh Wendy, this is my assistant, Linda."

The women exchanged greetings and handshakes.

"As soon as they finish with the furniture setups you can display the plants and flowers. As you see we needed to decrease the size of the patio because of a shortage of space, but I'm sure there's room for your plants. Hope you like the way it looks."

Wendy surveyed the area. "Yes, I do, it's great. Can't wait to put the greenery around."

Other showcases were setting up, like bedrooms, kitchens, and of course, other living rooms and dining rooms, but not many patio areas. Wendy knew a lot of money and time went into the plan for the execution of each designer's showcase. This showcase provided important publicity for all of them.

Their actual set up took a little over two hours. Claudia, Wendy, and Linda were relieved they could finish on the first day.

Early Wednesday Wendy returned to the Convention Center and placed a variety of plants on the patio and stood back to take stock. She changed the position of a few plants until she was comfortable with them. A red cordyline plant sat next to the wrought iron bench. A beautiful red and white Oriental Lily, along with a yellow one, sat in front of two palms near the outside entrance to the living room. The cushions on the love seat were soft, floral colors of pale green, yellow, tan, and peach. On the table she put a ground cover campanula with its pretty blue flowers.

She moved into the living room and dining room areas. On a table next to a cabinet, she placed a colorful coleus and on the dining table a small, very dainty maidenhair fern. On the coffee table she placed a smaller floral arrangement of miniature roses. By the inside sliding door to the patio, two red and white fuchsias stood on tall wrought iron stands. Wendy stood back from the display. The room looked alluring, a restful place to gather.

Before the show opened on Friday the three women walked around to see other displays. It fascinated Wendy to see so many interesting ways to decorate rooms. They stopped to chat with a couple of designers and returned to their set up shortly before the doors opened. The three of them were ready to answer any questions and hand out business cards.

The first person to ask Wendy a question was a tall, distinguished looking woman. "Excuse me, miss."

"Yes, did you have a question?"

"Actually, I do. Can you tell me about that fuchsia?" she asked as she pointed to it on the wrought iron stand.

"Well, their care is pretty easy. They prefer shade, north light is good, and they like to dry out a bit before re-watering. After they bloom, if you nip off the dead blooms, it encourages new growth and new blooms. They bloom from spring through summer. The popular colors are purple, red and pink."

"Thank you. I'm definitely looking into them."

"You're welcome. I'm sure you'll find them exceptional." That conversation reminded Wendy she needed to work on getting a blue fuchsia like her mom wanted.

It turned out many visitors asked questions. Wendy liked listening to the customers discuss their gardens. Some visitors went into greater detail. The description of their gardens and how they came up with their designs intrigued her. So many creative people impressed Wendy.

On the last day of the show, as the hours drifted away, the women agreed they were completely satisfied at the outcome of their design showcase. The next morning Linda arranged for the plants and other items to be returned to Claudia's warehouse. Charlie picked up Wendy's plants and returned them to the nursery.

Wendy beamed with pride for this achievement. It renewed confidence in her ability after the disastrous Fireplace Grill. She limited her activities for the next two days. She spent down time weeding her garden and working in the greenhouse.

One night she went to Cat and Mouse to listen to Matt. Cat and Mouse restaurant was busy, also the bar area. She stood in the bar entry for a minute. People there whispered to each other, no loud voices, nothing to interfere with the sheer joy Wendy experienced from the exceptional sound his calm voice brought. She couldn't believe she loved Matt's phenomenal voice as much as Brad's.

The piano bar was full, so she meandered to an empty table across from it. Matt looked up and nodded at her as she passed by him. She gave a little wave. The waitress took Wendy's drink order.

Another reason she liked Cat and Mouse was because of its more elegant look than the more casual Pirate's Cove, not in a snippy way though. The atmosphere seemed more like she was at a private party. The simple décor reflected the formality with the black velvet drapes around the windows. The tables were covered with small lavender and black plaid and the booths seats were solid black. It amused Wendy because the other times she was there she didn't pay much attention to much of the area.

The waitress brought her screwdriver and Wendy took several sips. She liked sitting at the table as an audience member. She never felt that way at the piano bar, where she only faced the entertainer. She cherished the songs, especially the one he now sang, James Taylor's, "Something in the Way She Moves."

At his break Matt stopped by her table.

"Hi. You haven't been in for a while, everything okay?"

"Been good. I was busy putting together an interior design show at The Convention Center."

"How sweet is that? How'd it go?"

"Terrific, actually. Thanks for asking."

"You're the creative type, huh?"

"I've been told, yeah."

"Keep it up," and with those words he wandered to chat with some others before returning for his next set.

Wendy sipped her drink as she experienced complete relaxation.

Alice, the friend she made the last time there, walked in and with a surprised look came over to Wendy.

"Haven't seen you in ages."

"I know. Wanna join me?"

Alice looked toward the piano bar, turned back and leaned into Wendy. "Thanks, but I'm going to sneak into the bar stool that just opened up."

"Okay, see ya later."

"Gotcha."

Wendy figured Alice did have the hots for Matt. Wendy put her drink down and sat back in her chair and mellowed out immersed in the lyrics. She stayed for the next set but when it finished, she decided to leave. She didn't get a chance to talk to Alice but waved to her as she left. Matt nodded as she strolled past him.

At home, she lit up a joint, sat back in a chair with her feet on the ottoman. She sat completely unwound, what a good day and evening.

CHAPTER 43

ON FRIDAY NIGHT, WENDY WENT TO THE COVE. Brad was on a break when she arrived. She noticed several empty seats at the piano bar and quickly hung her purse on the back of one of them.

Wendy wanted to talk to Rusty and was told he went to the office. She went through the kitchen and found the office door open.

Rusty saw her standing in the doorway.

"Hey, Rusty. Hope you don't mind my coming back."

"Of course not." He stood up from his desk and came around to her. "You're always welcome."

They stood facing each other.

"Thanks. I wanted to talk to you a minute."

"Sure, about what?"

Wendy closed the door. "I wanted your opinion about peyote, if you know anything, I mean. I hear you can really light up on it."

"Have a seat. What did you want to know?" He returned to his desk.

"Are you aware of its side effects?"

"Yes. Are you thinking of trying it?"

"I am intrigued. I've heard some of my customers share their experiences on it, their vision quest, as they say. I thought I'd like to give it a try."

"It does happen. If you want to try it, I have some dried mushrooms."

"No kidding." Wendy didn't hesitate. "May I come over?"

"Of course, I'm available next Wednesday night, if it works for you?"

"Yeah, I think it does, thanks."

She returned to the bar and her seat right in front of Brad.

Brad sang three songs in a row, all of which Wendy liked: "Incense and Peppermints," by the Strawberry Alarm Clock, followed by "Here Comes the Sun," by The Beatles and "Genii in Disguise," by the Stylistics. Out of nowhere a thought hit her: maybe she should proposition Brad. She shook the crazy idea from her head. She wanted him to want her.

She listened until Brad finished the set and then left.

At home she called Cindy. "Any interest in meeting for lunch tomorrow?"

"Sure, how about Hamburger Hamlet?"

"Meet you there at eleven thirty."

Wendy arrived at Hamburger Hamlet at eleven twenty. The hostess seated Wendy at a table where she could watch for Cindy while she looked over the menu.

Suddenly, Cindy plopped down across from her. "I forgot how much I liked this place."

Wendy looked around. "I like to come here because it's comfortable and I think homey."

Cindy put her menu down and brought up Scott and they briefly discussed Wendy's mixed thoughts toward him.

"So, what's with you and Scott?"

"Nothing, but we're friendly."

"Well, that's good."

"I guess. I'd rather not discuss him."

Cindy changed the subject. "So, tell me all about the design show. How did it go?"

"It was outta sight. Everything worked out with the furniture and plant arrangements. I handed out thirty business cards. I totally loved everyone else's designs. It gave me some ideas about changes I'd like to make in my house."

"That's primo."

They ate while they shared their missed times together.

In the evening Wendy headed for the Cove. She still liked Cat and Mouse a lot, but right now she wanted to be near Brad, and not think about the mention of Scott from Cindy. The thoughts about him were entrenched in her mind. Particularly, she dwelled on the conversation they shared about his new activities and lifestyle. He seemed so different, more like when they dated, but was he?

Brad's strong voice welcomed Wendy as she came in. There weren't any seats anywhere, so she stood next to an artificial fig tree near a few occupied tables. The waitress, Julie, came to Wendy and she ordered her usual screwdriver.

Brad sang Neil Diamond's, "Solitary Man." There were two couples on the dance floor, lots of conversations, and some like Wendy, watching Brad's every word and expression. He interpreted lyrics with such depth. She thought he must be a sensitive and caring man when with friends. Those two traits were ones Wendy admired in a man. She considered Scott might have those traits now.

The set finished with another Neil Diamond song, "Kentucky Woman." Brad came over to Wendy as he left the piano bar area.

"Hey, how you doin'?"

"Doing well, thanks."

"Good to hear. By the way, I like your top," he said as he moved away.

He liked her top. It wasn't anything special, a blue and turquoise print blouse. In all the time she'd known him he never commented on her clothes before, or anything else personal. She didn't know what to think about it, but it made her happy and put her on a natural high.

Wendy stayed for the next set and waved good-bye as she rose. Rusty stood at the bar. They confirmed Wednesday night at his place.

"May I ask a favor of you?"

"Maybe, it depends on the favor."

"When you're here would you mind turning the house music on and off when Brad's on breaks? It'd help me out because sometimes I can't get to it right away."

Calming her excitement she said, "No problem."

"Thanks. I appreciate it."

Turning the house music on and off was something Cindy used to do. Wendy said goodnight and left. It thrilled her to be involved in a Pirate's Cove activity.

CHAPTER 44

WENDY CAME INTO HER EMPTY HOUSE AND wished she could talk to someone about Brad, but there wasn't anyone. She couldn't even mention it to Cindy, although she could talk to her about Scott. She lit a joint and called.

"Hey, Cindy. Hope it isn't too late?"

"Nope, glad you called. I wanted to ask you why you didn't want a deeper discussion about Scott at lunch."

"Wow, that's actually why I called. I didn't want to talk when he came up because I was still thinking through a conversation I had with him. If it's okay, can we talk about him now?"

"For sure."

"I wanted to tell you he seems to have changed in a very good way, but I'm still leery about starting anything with him."

"I think you need to go slow in order to know if he is for real, maybe start with another lunch."

"I know I have to do something, but how do I go on dates without his thinking I want him back right away?"

"That's like, hard, maybe meet him somewhere casual once in a while for a soda or coffee and skip lunch at first."

"Yeah, it could work, but what reason do I give for the invitation?"

"Hmm…you need to think on that one."

"Yeah, thanks a lot."

"Glad to help. Stay cool, goodnight."

They hung up.

Cindy was right, Wendy thought as she went to her bedroom. She needed to go out with him.

At the beginning of August, she flipped on the TV to hear the news. Nixon announced his resignation effective the next day…beats impeachment. August 1974 was about to be a hotter one for more than just the weather. She relaxed in her living room chair smoking a joint.

After a quick breakfast the next morning Wendy left for work. She mulled over talking to Carol about her Scott situation, although they rarely talked personal life, but she knew Carol would listen and be honest.

Carol was busy with a customer when Wendy arrived, so she moved around the nursery trimming here and there. Her mind focused on Scott. She simply couldn't come up with any plan to engage him. She decided not to talk to Carol.

The next day the nursery was slow, so Wendy left at one to run some errands. She picked up the magazine, *Get Down*. The articles dealt with popular drugs. She took the magazine to a coffee shop and read through it while she ate lunch. The drugs discussed were LSD, cocaine, pcp, peyote, and weed. She concentrated on the information about peyote. She liked the description of peoples' highs when they were on it. Some talked about the silliness they experienced along with immense euphoria and fun hallucinations. A few commented negatively about the way they got hooked on it and a few disliked the hallucinations when they were ugly. Wendy's intention was not to get hooked on anything. Once in a while she just wanted to experience the euphoria she heard about, a chance to escape from her mind about both Brad and Scott and her loss of Elliott. She wanted a separate world where she could be somewhere else.

As per their plans Wendy arrived at Rusty's apartment in West Los Angeles, a few blocks south of Wilshire Blvd. He rented a small one bedroom, one bath, and Rusty showed good taste with the usual beach theme.

"Have a seat," he said as he indicated the dining room table. On it stood a jar with liquid that looked like tea. Rusty opened it, sniffed it, made an ugly face and held it toward Wendy. She sniffed it with the same reaction.

"How much do you know about peyote?" he asked.

"I knew a little when I talked to you, but I read up about it, in more detail, and understand it better."

"You know what can happen?"

"You bet."

"So, you're ready for this?"

"Let's rock on."

Rusty poured some of the tea in a glass. "To start, just take a little of it."

She smelled it again and scrunched her nose. She took a small sip, gagged and coughed. She sat up.

"You can have a little more."

Wendy took a longer drink, with less coughing.

"It's difficult to swallow, literally because of the pungent taste, but you'll get used to it."

Fifteen minutes later her neck and shoulder muscles relaxed, and she brightened with energy and became very talkative.

Rusty listened as Wendy rambled on about the nursery and Scott. She got up and started to sing and dance for a few minutes.

"So, what do you think?" Rusty asked as Wendy 'came down.'

"Like wow! Can I buy some from you?"

"I'll have to get some peyote buttons for you. I don't have enough to give away. I'll let you know. You need to heat the buttons and roots in water until it becomes a tea, or you can eat the buttons."

"Good to know. Thanks, Rusty. I really appreciate it."

They talked for a while and Wendy headed home.

The nursery was doing very well. She truly appreciated its naturalness and the display of the great variety of plants. The fact that many people kept returning let her know they enjoyed it.

On Thursday night Wendy went to Rusty's to get the peyote buttons.

"Thanks," Wendy said when Rusty handed her a plastic bag with a dozen buttons.

"You do know you have to be careful with this stuff, so you won't get hooked."

She let that go by her. "How long have you been using peyote?"

"A couple of years, but I use it sparingly and not a lot at one time."

"I'll certainly be careful." She looked at the buttons. "I appreciate the info. Mind if I indulge now?"

"No, go for it," Rusty encouraged.

"You want to join me?"

"No thanks, not in the mood." Rusty went to the kitchen for the tea and put it on the coffee table where they were seated. She only sipped a little, followed by a little more. It wasn't the same high she experienced before, but soon it became enough for her to feel renewed energy.

Half an hour later Wendy said, "I didn't feel the same exuberance as the last time. Why not?"

Wendy watched as Rusty got up, made himself a drink and came back to sit next to her. "Sometimes it's just the way your body reacts to it, and you didn't drink as much this time."

"Okay. I guess I'll try a bit more and find out?" she laughed.

"Wendy, take it easy," he cautioned, as she took a larger swallow.

"With you here I feel safe. You're a good friend." She felt a rush. "Rusty, come dance with me," she said as she pulled on his wrist.

"You think I should put some music on first?" he asked as he moved to the record player.

"Oh, yeah, that'd be rad."

They danced and when the high diminished, Wendy fell onto the sofa. Rusty turned the player off and sat next to her.

He asked, "Have you ever read the Bhagavad Gita?"

"No, but I'm familiar with its basic tenets about love."

"Really, I'm surprised."

"When I read and studied the women's lib movement and free speech, and religions, I delved into some eastern religions like Buddhism. I liked their Four Noble Truths about there being a path leading to the cessation of suffering. There were other interesting thoughts from different religions. They all seemed to say similar things about bringing tranquility into your life. I also appreciated the Divine Light Mission. It follows the Bhagavad Gita."

"And what are your thoughts about Bhagavad Gita?"

"Very straight forward as I recall and logical. I especially liked their idea about, 'don't put off until tomorrow what you can do today.' It's also about meditating to find inner peace, right?"

Rusty reassured her, "Pretty much. Do you meditate?"

"No," she said with regret. "I never really followed through with grasping their ideas. There were too many other things happening then."

"Do you have time now?"

"To meditate?"

"That and to learn more about their practices and beliefs. I think you'd like to know more because their ideas are calming, like drugs, only better for you."

"And exactly how could I learn about them?" She asked questioning how it could be possible.

"You can join me at an ashram."

Her eyes glowed with the fascinating idea. "There are ashrams around here?"

Oh yes, one in Venice, not far from Santa Monica. Are you open to trying it?"

"Yeah, sure, definitely. It's about finding enlightenment and inner peace. Boy, could I use some of that."

"How 'bout I pick you up on Saturday at one forty-five, the program starts at two. I have to be at work by four-thirty so it may be a short stint."

"It's fine. I'd like to see what it's about in person instead of reading about it. Thanks again for your friendship." She kissed his cheek, stood up, and grabbed her plastic bag with peyote.

Rusty saw her to the door.

As soon as she got home, she called Cindy to tell her she and Rusty were going to an ashram.

"An ashram...I know someone who went, and they found it the coolest thing."

"Hope they're right. I'm anxious for this."

Cindy chimed in. "I was going to call you too. I wanted to tell you about this guy I met in the rec. center downstairs. He's a part-time disc jockey and a writer. He's so intriguing and a fox."

"What's he write?"

"Mystery stories for magazines."

"I'm impressed. What's his name?"

"Bill Stephens. We're going to see a movie tonight."

"Sounds awesome. Hope you two work out, very exciting."

"It really is. Gotta go. Be cool."

"I will and keep me up to date."

"You bet."

Cindy finding a person to move on with made Wendy very happy.

Early the next morning Wendy sat in her office at the nursery. Her mind started to wander. There was so much good in her life, but her loneliness stood out. She so wanted Brad in her life, but any advancement toward him could end the comfortable and casual relationship she shared with him, not only with him, but with Pirate's Cove and the people she knew there.

Wendy felt a tightness in her chest. Scott truly sounded like he changed, and his personality had opened up. Good memories came into her mind…how much fun they had before his mental and physical dismissal of her. She just needed to know his improved attitude and interests were permanent. What if she went back to him and he didn't make the improvements? Taking a chance with him could be risky.

Closing time came and Wendy stayed at the nursery for a while. Carol and Jim finished unpacking some supplies. Wendy chewed on a peyote button as she looked at the twilight sky through the lattice. The colors were vibrant, rich reds, yellows, greens, blues and purples.

Wendy meandered around the nursery as she sang to herself. Carol stopped what she was doing and followed Wendy's voice.

"What's up?" Carol asked."

"Nothing, just enjoying the stunning serenity." Wendy's hands reached toward the glass ceiling.

"Wendy, what are you on?"

"Just a little peyote, an escape from the outside world…and the men in my life. I like this inside world better."

"I didn't know you did drugs besides pot."

"Just sometimes." Wendy took a three-hundred and sixty-degree turn. "This place is intoxicating. Look at the depth of that shiny yellow croton leaf over there." She pointed a few feet away. "Need to see it closer," she said, moving toward it and touching its shiny texture. Carol shook her head and returned to the counter.

When Wendy finished her inspection, she strolled up and down different paths. Suddenly Carol heard a scream and ran to Wendy who had tripped on a rock and fallen. Carol helped her get up.

"You okay?"

"Sure, sorry."

"Wendy, I'm not sure drugs are a good idea. Hallucinations can make problems."

"No hallucinations just slipped. I'm good." Wendy went to the gazebo where she sat for a while. Finally, she went to the office, grabbed her purse, and said good-bye to Carol.

Rusty picked Wendy up on Saturday as planned and drove them to a side street in an old area of Venice. It was filled with wooden bungalows, many built during the 1920's and 30's. The homes were close together and painted in subdued colors but the trim on many was outstanding…black, different shades of blue, yellow, and some brilliant colors. The houses were immensely appealing to Wendy, taking her back in time.

A man opened the door and greeted them with a bow of his head. The scent of incense filled the house. They followed the man to the back of the house and into a large room. A lot of people sat, most on the floor, some on pillows. The man indicated a space where they could sit.

Everyone seemed to be entranced by the speaker in the front. Rusty whispered to Wendy he was the guru, the leader. He was discussing the ultimate meaning of life.

"There will be times when you will feel deep sentiment for people, animals, and objects. Some of these will have more meaning than others. However, they should all be treated with equal respect."

The talk put Wendy at ease. The people she saw sat mesmerized by the guru as they sat with their legs crossed, their hands resting on their laps or on their thighs. Wendy put her hands in her lap. The words the guru spoke released tension inside of her. He continued to discuss family and its importance. Everything he said made sense. Wendy could feel the cohesiveness of the attendees. These were people devoted to a belief in gaining knowledge, so they could experience enlightenment. The guru emphasized the importance of everyone searching for their own freedom through meditation, family, and good work.

After the talk Rusty introduced Wendy to Jahad, a man Rusty knew from his visits to the ashram. Jahad explained the importance of kindness toward everyone.

"Do you know," Jahad said, "almost all the people in this room live in this house?"

"No, I didn't," Wendy said in surprise. It seemed too small to hold so many.

"We are devotees to what kinship and love are about. We practice this every day."

His words intrigued Wendy. "It sounds wonderful."

They visited for a little while until Jahad moved on.

Wendy never experienced anything so satisfying as what she heard. As Rusty drove back to Wendy's she understood why people went to the ashram.

"Rusty, thanks so much. Their beliefs are calming."

"That's why I wanted you to come, Wendy. I thought it might help you get through what's buggin' you."

"It gave me a lot to think about. I do like their philosophy of goodness, kindness, the importance of family and ways to bring tranquility to yourself."

Rusty dropped Wendy at her house and continued on to work. Wendy grabbed a bite, while thinking about the ashram and how inspired she was. Later she enjoyed part of a joint and watched TV.

CHAPTER 45

THE NEXT DAY WENDY INVITED CINDY FOR DINNER so they could relax and catch up. Wendy missed the comfort of their friendship.

The lasagna was almost done. She turned the oven down and prepared the salad.

Cindy wasn't expected for a while, so Wendy dropped into a living room chair and picked up the mail on the table next to her. After a brief examination, she tossed it back on the table and headed for her study.

She took out a peyote button and bit down on it. Twenty minutes later she floated down the hall into the kitchen and out the back door. In the silence, she heard crickets as she twirled on the patio and stepped onto the grass. She screamed at the sky, "Love you, beautiful stars, love me someone."

A bright light went on next door and a creaky door opened, but Wendy was oblivious to them; nor did she hear the doorbell ring, or Cindy's frantic knocking on the door.

Lying on the lawn in a drug induced stupor, Wendy was only vaguely aware of someone running over to her and yelling her name.

"Wendy, it's Cindy. Wake up."

Wendy blinked a few times, opened her eyes blinking several more times.

"Hold on. I'm going to get a wet towel."

Cindy wiped Wendy's face, but Wendy pushed the towel away.

"God, you scared the shit out of me. What happened to you?"

"Cindy, I..." Wendy realized she was lying on her lawn. She slowly sat up with Cindy's help. "I'm not sure."

"Let's go inside." Cindy steadied her as they moved through the kitchen into the living room. Cindy sat next to Wendy on the sofa.

"Now, tell me what happened."

"I, uh..."

"Damn it, get it together, talk to me."

"I'm not sure. I ate part of a peyote button and felt great. I don't know what happened."

"You're doing peyote? How long has this been going on? I thought you just did weed."

"Just on peyote for a short while, a few weeks."

"Are you stupid? You probably used too much."

"I'm usually careful with how much. I just wanted more of a thrill. I talked to the sky, that's what I remember. It was so beautiful up there." She indicated the ceiling in the living room.

"That's the problem with this shit. You're probably hooked. You need to go cold turkey now. Where do you keep it?"

Wendy hesitated. "I need it. I experience such wonderful vibes... it's transforming."

"Where!" Cindy belted. If looks could kill the one Cindy shot Wendy would have done the job.

Wendy hung her head. "Bedroom and fridge."

Cindy grabbed the bag on the dresser, and the container of the tea, and came back to Wendy. She shoved all of it in her face. "Either I flush this tea down the toilet and trash the buttons or I walk out of here, and I'll have nothing more to do with you."

Wendy stared at her best friend. Pain filled Wendy's eyes and her face flushed.

"Well?"

"I need it to help me get away from my mixed-up mind. It takes me somewhere else, to better times." Wendy burst into tears.

Cindy put down the items and threw her arms around Wendy. "Why didn't you tell me? We used to share so much, but you kept something inside tearing you up and didn't tell me. This is a treacherous path you're on."

Wendy pulled back. "People have their own problems. With the conflict going on in my head I need to work through mine too."

"Yeah, well, you aren't succeeding, that's apparent. Doing drugs doesn't help with your problems, it adds to them. Now, am I getting rid of this stuff?" Cindy grabbed the items and stood, glaring down at Wendy.

Wendy shifted on the sofa. Her tears slowed as she looked up at Cindy. "You're okay being here to help?"

"That's what friends do best. Now, let's hear what's been eating at you. And don't snow me with any crap," she said sitting back down.

"It's Scott. The talks we've had…he's made some major changes with his job, his life, his attitude toward different things. And everything he said is what I wanted in him all along.

"So, what's the problem?"

"I don't know if I can trust him."

"The question is, how do you find out the truth?"

"That's what I've been obsessing over for so long. I can't figure what to do."

"I said it before, the only way is you go out with him and get to know the new Scott. See what your gut feelings are. I think you'll know if he's leveling with you after a few dates. I'd hold off on the sex, otherwise your emotions will rule before your head finds the answer."

Wendy stood up and walked to the fireplace, looking down at the unlit logs. She turned to Cindy. "Of course, you're right. I'm really nervous about the idea of dating him and being with him for any length of time."

"Your other choice is to forget about him."

"I've given that idea too. Wendy went back over to Cindy. "Should I just enjoy the single life and have fun and maybe try to meet someone new to be with?"

"You have choices."

Wendy sat. "I know I have to decide. I can't go on the way I have been." Wendy agonized over her thoughts. "I do like this alternative lifestyle I've been living. But you're right, of course, the drugs don't give me any answers."

"You could make a list of pros and cons before you make a final decision about Scott."

"That was Dr. Lewis' suggestion too," although Wendy never did it. Wendy locked eyes with Cindy. She wanted to talk to Cindy about Brad too, but there wasn't any way they could talk about Brad and remain friends, and her friendship meant so much more.

"Thanks Cindy. I needed someone else's perspective. Your honesty has always been something I loved about you."

"No problem. Trash all of it?" Cindy asked gesturing toward the peyote and tea in her hands.

Wendy didn't hesitate, "Yes."

Cindy left soon after she disposed of the peyote and poured the tea down the toilet.

As Wendy crawled into bed, she tried to remember what she heard at the ashram about experience and gaining insight to help toward enlightenment. Maybe what happened to her on the lawn and what she learned at the ashram, were the experiences she needed to face Scott. She needed to take a chance but figuring out how to approach him was tough. She didn't know the right thing to say that might bring them together in a new kind of relationship…a relationship filled with good times and kindness.

CHAPTER 46

THE NEXT NIGHT SHE STILL WASN'T SURE HOW TO start a conversation with Scott. She decided to let the thoughts go and escape to the Cove. She needed it more than ever.

She arrived at eight and there weren't any seats at the piano bar, but she found a table nearby. It was a good crowd. Trudy, Wendy's favorite waitress, came toward her with a screwdriver in hand.

She set it in front of Wendy. "How's it going?" she asked.

"Fine Trudy. Thanks for the immediate service, you do know me."

"I know you're very nice to everyone and I admire kindness in today's funky world."

"Thanks, I appreciate it."

Trudy smiled and left. She reminded Wendy of someone from the Ashram. Most people rarely discuss being kind.

Brad was singing James Taylors', "Fire and Rain." He looked so sexy in the khaki pants and light blue floral shirt with a brown vest. Long, wavy sideburns framed his face.

Wendy took a few swallows of her screwdriver and watched the people at the piano bar as they visited with Brad between songs.

As Brad rose to take his break Wendy went to the counter to put the house music on, then went to chat with Rusty about the evening and about the great crowd.

"How ya doin'?"

"Good." She leaned into him to whisper, "In fact so good, I'm off the peyote."

"Really?"

"Yup, never again."

"And the weed?"

"No decision there yet."

Brad passed by them on the way back for another set and Wendy went to the counter to turn the music off. She leaned down to reach the controls and when she stood up Brad was on the other side of the counter facing her.

Wendy pulled back. "You startled me. I thought you were heading back."

"I am, but I have a question for you?"

"What's that?"

"That depends."

"On what?"

"On whether or not you'd like some company tomorrow."

Wendy was frozen. "That…would…I mean, I'd like it…sure."

"One o'clock, okay?"

She arched her eyebrows, "Fine."

He winked as he returned to the high stool to start his set. She stood there for a minute in complete disbelief and tripped on a chair leg as she headed back to her seat. Brad's singing of Neil Diamond's, "Girl, You'll Be a Woman Soon," brought her out of her stupor. She wanted to talk to Cindy, to Carol, to anyone who would listen and care. Wendy sat trying not to explode, but calmed herself, and used a little restraint to stop herself from screwing up this electrifying time. She wanted to savor the moment for as long as she could.

The evening ended, and Wendy drove home in the slow lane. She needed to concentrate on her driving, not on what was deep in her heart. Brad finally found her desirable. She would have time alone with the man she hungered after for so long.

She moved through her house and fell onto the bed. She couldn't believe it finally happened. Brad wanted her, but she wondered why now?

The next day at The Shade House Wendy couldn't contain her excitement and practically blurted the news to Carol.

"Holy shit, after all this time."

"I know. I'm...I don't even have words to describe how I feel. It's undeniably, well, outta site, a mystical happening."

"I'm really happy for you."

"Thanks. I have to plan for tomorrow. I need to decide what to wear, what music to play..."

Carol went to help a customer as Wendy sat in her office re-thinking last night. Was it what she wore that did it? Her hair and makeup were the same. She just couldn't imagine why now. Oh, how she wished she could share this with Cindy, but what a ridiculous idea. She didn't want to hurt Cindy. Wendy felt guilt, she wanted him so much, but since he and Cindy split, maybe she'd understand.

To stop her head from spinning she started looking through the receipts. She saw a drop in profits. But, what to do about it was the question. She thought for a few minutes, and it came to her, she'd have an Open House. Yes, she liked the idea. She pictured the set up. She could serve snacks, have soft music, and offer new plant varieties. With growing excitement, she scanned through the plant catalogues.

Half an hour later she completed a list of sixteen new plants to order. She'd work on advertising tomorrow.

She left the office and told Carol about her plans. Although surprised Carol liked the idea. They'd discuss the details later as they noticed many customers roaming around and went to assist them.

CHAPTER 47

THE PARTIALLY CLOSED BLINDS ADDED ENOUGH darkness to set a romantic mood. "A Quiet Afternoon," played softly on the record player. Wendy moved three candles to the right of the coffee table. In the kitchen, she checked to be sure the bottle of Chardonnay had chilled. It had, but since Brad wouldn't be there for another hour, she shoved the bottle back into the fridge. She leaned against it. Unrelenting nervousness consumed her. She didn't know what to expect.

She brushed her teeth and, in the bedroom, examined herself in the full-length mirror. Admittedly, Wendy's stature was not that of a model, but she had lost fifteen pounds since she first knew Brad and she knew she looked good. In her off-white, jersey lounge dress, she felt very sexy, especially since the dress exposed the tops of, what someone told her were 'ample breasts.' She continued to look at herself, finding it difficult to grasp this was about to be the moment she longed for and dreamt about for two years.

She parted her hair in the middle, and it hung down her back. She used sparse makeup, but the soft, green eye shadow brought out the green in her hazel eyes.

Just before one o'clock she again ran the brush through her hair. She stood in front of the mirror, smiled at herself, and went out to the living room where she lit the candles and put the album on the record player. The doorbell rang.

She rushed toward the door, stopping for a moment to run her fingers through the sides of her hair. When she opened the door, there he stood, in stonewashed jeans, a silky, blue shirt, and in his hands a potted palm.

"Hi," she smiled.

"Hi," he said as he entered and handed her the gift. "Hope you like plants." He laughed and she joined him.

She couldn't imagine he took gifts to everyone he saw. "Thank you, this is so nice."

"You're welcome. I like your house, it looks very cozy," he said as he surveyed it.

"Thanks." She placed the palm on the end table. "Would you like a glass of wine?"

"That'd be great."

"Go ahead and sit down. I'll be back in a minute. Is Chardonnay okay?"

"That's good."

She pulled the cork and wrapped a towel around the chilled wine to keep the condensation from dripping.

She set the wine and two glasses on the coffee table. She hoped she looked calm because her racing heart was anything but. She sat next to him on the sofa and watched as he slowly poured them each a glass. She took small sips, relishing the strong, dry taste as it lingered on her lips. They chatted about some of the regulars who came into the bar and about an opportunity he was offered to audition for a movie soundtrack.

Being the first time alone with him made her intense. It was unnerving to feel his tight, muscular leg against hers. His eyes were truly aquamarine, and she studied them for what she thought too long. Her head spun like a ball. So hard to believe her fantasy of being with Brad unfolded before her.

After drinking some more wine, she finally felt relaxed, but she needed to slow down before she did something foolish like grab him and kiss his beautiful full lips.

"You really look terrific," he said. "It's funny, when I saw you last night I thought, 'she's looking great.' And, it isn't just your attractive body, you're a good person," he said as he fingered the side of her hair.

She again stopped herself from grabbing and kissing him.

"And besides you seem different somehow; I think your personality has opened up more than in the past. You're less shy."

Wendy wasn't sure how to respond, so she smiled and said, "I have made some changes. Glad you like them."

Brad put their glasses down and turned her to him. She melted into his arms. He pushed hard against her lips, pushing them open with his tongue, searching the highs and lows of her mouth. Her entire body trembled. She ran her hands through his long, dark, wavy hair and down his back, relishing the taut skin beneath her fingers. Her eyes were shut when his hand moved to her breast.

He pulled away, "Perhaps we could go to the bedroom."

He certainly didn't mince words...not that Wendy cared. She stood and Brad followed her. As soon as they reached the bedroom, he began to undress her. "I want to see all of your body." As he said the words, he slipped the dress off her shoulders and down, pushing it over her hips. She didn't have a bra on. She stepped out of the dress.

"Great body, very nice." He said the words with a softness he used for those special ballads he sang.

Wendy loved the words and savored them, but she realized he'd probably said the same thing to other women. She blinked her eyes to erase the dismal idea and watched from the edge of the bed as he unveiled his gorgeous frame. She should have known it would be flawless, except for two small birthmarks on his shoulder that were cute in themselves, like beauty marks.

She stood up after he finished undressing and held him tightly as they kissed. He helped her onto the bed. His hands began roving over her body, constantly moving. She held him, as she ran her hands down his spine and up through his hair. He slipped on a condom.

Wendy's mind floated, almost as if it were outside of her. His hands moved over her entire body, like she imagined, but after a few minutes she became aware…his fingers never lingered in any of the areas she always responded to so willingly. He touched her everywhere, but he didn't caress any part of her body or spend enough time in the one area where she could climax.

She felt the strength of his shoulders when he moved on top of her. With a few quick movements, it ended. He kissed her gently on the lips as he rolled off her. Wendy lay still, staring at the blank ceiling, trying to understand what just transpired.

"You're great, Wendy. Hope we can do this again." With those words he got up, grabbed his clothes, went into the bathroom where he disposed of the condom and ran his fingers through his hair. Wendy stood by the bed and slipped into a robe she laid out.

Brad came back all dressed. "Sorry I can't stay longer, but I have to spend time with my kids."

Wendy knew they lived with his ex-wife.

"Really, that was great, I look forward to more sweet times."

"Thanks."

Wendy walked with him to the door.

He gave her a quick goodbye kiss. "I'll see you at the Cove," he said as he scooted out.

Wendy went to the sofa, flopped down, and blew out the candles. She sipped the remaining wine in her glass.

He's a surface person, she decided. He lives in his inner world. No one really knows him. The foreplay was minimum, and the sex ended before she knew it. She was thrilled he even wanted her and asked to get together again, but now Wendy wasn't sure she wanted him. His movements were almost mechanical. Was it a routine he developed? Where were the deep penetrating hands that always stimulated her until she enjoyed the wonderful sensations of the climax? She so badly wanted to feel the warmth of his hands, the feeling she got when someone really cared about her. She tried to grasp the reality of why a wonderfully, talented hunk of a man proved such a disappointment. After all this time, all those daydreams and then to discover he was...well, it was laughable when she remembered how she envied all those women he slept with, only to discover what she needed and wanted Brad didn't have. There were no true feelings for her.

CHAPTER 48

THANKFULLY, THE NEXT DAY, BEING MONDAY Brad had it off. Wendy needed time to decide how she would act around him now. Her attitude toward him changed, and she wasn't sure how it might impact how she behaved or looked at him, especially if she sat right in front of him. She now realized the warmth he showed when he sang didn't exist. He not only sang to the audience, but he acted for them. She would continue to enjoy his voice, but less frequently. Wendy felt no desire to be in bed with him. She wondered why some of the women he bedded continued to want him. Did he perform differently for them, or did they just want to brag such a talented and sexy guy wanted them? Wendy hadn't desired him for just his talent and looks but for a man she hoped would appreciate and care about her.

At work it would be hard to tell Carol the truth. Wendy felt like a fool for having been wrapped up in him for so long and now having to tell Carol how disappointing he performed, it embarrassed her.

"So, tell me," Carol insisted almost immediately after Wendy's entrance.

"Let me get settled," Wendy said as she went into her office, brooding about what to say.

Carol followed her in. "Okay, you're settled, so talk."

Wendy stepped out of the office and Carol followed. They stood behind the counter as they faced each other. "It wasn't good. His idea of intimacy is do it and be done. It's like he added another notch on his belt."

Carol patted Wendy on the shoulder. "I'm so sorry. I know how long you've wanted to be with him."

"Thank you. It's a lesson learned. I think I loved what he stood for-talent and looks. I wanted to be part of his adoring groupie… how stupid."

"I'm proud that you're able to put it in perspective."

"Thanks. Do you ever hang out in bars?"

"No, the bar scene isn't me."

A long time ago Wendy remembered having the same thoughts.

Wendy and Carol took some time between customers to discuss the Open House. They talked about the refreshments and where they could fit small benches along the paths so people could sit and eat.

"We can put bridge chairs in the wider paths and set up the TV trays and chairs by the stream," Wendy decided. "Could you work out a menu with a caterer?"

"I'll get a detailed plan down."

"Great, thanks."

They put a flyer together to post in grocery stores and other places and some for the counter where they could point them out to customers. The ad would mention the new plant varieties available starting the day of the Open House. Enticing old customers, as well as new ones, was the plan.

She wanted to talk to Cindy about Brad but didn't know how it might affect their relationship. Wendy wanted to know what Cindy thought of his performances. Maybe Brad was great with her. Maybe his sexual interactions were never the same. Wendy didn't know how to ask Cindy, or should she just let it go and push her disappointment deep inside? She couldn't decide. Cindy might be furious if Wendy told her what happened.

At night she made herself an omelet for dinner and later in her study she lit up a joint. She stared at the phone and put the weed out. What could she say to Cindy? She stood up and walked around the house trying to get the nerve to call her. She finally stopped, hesitated and dialed her number.

"Hey, glad you called I was going to ask you about going to a new place tomorrow night for dinner and entertainment."

"Sounds good, but first I need to talk to you and ask you something. May I come over?"

"Now?"

"Yes."

"Sure."

"See you in a few."

They hung up and Wendy drove the fifteen minutes to Cindy's. She knew telling Cindy would be awkward, strange, and difficult. But, since Cindy didn't care about Brad anymore, she hoped she'd be okay with Wendy's news.

"So, what's going on?" Cindy asked as soon as Wendy came in.

"You have some wine?"

"Sure, hang on."

Cindy returned from the kitchen with two glasses of Merlot.

They sat next to each other on the sofa.

"Thanks." Wendy took a swallow.

"So?"

Wendy set the wine on the coffee table and turned to Cindy. "This is hard, and I feel completely weird telling you, but you said I should come to you whenever I didn't know what to do about something, right?"

"Yes."

"It isn't exactly that but..."

"Get to the fucking point."

"Brad and I…" She didn't know how to say it…"the fucking point is, we fucked."

"You and Brad?" Cindy sat upright.

Wendy nodded.

Cindy collapsed against the sofa, staring at Wendy and finally sitting up. "That was the first time, or has he been screwing you all along, while screwing me, and you just didn't tell me?"

"No, no. This was the first and only time. I was totally shocked when he asked, but Cindy…I have desired him for a very long time. I just never told you…I couldn't. I loved him. At least I thought I did. He was the type of man I always wanted to love and be loved by. His talent, his body, his personality-I saw it all in Brad. He never showed any interest, but I just dreamt about him until two nights ago."

"Wow! And all this time…you never talked about him except as a singer."

"I couldn't. He suddenly asked me. I know you feel he was part of the reason you left, but since you stopped seeing him…I hoped maybe we could talk about this. I didn't want to be deceitful and not tell you. I'm sorry if this hurts. I didn't want to be friends and keep it from you."

"It's okay. I stopped caring about him quite a while ago. I'm not mad, and I'm glad about you're being honest."

"At the ashram they talked about the importance of family, friends and kindness. I've been thinking about those things a lot."

"Wow, tell me what the ashram was like?"

I enjoyed it immensely and like I said I learned a lot about people and letting go of hang ups and not freaking out over things I can't control. I'm working on it."

"Maybe someday we can go to one."

"Sure, an amazing experience."

"So, how did you like the sex?"

Wendy didn't hesitate. "I didn't."

Cindy burst into wild laughter.

Wendy's eyes widened and her face showed confusion.

"It's okay Wendy. I never thought he was good either." They both laughed.

Wendy told Cindy everything from when Brad asked her out, to how the evening ended.

"He is the worst lover I've ever had," Cindy admitted. "I think I so wanted to be one of his girls that I kept it up to feel important. Right after my job ended…I was, well, relieved I no longer needed to pretend he impressed me."

"Oh, Cindy, I feel so much better. He was only interested in fucking, not in me. I was obsessed with him. Do you think he's a nymphomaniac?"

"I'm not sure about that. I think he just needs to know he can have whomever he wants. It's an ego thing."

"What I don't get is why did he ask me now? I haven't changed anything about myself for ages."

Cindy took Wendy's hands, "Because he hadn't had you, and I suppose his character, or lack thereof, needed to add you to his list."

"You're right, that makes sense. I don't know how to act around him now. I was so taken with him all this time…I longed to share my deep feelings with him, but the other night I realized he didn't have deep feelings. My desire for him vanished, although I still love his voice…sorry for rambling."

"It's fine. This question will sound odd, but have you put off getting back with Scott because you thought Brad would want you? I mean, he might consider you special once you got together and you'd see him often."

Wendy frowned at Cindy, stood up and stepped across the room. She leaned against a bookcase. Cindy watched and waited. Wendy looked over at her friend and came back and sat down.

"I just want to be sure the changes Scott showed were real, but you might be right. I've worked a long time, to make myself look sharp, so Brad would want me as someone special. All the changes I made were with him in mind. My thoughts were always about being with him. How wrong I've been."

"I'm glad you found out the truth about Brad." Cindy waited a second before she asked, "Do you want to get back with Scott?"

Wendy didn't hesitate. "Yes, I do, especially since I've seen and heard so much change in him. I'm determined to find out if it's for real so I will have to go out with him.

"I don't know how to thank you, you're truly a great friend."

"And so are you. It took guts to tell me about you and Brad. Our friendship was most important to you. I think we'll always be good friends, family for life."

"And, if I can ever help you, I'll be there."

"I know you will."

They hugged tightly.

Wendy realized she was transforming into someone she liked. Being 'in style' wasn't important. Knowing what's right and what's wrong was important. She no longer needed to impress anyone and if they didn't like her then too bad. Friendship and kindness were what mattered.

At home, she went to the study where Brad's framed picture stood on her desk. She picked up the picture, shook her head and removed it from the frame. Without a second look, she ripped up the picture and tossed it into the trash. She leaned down next to her desk and picked up the marijuana container with all its paraphernalia. She went into the bathroom where she tore the wrappers from the joints and slowly flushed the marijuana down the toilet.

In her bedroom she leaned back against the pillows on her headboard and reminisced about all she'd been through and experienced in the almost two years since Scott and she separated. She was proud of her successful business and her contribution to the Showcase at the Los Angeles Convention Center. The partnering with Jake was a disaster but she finally accepted the fact it wasn't her fault and let it go. Her personal life was filled with other memories, some good and some bad. Marty's using her and the drugs that drove Elliott away were part of the reason her life had tumbled downward. She learned some things the hard way. Most importantly, she was lucky to have Cindy as such a great friend. In the end, her greatest lesson was from Brad. She learned sometimes people aren't all they seem to be, but she hoped Scott was now all he seemed to be.

CHAPTER 49

WENDY SPENT A FEW DAYS WORKING IN HER garden still thinking about Brad and remembering how desperately she wanted him. She laughed as she swept grass off her patio and erased the disillusioned mistake out of her head.

She returned to the nursery and continued the planning for the Open House. Carol found a caterer who would set everything up, including coffee, plates, utensils, and iced tea. Wendy was excited about what was to come.

September started with Wendy's calm reflections about the past she left behind. It was the day before the Saturday Open House and Wendy strolled around the nursery to see if she wanted to make any final changes of plant locations but decided she liked the way all the plants looked. Carol and Wendy set up the chairs with TV trays along the stream as planned. They placed a few benches around the nursery.

On Saturday, both Wendy and Carol arrived at The Shade House at eight. The caterers brought the food, dishes, coffee, and all necessary supplies. They set up everything on two folding tables covered in yellow and green floral tablecloths.

At nine Carol opened the door and stood aside to greet people for a few minutes before going to the tables as hostess. Wendy moved around mingling with both old and new visitors. Early afternoon Cindy came in with a cheerful look. She strolled around with Wendy, complimented her again on her nursery, stayed for a short visit and left.

Wendy passed the stream area, where she chatted with a man and woman as they discussed a begonia they bought. That's when she noticed Scott come toward her. Wendy stared as a shiver ran down her spine.

"Hi," was all Wendy could get out as she observed how good he looked. She excused herself from the couple and turned to Scott. He lost some weight since Wendy last saw him, not that he really needed to, and he wore his hair differently, parted on the opposite side from where it used to be. Somehow it gave him an even more appealing look.

"Seems like a good size crowd. The parking lot is pretty full."

"Thanks, Scott. You knew about this?"

"I saw the ad in the Santa Monica paper. I'm glad I came. Are congratulations due?"

"For what?"

"I figured this was a celebration for something special."

She smiled and lowered her voice. "I did it purely to bring new people into the nursery in hopes they'd come back and bring friends."

"So, business is doing…?"

Wendy could tell he didn't know if the need for publicity was normal, or business wasn't doing well.

"No, no, business is good, but it never hurts to have new customers."

"True and I'm relieved. I couldn't tell."

"I can understand. Businesses have parties to drum up more clientele to keep their enterprises flourishing."

Scott smiled at Wendy, "Makes good sense."

"Did you want some refreshments?" Wendy asked not knowing what to say next.

"Sure."

Scott followed Wendy to the food tables. Carol came over to say hi. Scott gave a big grin, and a hi back.

Wendy took a small plate and put some chips and dip on it. Scott's plate was filled with guacamole and crackers. They each took a cup of coffee and Wendy led the way to two chairs by the potting area.

"What's been happening with you?" Wendy asked. She hadn't forgotten their lunch visit and wondered if his viewpoints continued to change.

"Well, my job has changed recently."

"Really, how?" she asked sipping her coffee.

"Do you remember I told you I only handled the import aspect?"

"Yes."

"I was promoted. And guess what? I don't travel at all."

"How did this come about?"

The company asked if I was interested in handling the marketing. Since my old job involved marketing with the import/export business I possessed the confidence and good marketing skills to successfully execute the job."

Although it sounded a bit arrogant Wendy was impressed. "That's wonderful, Scott. Do you like it?"

"Love it. It gives me a chance to share creative ideas with different advertisers."

"I'm really happy for you." Wendy's voice filled with enthusiasm.

At that moment a customer came over to discuss a plant she was interested in. Wendy set her cup and plate on the seat, excused herself from Scott and strode with the woman as they talked.

Scott remained in the same spot when Wendy returned.

"Listen, I know you're busy, so I won't keep you any longer," he said as he stood.

"It's been a little crazy today, but in a good way," she assured him. With conviction she added. "I'm glad you stopped by…it was very nice." It was the first time she had said anything encouraging to him.

"I'm glad I did too."

Wendy followed Scott as he put his coffee cup and plate down and headed for the door.

"See you later," he said as he left.

Wendy watched as he walked out. She took a break from the festivities and went into her office, closed the door, collapsing into her chair. He made major changes and talked more, the way he was when they dated and during the first part of their marriage. She now saw him with renewed interest, more than the last time they talked. She liked his new job and his attitude toward it. The question was, would the conversations stay as stimulating if they got back together? Would they stay in "feel" with each other?

Wendy left the office and went to speak with some familiar customers. Two men stood next to her as she visited with a customer who was interested in a hanging plant she held. When the conversation ended the men asked if they could talk to her a minute. She went with them to the counter.

"Hi, my name is Mitchell, and this is Alan."

"Nice to meet you both."

Mitchell spoke, "I understand you are the owner and designer of this nursery."

"Yes, I'm Wendy Murray."

"Alan and I represent the California Shade Plant Association. A while ago we visited your nursery when we read about it in the paper."

Alan continued, "We found your nursery a unique design and a lush haven. It looks even more incredible now."

"Thank you so much."

The men looked at each other for just a second. Mitchell spoke, "We would like to nominate your shade plant nursery for a special award from our association. It's called 'Best Shade Plant Garden of California.' We include indoor spaces if they look as amazing as yours."

Stunned and speechless Wendy finally spoke, "I don't know what to say. This is such an honor for me and my nursery. So nice of you to consider it."

"Just so you understand," Alan said, "You're one of five nominated. If it's okay, we will take some pictures and a short film to share with the nominating committee."

"Yes, of course."

Mitchell added, "The committee will vote in about two weeks. There will be an Award's ceremony at the Los Angeles Hotel downtown. If possible, we'd like all the nominees to attend."

"Amazing, this is a lot to take in. I'm very gratified you find my nursery to be worthy of a nomination. And, of course, I will attend the Award's ceremony. Once again, thank you."

Each man shook her hand and said, "You're welcome."

Wendy's eyes followed both Mitchell and Alan as they strolled around the nursery and took pictures of many areas, including the inner bark paths where many plants were. She watched them recording the nursery as they proceeded toward the stream and finally turned to the gazebo.

"Thank you again for your creation."

Wendy went with them to the door.

"We'll be in touch," Mitchell said as they left.

The first thing she thought when they left was that she'd invite Scott to the Award's ceremony.

Near the end of the day the number of people dwindled, and Wendy immediately went to Carol to tell her the news.

"Oh, wow. I don't know what to say, what a great honor."

"I know. This is unbelievable." Wendy's eyes danced.

"But you do know you deserve it. All the work you put into the design and its final appearance…it is a kind of fairy land."

"You've been a great supporter all along, thank you."

CHAPTER 50

AFTER THE OPEN HOUSE WENDY AGAIN TOOK time to work in her garden and even wandered around her neighborhood trying to think clearly about Scott. She strolled several blocks before returning home. As she came in the phone started ringing. It was Mitchell from the Shade Plant Association. He announced her nomination. What a surprise, especially since he said the committee would meet in two weeks and it had only been a week. What an incredible honor and in three weeks would be the banquet. Wendy couldn't have been more ecstatic. She called Cindy and Carol and then Jake. They were all enthusiastic about her accomplishment.

Wendy surprised herself when she called Scott and asked him out for dinner, her treat. She picked Cat and Mouse because she liked the music, the quiet, and the atmosphere.

Scott picked Wendy up at seven.

"Hope you like this place. They have a nice bar and a very good piano player with a dynamic voice."

Scott looked around the restaurant as they sat across from each other at a table. "I do like it so far. Thanks for inviting me. I was pretty surprised."

"I invited you to help me celebrate."

"Celebrate what?"

"My nursery being nominated as one of the five best shade plant gardens by the California Shade Plant Association. There's a banquet in a few weeks."

Scott's hand reached out to Wendy's as a way of saying, how wonderful. Wendy looked at their hands together and up at Scott. They smiled. His action reminded her of how sweet and warm he was before their marriage began to crumble. They pulled their hands apart.

"Now, that's extraordinary. I mean, I think you deserve it, but to be nominated as one out of five in California, I'm so happy for you."

"Thanks, I truly appreciate it. There is another reason I invited you out tonight. I must be honest. I needed time to see if all you've said about yourself is true. You do seem different, wonderfully different."

"I can understand where you're coming from, and why you may not trust what I've told you, but it's all true. As I said, my job has no traveling component and the promotion as Marketing Director at this new company allowed me to see that I am a successful person. I've needed to know that for a very long time. I want to spend my life with you…traveling, going to movies, dances and whatever you want. It's taken me a long time to realize what an ass I was, not just to you but to others."

"I think we've both changed. It's taken me a long time to figure out what direction I wanted. I know now."

They smiled at each other and finally looked at their menus. A short time later the waiter took their orders.

Scott continued after the waiter left. "I admit during our marriage I spent a lot of my time on myself and what I wanted, or what I thought I wanted. When you left it didn't take long for me to realize you were what I really wanted."

"Oh, Scott." The powerful tension she used to experience around him evaporated. "I pray we can make us work, but like I said, I will need time."

"I do understand."

The waiter returned with their dinners.

"Hey, you," Scott said as the waiter started to turn away.

The waiter turned back to Scott.

"Yes, sir."

"You spilled the gravy, now why don't you clean it up, it's disgusting?"

Wendy shook her head at the terrible way he spoke. Her face contorted. He was gruff and mean.

"I'll be right back with a rag."

"Make it fast."

The waiter left and Wendy glared at Scott. "What in the hell? How you talked to him was demeaning. I can't believe what you said."

"Well, he did deserve it. He should have cleaned it right there."

Wendy's face turned red. "As he said, he didn't have a rag." Her voice cracked. "You didn't give him a chance to get one. I thought you had changed. You sounded like you changed, but now I know you haven't."

"I have changed but what he did angered me, like we weren't good enough to be treated with respect."

"You didn't give him a chance to clean up. He didn't have a rag with him so how could he clean up right then? You weren't treating him with respect."

"Bullshit. I was standing up for what was right."

Her words hardened. "You could have asked him in a nicer way. I am totally surprised by your shameful behavior right after telling me you had changed!" She shook her head. "I'm not hungry anymore, please take me home."

"Well, if that's the way you want it, fine."

Neither spoke as Scott drove her home. He pulled in front of her house. Before letting herself out of the car, she turned and said, "Great performances you've shown me, but the truth showed itself, goodbye."

Scott drove off.

She crashed onto her bed and cried herself to sleep.

The next morning, Wendy went to Cindy's and explained what happened. Within minutes of sitting with Cindy, Wendy began crying. "It was like he always was-mean, disrespectful and critical… she screwed up her face, he angered me like I've never been angry."

"I'm so sorry. Please try to calm yourself." Cindy held Wendy.

Tears continued to trickle down her cheeks.

Cindy pulled back. "I feel so sad myself. I was so hoping it would work out and he had changed."

"It's the realization that all along he wasn't honest. He played me to get me back, but why?"

"You told me he said he loved you and realized how shamelessly he treated you. He seemed to want you back. Maybe that part was true. He did love you but for some reason what the waiter did set him off and he showed his true colors."

"If that incident hadn't happened and I went back to him, I know that some of his other negative traits would have returned. I told him good-bye."

"I'm so mad at how he hurt you and caused you more pain."

An hour later Wendy calmed down and left. She went to her backyard and sat in a chair admiring the beauty of her garden.

The next day at The Shade House, she walked around until she came to the window at the forest end where Elliott commented on the light in the window hitting the orchid. She thought about that first meeting with him and how wonderful he was to her, not just then but from then on. She loved him and he loved her, but she blew it with drugs and booze. She stared up at the window, 'I still love you…sorry I was such an idiot.' Of course, the apology wasn't really to Elliott. She went to the gazebo and sat. She wondered if there was a way to tell him what a fool she had been and how she had stopped the drugs. Would he be interested in trying again? She didn't know how to contact him comfortably, and he may be with someone else. Her mind shut down and she went to help a customer.

At night she called Cindy, and they discussed what Wendy wanted to do and how much she still loved Elliott.

Cindy didn't hesitate, "I think you should try to find him and see if he'll talk to you. He's a great guy."

"Should I call him?"

"Seems like the best way."

"Okay, I will, thanks."

When they hung up Wendy went to her comfy living room chair, put her foot up on the ottoman and let her mind wander. Thinking about making the phone call made her extremely nervous and thinking what his reaction might be made her fearful. She went to the kitchen phone and sat down at the table. She didn't remember his number but pulled her address book from a counter drawer and stared at the page. 'I have to do this, or I'll regret it forever' was what ran through her head.

She dialed. The phone rang and she started to hang up but then she heard his voice, "Hello."

"Hi Elliott, this is Wendy."

"Wendy, well, I'm surprised."

"I don't blame you. I was wondering if we could meet somewhere and talk."

"Talk about what?"

"What a horrid person I was and how my terrible behavior made me realize I wasn't living the life I really wanted." She took a breath. "I was out of control."

"Well, you can say that. You feel you've changed…how could I know if what you tell me is the truth?"

"I'd never lie to you…I didn't in the past."

"That's true. Okay, I need to leave. I will call you back, bye."

"Bye," she said as she pulled the phone from her ear and set it down. She worried about the abrupt ending, maybe he was meeting someone, or maybe he didn't know what to make of her confession and needed to think about it. All she could do was wait.

At the nursery she continued to think about Elliott and what he must have thought about what she said. Her thoughts got interrupted by a customer walking toward her holding a fern.

"May I help you?"

"Yes, I love this plant, please tell me about it."

She explained the plant and the woman paid and left.

Two days had passed since the phone call. She figured he must be too angry to trust her, the same way she felt about Scott, so Wendy understood. Passing into her bedroom she kicked the bottom of the door angry at herself for being such a fool.

She hadn't been to Cat and Mouse since Scott's outrageous behavior. She would apologize to the waiter if he was there, although it had been quite a while, but she needed to escape from her anguished thoughts about Elliott. She walked toward a table and Matt smiled at her. Maybe he didn't know about Scott's mouthing off. She listened to the music. He sang, "What the World Needs Now is Love." What great timing for that song.

Matt visited with her at his break. After he walked away the waiter who served Scott and her came by. Wendy stopped him. "Sir, I don't know if you remember but I was here with a guy who treated you rudely."

He arched his eyebrows. "Oh, I remember."

"I'm so sorry he treated you so mean. He'll never be back."

"Thank you, I appreciate your apology."

She smiled as he moved away. She felt relief at having talked to him.

The next night was Sunday. She decided to stay home and read a book. She liked mystery stories. The one she was reading, *Come See Her* turned into a good read. She took it with her to the kitchen where she grabbed a mug and poured herself some coffee. She was about to go back to the living room when the phone rang. She thought it was Cindy because they hadn't talked for a while.

"Hello."

"Hi Wendy."

She couldn't believe it. "Hi Elliott," She put the book and mug down.

"I've given your phone call a lot of thought. I would like to hear about what happened to you and how you think you've changed. You want to meet somewhere?"

Wendy held her excitement in abeyance. "Yes, I'd like to."

"Okay, there's Robin's House on Westwood Blvd, north of Wilshire. What's a good day and time?"

"With Carol at the nursery I can pretty much go anytime, I'm open."

"How about tomorrow at 12:30?"

"Sure, thanks."

"See you then, goodbye."

Wendy didn't know how to calm herself. She put her head on the table, then jumped up and went to the living room where she fell onto the sofa. All she could think about was how happy she felt that he wanted to talk everything out. The concern now, how to tell him what she needed to say.

At the nursery the next day she pulled dead leaves as usual and kept herself busy until noon. She went to the gazebo and sat. She tried to think of ways to start the conversation. Nothing came to mind.

"I'm really excited for you," Carol said as Wendy grabbed her purse. "I hope everything goes the way you want."

"Thanks, I hope so too."

Wendy pulled into the parking lot next to the restaurant. Elliott waited in the entry. "Hi," was all she could say.

"Hi. They're holding a table for us."

She followed him to the table where they sat across from each other.

As soon as they settled in. "I have to tell you, Wendy, I was very conflicted about meeting you, but I want to hear what you have to say."

"I can understand your hesitancy." She stopped when the waitress came over and set down the menus. "I don't know where to start."

"Want to look at the menus first?"

"Sure." A nice gesture since he obviously knew she was nervous and not sure how to start. She didn't look at the menu long…just decided on soup and a roll. Soon the waitress returned with water, and they ordered.

When she left, Wendy looked Elliott straight in the eyes. Her body stiffened, "What happened to me, I tried to forget the pain I was feeling about Scott, the failure of the Fireplace Grill, and my feelings toward you. At the time, I was also interested in Brad. My mind couldn't seem to concentrate even after I visited Dr. Lewis. I got completely taken away by the bar scene and all the fun it offered me. But I changed so much and apparently couldn't deal with the consequences of my behavior. I turned to drugs as an escape. I wanted to fit in with the new world I was experiencing. My conservative lifestyle was turned upside down when I made changes to myself, and men looked at me for the first time like I was…sexy and I finally felt appreciated. I'm so sorry about everything."

"It's ok. I want to hear the truth."

She waited until the waitress set their dinners down.

"It all began with my dad…how critical he used to be to me and then Scott was too. I know I mentioned this a long time ago, their treatment of me really left me feeling unloved and uncared for. They destroyed my self-confidence. You made me feel the opposite. I loved being with you because you," she shook her head and then refocused her eyes on him, "always showed you cared about me." As her eyes continued to focus on him, she gulped some air. "I should have never turned to drugs, but at that point in my life, I needed an escape into a world I didn't know how to deal with. I've been off drugs for over five months. I've learned to deal with problems in a more practical and sane way." Her face flushed and beads of sweat ran down her face.

Elliott looked at her with admiring eyes. With a quick movement of his hands, he held hers. "For the most part I knew and understood what was happening. I just couldn't stay around and watch you continue to fall apart. I couldn't deal with what was happening to you and the changes that I found disturbing."

Wendy looked down and tears dripped. Elliott lifted her chin and brushed them away. "I'm sorry you went through what you did, especially how your dad and husband treated you. But I appreciate your candor and I believe you have changed. I do want to remind you that some of your changes were good. You are very creative… look at your nursery and the House Retreats projects, a lot of hard work and great accomplishments. What I see in you is a woman who is smart, creative, and learned the hard way to deal with issues in a more practical way."

"It helped that Cindy was there for me. She's such a great friend."

"And I know you feel the same about her."

"Thank you. One of your traits that helped me was that you never criticized me until I made a fool of myself that night. I will always regret it."

"There are things I regret too, but that's how we learn, sometimes the hard way, but look at yourself now. You've obviously came to terms with everything that was bothering you and are ready to appreciate your new outlook. Groovy."

Wendy laughed at the word he never used when they were together. He laughed too.

"I don't know what to say. I embarrassed myself and you that night. Nothing like that will ever happen again."

Elliott grinned. "I know. I can tell you have changed in a good way."

Wendy's forlorn look turned into an endearing smile.

Elliott stroked her hair. "I'd like to give us a chance to start over."

"Oh Elliott, thank you for believing in me. I know I won't screw up again."

"Well, we all screw up, but now, maybe in less traumatic ways." Elliott smiled.

Wendy looked at their plates and laughed.

"What's so funny?"

"Neither one of us has eaten anything."

They both laughed.

"I want to tell you my nursery was nominated as one of five by the California Shade Plant Association."

"That's terrific!"

"Thanks. There's an awards banquet where they will announce the winner. Can I interest you in joining me?"

He ran a hand down the side of her hair and took her hands in his, "I'd like that."